LINDA BENNETT PENNELL

GILEAD'S PHYSICIAN

Black Rose Writing | Texas

ISBN: 978-1-68513-643-7
LIBRARY OF CONGRESS CONTROL NUMBER: 2025932630
PUBLISHED BY BLACK ROSE WRITING
www.blackrosewriting.com

Printed in the United States of America
Suggested Retail Price (SRP) $21.95

Gilead's Physician is printed in Baskerville

*As a planet-friendly publisher, Black Rose Writing does its best to eliminate unnecessary waste to reduce paper usage and energy costs, while never compromising the reading experience. As a result, the final word count vs. page count may not meet common expectations.

PRAISE FOR
GILEAD'S PHYSICIAN

Finalist in The Writer's League of Texas Manuscript Contest

"Gilead's Physician is a sweeping, heartfelt tribute to the quiet heroism of rural doctors and the communities they serve. A beautifully rendered and accurate historical fiction of grit, grace, and the price of one man's calling to care and heal."
–Janis Robinson Daly, award-winning, best-selling author of *The Unlocked Path* and *The Path Beneath Her Feet.*

"With its historical details and profoundly moving characters, Gilead's Physician is about resilience, love, and the fight to make a difference in a world that doesn't always welcome change."
–Manik Chaturmutha for *Readers' Favorite*

"Gilead's Physician creates the world of Appalachia at the turn of the 20th century with great sensitivity to time and place."
–C.R. Hurst for *Readers' Favorite*

"Pennell's close narration shows us the heavy emotional toll of selfless service, making the book both inspiring and heart-wrenching from cover to cover... Gilead's Physician is a compelling historical read that I would highly recommend."
– K.C. Finn for *Readers' Favorite*

DIALECT, DEFINITION, AND PRONUNCIATION GUIDE

Some of the novel's characters do not speak in a grammatically correct manner. If they had any schooling, it usually ended at 8th grade or earlier. Some are illiterate. They speak an older form of English that includes archaic words, usages, and conjugations. The isolation in which they lived and the lack of formal education preserved the language of their ancestors, many of whom were Highland Scots and Scots Irish.

Thay's	There is	Not to be confused with the pronoun "they"
Wyy	An expression of surprise or used to emphasize a point, etc.	Not to be confused with the word "why." Wyy is pronounced exactly like it is spelled.
To help	Conjugated as help, holp, holpen	An archaic conjugation until recently heard among the oldest residents of Appalachia
To tell	Conjugated as tell, tolt, done tolt	
To eat	Conjugated as eat, ett, done ett	
Sorry	Describing someone as sorry means they are useless, incompetent, lazy, and/or of low moral character	Often accompanied by "no account." Ex: "He's sorry and no account."

Folkses, deskses, etc.	Folks, desks, etc.	The people of this area, until recently, added the extra "es" for some unknown reason.
You'uns	You ones. A contraction of "you ones" that was first recorded in 1805-1810 in the spelling "youns."	Pronounced "yuhnz" or "yoo-uhnz". Sometimes used in direct address, usually to two or more people. Common in Appalachia and some dialects of the Ozarks and Great Smoky Mountains. A slight shortening of the Scottish "you ones."
If'n	Archaic word that's a negative particle of intention of purpose. Sometimes spelled "iffen" or "effen."	Used to introduce a clause that expresses something to be. Extracted from conjunctional uses of words like "considering" and "excepting."
Off'n	Off of	American Southern dialect as in, "He fell off'n his horse."
Out'n	Out of	
Dinner	Noon meal	
Supper	Evening meal	
Pie Safe	A freestanding cabinet with doors made of pierced tin that allow air to circulate but keep insects away from food.	

| **Childern** | Children | Intentional spellings to represent mispronunciations that were once common in the area in which the story is set |

GILEAD'S

PHYSICIAN

PROLOGUE

"Is there no balm in Gilead?
Can no physician there be found?
Why has healing not yet
Come to my poor people?"
NEVI'IM JEREMIAH 8:22

Freeman leaned on his hoe and tugged a sodden rag from his hip pocket. He ran it over his face, for all the good it would do, as he stretched his back and rolled his shoulders. When the boy finished that last row, they would be finished chopping cotton for a while.

Please, Lord, let this harvest be a good one.

He watched his son carefully extract weeds and remove the least healthy cotton plants. The boy was a hard worker. Everybody said so. And he was smart. Book learning and figuring came easy to him. Freeman squinted into the late afternoon sun while he wiped the sweat trickling from his forehead. Maybe it was time to ask the question that had been brewing. If he waited for James to speak, it might never happen. The boy might have learned the lesson about respecting his elders a little too well.

Freeman beckoned with a raised hand. "James, let's stop for now. You can finish the row in the morning." His shout echoed from the surrounding mountains.

The boy looked up in surprise and yelled back, "But I only got this row left."

"Come on now. It'll wait."

The boy wove his way through the rows. When he reached his father, his expression darkened. "You okay? You look pure whipped."

"I'll make it. My age is just showing a bit."

"What's so important you had me quit before the job's done?" James's voice held a touch of irritation.

Freeman chewed on his tobacco wad and spit. He watched the dark brown liquid soak into the soil near his feet. James needed for him to ask the question. That much was clear. Freeman had watched his only son growing ever more restless with each passing month since he finished his schooling. The boy worked the farm with the strength of two men, but his heart simply wasn't in it.

James shifted from one foot to the other. "Papa?"

Freeman met his son's eyes. "You'll be fifteen soon." The boy nodded. "You're almost a man. You give any thought to what you want to do with your life?"

James's eyes widened. "I have. It's all I can think about, but I don't want you and Mama to take it the wrong way."

The old man kicked at the dab of mud created by his spit. "Say what's on your mind."

James let his gaze wander to the mountains rising on the far side of the valley. "I don't want to farm. I feel like I'm supposed to do something else." A red flush crept across his face.

Freeman eyed his son. "Go on. Out with it. I wouldn't have asked if I didn't want to hear your answer."

James rammed his fists into the pockets of his overalls and dropped his head. "Farming is a fine profession and all, but I don't want to be a farmer." His voice was so quiet it was almost a whisper.

Freeman put a hand on James's shoulder and leaned in. "It'll be all right, son. Just speak your piece."

James met his father's eyes. "Do you believe some men are called to do certain work?"

Freeman nodded. "I suppose so."

"Well, I feel like I'm being called to help our people, to give them the care they don't get here in these mountains. I want to be a doctor."

Freeman stroked his chin while he studied his son. "That's gonna take money for a lot more schooling than you got right now. Are you sure about this?"

James squared his shoulders. His mouth formed a firm line. "As sure as I am that we're standing here in this field." His voice softened as though he was not sure how his father would react to what he said next. "If I can find a way to become a doctor, I'll never refuse anyone care no matter what it takes. It's a promise I've made to myself and the Almighty."

Freeman sucked on his lower lip for several moments then nodded. "Well, then. I guess we'll have to see what we can do to make that happen."

CHAPTER 1

July 1890, Salacoa Valley, Cherokee County, Georgia
James wrapped his horse's reins around a fence post and dashed toward the church steps breathing hard. He was late. The service had been underway for at least fifteen minutes. Coaxing a reluctant baby into the world had taken all night and most of the morning. If it hadn't been Mr. Sinclair's funeral, he probably would have gone straight home. As it was, he arrived with a day's growth of beard and in a wrinkled, stained shirt. With luck, his suit coat covered the worst of the blood. He could not miss the service no matter how exhausted or dirty he was.

He pushed the door closed with a little more force than intended and winced at the echo he created in the sanctuary where the only other sound was the preacher praying. Several bowed heads opened their eyes and glared while a small form sitting two pews ahead jumped and glanced over her shoulder. The young woman peeking at him from beneath the brim of her straw hat paused for just a moment then smiled. He gave her a slightly puzzled nod and saw her long-lashed eyes twinkle with amusement. With standing room only, he slid into an open space against the back wall but continued to glance in the girl's direction long after she returned to her private devotion. From his vantage, he could see her in tantalizing profile. She looked vaguely familiar, but he just couldn't place her.

With the prayer ended, the opening chords of "Rock of Ages" floated from the pump organ down front. James peered over a shared hymnal toward the song leader's waving hands, but the girl captured his attention once more. Her smooth peaches-and-cream complexion glowed in the afternoon sunlight streaming through the open windows. He thought she must be rather petite because the women who sat on either side of her towered in comparison. She was a striking vision in a sea of otherwise drab, weather-beaten faces. She was probably one of many who had been children when he left for college eight years ago, but she had grown up beautifully in the intervening years. A small smile lifted the corners of his mouth. No doubt his older sister, Elizabeth, would know who the girl was.

If he had not been standing among mourners at a funeral, he would have laughed aloud at the long-suppressed feelings now stirring. He had almost forgotten what it was like to admire a pretty girl. While pursuing his medical degree, he hadn't had much time to think about girls nor the money it took to walk out with one. His courting days were clearly long overdue. As the service progressed, difficulty in giving it his full attention only increased. A shiny chestnut curl peeping from under the girl's hat and dancing at the nape of her beautifully shaped neck kept distracting him.

The pastor gave the benediction and the pallbearers carried the casket from the sanctuary. The congregation followed them up the hill behind the church to the cemetery for the graveside portion of the service. Afterward, people stood in small groups sharing their memories of the deceased. Laughter occasionally erupted as someone regaled his listeners with memories of Mr. Sinclair and some of his more humorous quirks.

James's throat tightened as he recalled Mr. Sinclair's impact on his own life. The recurring nightmare from his medical school days, the one asking who would help the people of his mountain home if he couldn't finish his degree, had miraculously disappeared with a loan after the old man learned James was unable to pay his tuition. Then, shortly before his graduation, James and his sisters were forced to make a painful decision. Their parents died during a virulent flu outbreak and selling the family farm had become necessary. As sad as he was to see the land pass out of the family, the sale had enabled James to repay Mr. Sinclair. Even with loans no longer binding them, their friendship continued to the end of the old man's ninety-six years. James would miss his friend's advice and wisdom more than words could express. He paused by the grave to say his own silent farewell and then went in search of Elizabeth.

He spotted his sister and started working his way over to her but was waylaid by friends who had not seen him since his return to the valley. When he finally slipped up by her side, she was deep in conversation with a neighbor. The elderly woman shouted her conversation at all interlocutors in the firm conviction that they needed the volume as much as she did. Since there were never any secrets around this lady, James kept his thoughts to himself.

Elizabeth smiled politely while the neighbor held forth. "Thay's something got to be done about them childern. Wyy, it's a disgrace the way they tear around these roads in them buggies. Somebody's gonna get hurt. You mark my words."

While the neighbor droned on, James's gaze swept over the crowd, searching for the straw hat covering the lovely chestnut curls. He found the girl being helped into a buggy by a man he did not recognize. James stiffened and then shifted from one foot to the other like the small boy Elizabeth had once looked after. She must have sensed his distress for she glanced at him and suddenly gave her conversational partner a broad smile.

"Now, it don't matter to me . . ." rang out as Elizabeth yanked James's arm and pulled him backward as he spluttered a hasty goodbye to the considerably surprised neighbor.

Elizabeth was his third eldest sister and the one James had cried after when he was a baby. His care had been her responsibility while their mother attended to household chores. As a result, they were particularly close and she still looked on him as her baby brother despite his college degrees and age. With the skill of a mother soothing a fretful child, she patted his arm as she pulled him away from the crowd.

"James, is everything all right?" Elizabeth asked. "I noticed you were late to the service."

"I was at the Locklin's this morning. I couldn't leave until she had the baby. I . . . I . . . was . . . just wondering . . ." James stammered around searching for the words that would extract the desired information without causing too much comment. He was seven years old again and asking Liz for the last piece of sweet potato pie.

When he saw the stranger climb into the buggy and take the reins, James pointed and blurted out, "Who's that girl over there?"

If Elizabeth was surprised by James's behavior, she didn't show it. Instead, she glanced up at her brother from beneath her lashes, smiled, and then looked in the general direction in which James was staring.

"What girl?" she enquired as she slyly peered at every conveyance in the yard except the one of such interest to James.

The buggy bearing the girl began moving when the stranger flicked the reins on the horse's rump. Ignoring good manners and abandoning dignity completely, James gestured even more emphatically. "The one over yonder in the buggy leaving from under the big oak . . . The one with . . ."

Feeling rather frantic, James looked down at Liz and saw the humor dancing in his sister's eyes. He smiled sheepishly and continued more calmly, "That girl right over there. The one in the blue dress. And who's driving the buggy?"

"That girl, as you say, would be Bud Campbell's oldest girl, Mary Alice. You probably remember her as just a little thing with long braids. And the man at the reins would be her gentleman caller, the schoolteacher. He's been at the school for about a year now and been walking out with Mary Alice for a while. Thay's talk he's popped the question, but she ain't give him her answer."

As if she felt their regard, the girl suddenly glanced over her shoulder. She seemed a little startled that they appeared to be watching her, but also pleased for she smiled and lifted her hand. She then quickly turned away as the buggy picked up speed. James stared after them until they disappeared around the curve in the road.

He tapped Elizabeth's shoulder. "Are you sure they aren't promised?"

Elizabeth raised a brow and tilted her head. "Well, now, Miss Mary Alice Campbell ain't confided the deepest secrets of her heart to me, but I'd say he's more interested than she is. She don't have the look of a girl in love. But mind you, that's just my opinion." Liz became quiet and all humor disappeared from her expression. She looked up at James with a small frown. "Little Brother, if you've got your eye set on that girl, you best recall the war. Bud Campbell may not take kindly to a pro-Union man's son coming to call, even if you was born and bred here in the valley. Bud ain't never forgive the way he was treated at that prisoner of war camp outside Chicago."

James's only reply was a crooked smile and a determined gleam in his eyes.

CHAPTER 2

A month passed before James caught sight of Mary Alice again, a month during which he unaccountably expected to see her pretty face at every turn of the road or sound of approaching footsteps. While he waited for the next encounter, he worked hard to help everyone in need and was rewarded with a growing reputation as a healer. He was gradually taking over from the local midwife as the first choice of laboring mothers. He had feared Maggie, who helped his own mother deliver all seven of her children, would be offended, but she had recently confided to him that she was too old to sit up all night waiting for a reluctant baby to make its appearance and she was glad to leave it to him. He had also set a broken arm, popped a dislocated shoulder back into place, and made and administered medicine for the whooping cough making the rounds of the valley's children. So far, his efforts had produced $5.00 cash, a dozen eggs, two crocks of pickled beans, a quarter pork shoulder, and a peck of corn for his horse.

Today was the second Sunday and the whole community was turning out for the monthly service. James peered in anticipation as the Campbell wagon lumbered into the yard, coming to rest under the ancient oak whose canopy shaded the whole area. His heart skipped a beat when he glimpsed Mary Alice climbing down after her siblings. If possible, she was even prettier than he remembered.

James stood on the porch socializing but kept an eye on Mary Alice while she and her family approached. He was rewarded by a quick smile directed solely at him when the Campbell family passed into the sanctuary. He discreetly followed, his gaze trailing after Mary Alice and her mother as their long skirts swished toward their customary seats. New Canaan Baptist Church followed the traditional form of congregational seating with men sitting together on the right side of the sanctuary and women on the left. Even married couples parted company at the church door. In irritation at what he suddenly deemed an unreasonable arrangement, James cast about for an empty seat.

The Campbell women were now settled into their usual pew close to the front. James grinned when he saw an opening next to Mr. Wilson. He elicited the old man's indignation by squeezing past the other's girth and sitting next to him in the second pew of the "amen corner," which was at a right angle and perpendicular to the main men's set of pews. This gave James a beeline view of Mary Alice, and potentially, she of him. If she looked his way, Mr. Wilson's ill will would be a small price.

Circuit-riding pastors had access to each congregation only once per month and generally felt it their duty to give a full measure of hellfire and brimstone before the benediction was said. The congregation would probably be held captive for two hours or more, the majority of which would be filled with hymn singing and the preacher's loud exhortations, before James would be able to approach Mary Alice.

The preacher delivered himself of a particularly fine sermon based on Revelation, stirring the congregational spirit in anticipation of the coming week's revival. A guilty pleasure coursed through James as he thought about the multiple opportunities this afforded him to encounter the object of his desire. He was falling short of a properly reverential attitude, but surely he might be forgiven this small failing. It had become evident he needed to act quickly if he was to separate Miss Campbell from the schoolteacher. Too many people were saying the couple would marry in the coming year. He would enlist Elizabeth's aid in his plan to become re-acquainted with this grown-up version of the little girl who used to have heavy plaits swinging down her back. It was convenient that the Buchanan women sat directly behind the Campbells. The women had resumed their friendship after the war despite the continued animosities between their men.

When the preacher finally concluded no additional good could be gotten by singing the invitational hymn again and the benediction was pronounced, James squeezed from the pew in a dash for Elizabeth, causing Mr. Wilson to emit a loud harrumph and glare once more. Conveniently, Liz had engaged Mary Alice and her mother in conversation.

Elizabeth paused, took James's arm, and pulled him into the circle. "Miz Campbell, Mary Alice, I'm sure you remember my brother, James Hiram?"

"Course we do. James, good to see you again." Mrs. Campbell gave him a sincere smile. "It ain't every boy what makes a doctor and I know your parents would've been proud you set up here where you was born and bred."

The two older women chatted for several minutes while James stole glances at Mary Alice. She blushed and returned them.

Mrs. Campbell must have noticed the silent interaction, for she suddenly turned her full attention on him. "How long was you gone from the valley, James?"

Heat rose in his face and his voice cracked a little under such scrutiny. "Eight years, give or take a few weeks."

"How're you making it since you got back?" It could have been James's imagination, but Mrs. Campbell's questions sounded more like interrogation than a neighborly inquiry.

James tried to sound modest. "I'm doing well, and my practice is growing."

"See much difference in the valley?"

"Well, New Canaan wasn't here when I left for school, and there're several new families who've moved in." James paused for a moment and then looked directly at Mary Alice. "Other than that, it's pretty much the same, except for the children who've grown up while I was gone."

The girl's smile brightened then she dropped her eyes.

It was now or never. James ran a finger around under his collar and swallowed hard. He bent his knees a little so he would not tower so over the women. "Miz Campbell, I was wondering if you and Mr. Campbell would mind if I called on Miss Mary Alice this afternoon?"

Mrs. Campbell looked sidelong at her daughter. "Well, I guess that's up to her."

They all turned toward the girl, who simply smiled and nodded.

Mrs. Campbell cocked her head to one side. "It's getting on dinnertime and the menfolk don't like to be kept waiting. Goodbye, Elizabeth." She then cast her gaze over James. "I guess we'll be seeing you again sometime this afternoon." With a farewell nod, she herded her family down the center aisle.

Grinning broadly, James watched the Campbell women sweep through the door.

Elizabeth nudged him in the ribs. "You look pleased with yourself."

He chuckled and grabbed her hand. "That went rather well, if I do say so. She's a wonderful girl."

"Yes, she is." Liz pursed her lips and emitted a grunt tinted with irony. "And quiet, too."

At her tone, James shot his sister a quizzical look. It was then he realized Mary Alice had yet to utter a single word to him.

***

Mary Alice glanced back over her shoulder as she climbed into the wagon. From the corner of her eye she saw Dr. Buchanan watching her from the church steps. He was certainly a handsome man with his dark hair and startlingly blue eyes. And he must be smart too. Salacoa School only went through eighth grade, meaning he had entered college with only an eighth-grade education. Memories of him as a boy played through her mind. He had been a jolly sort who enjoyed harmless jokes among his peers but was always kind to younger children.

Mr. Thompson, the schoolteacher, was a nice man and he would give her a peaceful, respectable life, but she couldn't say she was passionately in love with him. Mama and Papa liked him a lot and urged her to accept his proposal before he changed his mind. Perhaps they were right, but didn't passion mean something in a marriage? Shouldn't the couple feel an attraction to one another? She sighed quietly. It was so hard to know what was best. It might be easier if the decision didn't determine how she would spend the rest of her life.

Mary Alice settled herself on the seat between her youngest brothers to keep them from pushing and shoving one another. Papa flicked the reins and the horse pulled them forward toward the road home.

With a final glance sneaked from beneath her lashes, Mary Alice searched for James. Yes, there he was on the steps still watching as they left the church yard. Maybe his visit this afternoon would help her understand her own mind and sort out her heart.

CHAPTER 3

The afternoon settled in like all those of previous Augusts . . . hot, humid, and still. James tied his horse's reins to the post by the Campbell's front gate and walked through the opening in the picket fence. He looked around for a moment, taking in the changes to the old pine-log homestead that had occurred in his absence. At some point, clapboard had been added to the exterior walls. It had been up long enough to turn a weathered, silvery gray.

The daily accumulation of debris blown in by a breeze or dropped by free roaming hens had been recently removed from the dirt yard. The switch marks from today's sweeping with the besom were still fresh. Hopefully, this was a sign that James was welcome. He had not personally spoken with Archibald Campbell since returning to the valley. There was no telling how Mary Alice's father would look on his coming to call.

Mr. Campbell had been captured at Vicksburg along with many of his Confederate unit and the difficult years of imprisonment in Camp Douglas on Chicago's south side had left him with an abiding hatred of all things Republican. With luck, Mr. Campbell would set politics aside and overlook James's devotion to the Republican Party, which grew from his own family's Union sympathies during the war.

Hat in hand, James mounted the steps and knocked on the open door. Archibald, or Bud as his friends and family called him, answered.

James extended his hand with what he hoped was a winning smile. "Mr. Campbell, I hope y'all are having a good afternoon. I've come to call on Miss Mary Alice, if you'll permit it."

Bud Campbell ignored James's hand and paused in the doorway, looking James up and down like he might be seeing something he didn't want on his porch. He finally extended his hand and responded, "Mary Alice don't seem to have no objections even though you're a Republican. I heared you made a medical man."

"Yes, sir. I hope to be of service to the community for a long time." James's words sounded stiff in his own ears, and he wondered if his smile looked as tight as it felt.

Bud didn't respond, leaving James grinning and feeling as though he must look a fool.

When Bud finally spoke, his tone still lacked the warmth of welcome. "Well, I guess I'd better fetch Mary Alice since it ain't me you come to see." With a frown, Bud entered the house, leaving James waiting by the door.

"Good afternoon, Dr. Buchanan." Mary Alice appeared quietly, wearing a dark flowing skirt and white blouse. Her uncovered hair was pinned up in a tyle ending in a knot on top of her head. A few shiny chestnut tendrils had escaped and curled around her face, giving her a rather angelic appearance. She looked fresh and pretty despite the heat.

Smiling demurely, she continued. "Won't you sit here on the porch? Can I offer you a glass of iced tea? The ice man came just yesterday."

James seated himself in one of two bent willow porch rockers as Mary Alice disappeared into the front room's dark interior.

This house and its outlying area brought bittersweet memories of his childhood home. Watching his parents' farm being sold had been painful, but James's portion of the proceeds had been a godsend for it solved his financial woes. But his initial relief had evolved into guilt at profiting from their tragedy and a sense of increased obligation. He left for Salacoa on graduation day feeling an urgency to establish his practice that he had not observed in his classmates.

James glanced around the Campbell yard while he rocked and waited. Cicadas sawed away in full chorus from the trunks of the old oaks surrounding the house. Largish clumps of tall tiger lilies stood on either side of the front steps, their orange heads nodding in a welcome breeze floating in from distant thunderheads gathering in the west. At a corner of the porch, a climbing rose spread its pink petals and sweet scent. There might be a pleasanter place to while away a Sunday afternoon, but James couldn't think of one.

Mary Alice appeared once more, tray in hand. It was crowded with a plump pitcher of dark amber sweet tea, two tall glasses filled with chipped ice, and a plate piled with fresh teacakes. James jumped to his feet and relieved Mary Alice of her burden, setting it on the table between the two strategically placed porch rockers.

They chatted for a while about mutual acquaintances and then lapsed into silence as they sipped and rocked. Instead of being awkward, the silence was both easy and companionable. The light breeze lifted the curls around Mary Alice's face and made the thin white lawn fabric of her leg-o-mutton sleeves flutter. She looked as fresh and lovely as a spring morning, despite the August heat. Her quiet gentle confidence made her company a comfortable pleasure. James had not felt this at peace in years. This girl was not only lovely to look at, but also seemed to have a restorative effect on the spirit. He gazed at her for an improperly long moment and concluded it would be a fortunate man who captured her heart. Without conscious thought or hesitation, James suddenly realized he was determined to be that man.

He needed movement after sitting for so long and very much wanted to be alone with her. "Miss Mary Alice, I believe there's a path running from here down to the creek and is a right pretty walk." James hesitated because what he was about to ask was not totally appropriate since they had spent so little time together under the supervision of parental chaperones. "Could I ask you to take a turn with me?"

Mary Alice studied James and then called, "Papa, could you come out here to the porch, please?" Mr. Campbell must have been very close at hand for he appeared almost instantly.

"Papa, Dr. Buchanan would like to take a walk by the creek. I hope you won't mind." She smiled up at her father with the confidence of a beloved child.

Bud once again cast an evaluative gaze on James, fixing him with a baleful glare before coming straight to the point. "Young man, Mary Alice is my eldest child and the treasure of my heart. I won't hold with dalliance. And you might as well know I don't like your family's politics any more now than I did back in '60. It'll go real hard if you toy with her affections, and I ain't the kind who forgives easy."

James didn't know what he had expected, but threats from Mary Alice's father hadn't been part of the scene he had envisioned. He hoped his voice sounded more confident than he felt. "Mr. Campbell, please believe I have only the most honorable intentions toward Miss Campbell. I would like your permission to walk out with her, if she's agreeable."

Mr. Campbell turned to his daughter. "Mary Alice, is this what you want?"

She nodded and smiled at James. "Dr. Buchanan would be welcome to call again." She seemed completely unperturbed, even indifferent to the little scene that was playing out.

Bud huffed a grunt from between his teeth. "Well then, I guess a short walk by the creek cain't come to no harm. Mind, you keep an eye on them clouds. I won't take kindly to my girl catching her death 'cause you kept her out in the rain." Mr. Campbell glared at James for another uncomfortably long moment before turning back though the door.

James and Mary Alice walked in silence through the yard and out the side gate. When they were finally out of earshot of the house, Mary Alice giggled. "Don't be put off by Papa. I think he likes you even though he's having trouble with your politics."

James gave her a rueful smile. "I'd hate to see what happens when he doesn't like your caller. May I offer you my arm?"

Mary Alice smiled up at him and placed her small hand in the crook of his elbow. As they walked, James was stunned by how truly perfect and tiny she was. The top of her head came only to his shoulder. He could put his hands, fingers and thumbs tip to tip, around her small waist, which was an unsuitably tempting thought.

They crossed the kitchen garden and walked into the shade of the hickories and poplars lining the sides of the clear rushing creek. The sound of the water as it splashed over rocks and flashed in the sunlight streaming through the trees created a soothing background for their conversation. A few minutes' stroll brought them to the baptismal pool. It was just a wide place in the creek where the preacher could stand waist deep and lower new converts backward into the water. When not in use for spiritual purposes, it served as a picnic site for families and as the swimming hole for the local boys. It was an altogether lovely place to stop and sit a spell.

As they watched the water swirling away into the western valley, an internal struggle gripped James. He very much wanted to declare his intentions, but feared his haste might offend her, so he settled on simply asking, "Miss Mary Alice, it would be a great pleasure and honor if you would allow me to walk you home from services this week."

Mary Alice paused for a moment before answering. "Dr. Buchanan, I would like nothing better, but I'm afraid I've already promised someone else to take me home after services."

A rush of disappointment darkened James's mood, but a glimmer of hope dawned when she looked up at him with regret clearly visible in her eyes.

Encouraged, James decided he would not let the moment pass. He took her hand in his and looked into her eyes. "Mary Alice, I hope you'll forgive my boldness, but I can't let this afternoon end without speaking my mind. I'm very taken with you. My intentions are of the most serious kind. Before you make a special promise to another man, I hope you'll consider what I've said. I know we haven't spent time together, but I know a pearl when I see one. And please call me James. You did when you were younger, and calling me Dr. Buchanan makes me feel old enough to be your father, which I'm not and—"

James's words skidded to a halt because he could think of nothing else sensible or appropriate to say. He had already violated all bounds of propriety by speaking his mind at the very beginning of a courtship.

Mary Alice was silent for so long James feared he had ruined himself with her by being too forthright, or worse, possibly frightened her.

He couldn't bear her silence any longer and was preparing to walk her home without any hope when she finally replied, "I'll gladly call you by your Christian name, and I will consider what you've asked." She stopped speaking as though lost in thought, finally placed her hand on his arm, and then looked directly into his eyes. James could have sworn lightning passed between them as Mary Alice continued, "I'm not promising, mind you, but I'll think about what you've asked."

This must be how a prisoner felt when receiving a reprieve from the hangman's noose. Mary Alice had not made anything like a firm commitment, but she had not refused him outright either.

***

Mary Alice's pulse quickened as they walked back to the house. James had not wasted any time in declaring himself. It sort of scared her and excited her at the same time. To be courted by two educated men, both with good futures, would be considered quite a coup by her mother's sisters. The spinster aunts held the family's social position in a death grip and made it their mission to protect it at all costs. Which man would they choose? Mary Alice's mouth lifted slightly with a private smile. It would be interesting to watch their reactions when they realized they would have no say in Mary Alice's choice. As to which man would gain her hand, she feared she would struggle with the answer. In this matter, would her head or her heart rule?

As a schoolteacher, Mr. Thompson offered a secure, calm life. With him, things would be predictable and sedate. His schedule would be dictated by the school calendar and the rolling seasons. She would never have any doubt as to his whereabouts or daily activities. In addition, he was capable and smart. There was already talk that he would one day have an elevated position, perhaps rising to superintendent of schools or something similar. He was offering the life her parents wanted for her.

With James, her life would be far less predictable. She knew this because her uncle was a doctor on the eastern side of the county. Her aunt never knew when her husband would be called away or how long he would be gone. She never knew when she put food on the table if her husband would be there to eat it. As a doctor's wife, life would be a never-ending clash of domestic needs versus the needs of patients.

It did not help James's cause that his family had supported the Union when Georgia seceded and joined the Confederacy. His father had said he had no intention of fighting for someone else's way of life or in being a traitor to his country, that mountain people had no reason to support the big plantation owners. Papa took the opposite view of loyalty to the state over the nation. In some ways, the War Between the States was not over and might not be until all the old soldiers were gone.

Mary Alice sighed. She had much to consider. All these jumbled up thoughts and emotions drew her attention away from the path, causing her to stumble over a tree root. When her grip on James's arm tightened, he looked down in some surprise then he grinned and patted her hand.

CHAPTER 4

October 1890

A blazing fire thawed James as he stretched tired muscles and relaxed for the first time in what seemed like weeks. The wind picked up to a howl and rain beat on the tin roof in earnest. It was good to finally be in for the night on this unseasonably cold evening. The long day calling on his growing list of patients had been made even longer by heavy rainfall, lightning, and thunder. Fording the creek had been difficult, causing his horse to take every excuse to shy and balk. James planned to turn in early tonight because he had been up most of the previous one tending an elderly stroke victim. He would call on his patient again in the morning, but until then, catching up on his sleep topped his agenda. As his thoughts drifted, they settled, as they usually did these days, on Miss Mary Alice Campbell. Her mother had invited him to supper the following evening. James relaxed at the thought of a home-cooked meal, which was almost as tempting as the idea of spending several hours in Mary Alice's company. His growing practice left little time to prepare meals, which was no great loss since he was a terrible cook.

His mind wandered to that Sunday afternoon by the creek last August when he had declared his intentions. He smiled as he considered the fruit it had borne. While Mary Alice still wasn't walking out with him exclusively, she was certainly seeing the schoolteacher less often. In fact, he strongly suspected she had recently refused several of the teacher's invitations in hope of one from James, and he had done his best not to disappoint her, even though his patients' needs sometimes got in the way. The spark of attraction that had ignited between them since his return to the valley was now a glowing, healthy flame. Life altogether seemed to be going his way. He tossed another log on the fire and settled back to go over patient notes in his journal.

James's head had begun to nod when a violent pounding rattled the front door, jerking him back from the edge of sleep. Someone was calling frantically for him to come quickly. He reluctantly rose to his feet and struggled to shake off his body's demand for rest. He fumbled with the knob and finally managed to fling the door open, finding a soaked and shivering Johnny Blalock standing on the porch.

Johnny didn't wait for James to speak. "You got to come quick. Part of the road done washed away down the bottom of the hill and a whole wagonload of folkses has been pitched off in the creek. Me and my boys helped them up to Charles Sinclair's house. Thay's one what's hurt real bad. I brung a extra horse already saddled."

James blinked several times to make his eyes focus while the chill night air jolted him fully awake. Between thinned lips, he muttered, "Of all the nights to be out on the road . . . Give me a minute to restock my medical packs and then we can be off."

Packs replenished, James tugged on his oilskin and followed Johnny to the waiting horses. They set off in a blowing rain that soon chilled to the bone. Rain poured from the brim of his hat and trickled down under the collar of his oilskin. James kicked his mount's flanks to force it forward. The horses' hooves made sucking sounds as they struggled through the deeply rutted mud pit the road had become, bogging to their hocks in several places and needing serious encouragement to move on.

The creek, which lay between them and the accident victims, was at flood stage when James and Johnny urged their reluctant mounts into the roiling water. It roared past the accident victim's overturned wagon, which looked as though it would be swept away at any minute. The horses shied and struggled to maintain their balance against the strong currents and to dodge swirling debris while crossing what would normally have been a gentle stream. As his horse slipped and slid its way onto the far bank, James could just make out the silhouette of the Sinclair house at the top of the rise. Lights blazed from the front windows.

Once they cleared the creek, James and Johnny turned up a single lane and made for the house. They pulled the horses to a stop by the front steps, slid from the saddles, and threw the reins to the eldest Sinclair boy who stood waiting with a lantern, bundled tightly against the weather. The horses were being led away to the barn as James ran up the front steps and was ushered into a scene of controlled chaos. In the front room, four young men in their late teens or early twenties, covered in mud and wet through, were stretched out on the floor near the fireplace. James made a quick visual assessment. Three boys groaned softly and shifted around trying to find more comfortable positions. Their injuries appeared painful, but not life threatening. They could wait. The fourth lay unconscious with a jagged gash running from his right ear to the hairline above his right temple. James's pulse quickened. Head injuries were dangerous and this one looked bad.

James's training took over, replacing the emotional response with calm professionalism. He called for a basin of hot water and soap. After scrubbing his hands and arms to the elbows, he gently ran his finger along the wound. A particularly sharp blow must have made the slight depression in the area under the upper hairline. Holding an oil lamp above the young man's head, he raised the right eyelid. The pupil was enlarged and fixed. James checked the other eye. It was responsive to light. With luck, the subdural bleeding was slight. James next ran his fingers along the neck and back as best he could without moving the boy. His neck and spine seemed to have survived the accident unharmed, but the prognosis was still uncertain.

James cleaned the wound and wrapped the boy's head, then turned to Mrs. Sinclair. "Sarah, I'm afraid there's no way we're going to be able to take this boy anywhere for a while. The ride over the roads the way they are right now would most likely kill him. He's got to be kept quiet until he has a chance to heal some and he needs to be off this cold floor. Do you have a bed we could move him to?"

Sarah nodded. "We'll put him in the east room where the boys sleep. They can bunk on pallets in our room until he's well enough to go home."

James smiled his thanks and then turned to her husband. "Charles, do you have a wide board about the place we could use as a stretcher? We need to be careful how we move him."

With his most seriously injured patient safely ensconced in the Sinclair boys' bedroom, James turned his attention to the scrapes, sprains, cracked ribs, and broken arm suffered by the other three.

As he worked, James observed his patients' general demeanor. Furtive was the best description he could come up with. Keeping his tone neutral, he said, "I don't believe we've met before tonight. May I ask who I'm treating and why you're traveling on a night like this?"

The one who appeared to be the eldest chose to be the spokesman. "We was going t'other side of the valley on business for our pa. Our name's Harbin. We live over on Pine Log Mountain."

James tried not to let his reaction show. He recognized the name. Everyone had heard of the Harbins. They were a fractious clan, and if the talk was true, they made and distributed corn liquor to half the county and cussed and fought with the other half. They were also rumored to be responsible for a recent barn fire at the home of a man with whom they had fallen out. The Harbins were not the type of people one wanted for enemies.

These boys must have been pursuing a very lucrative opportunity to be out in such weather.

Another boy raised up on an elbow. "You think our brother'll be good to travel in the morning?"

James eyed him for a moment. There was an odd note in the boy's voice, as though he asked more out of fear than concern for his brother's well-being. "I'm sure he won't be. His injury is serious. The next few days will give me some idea of how bad his condition is."

"Doc, we cain't lay around here waiting for Joe to get better. We gotta be going in the morning." A contemptuous smile curled the eldest boy's lips as his glare took in his brothers as well as James. "You'uns here on Salacoa may not have to see to work tomorrow, but we got to get home. Our pa's expecting us and we best not be late."

James's breathing increased while he considered how to explain Joe's condition. These boys would not want the truth, but he could not let them move their brother so soon. He ran a hand over his face to clear his sleep deprived mind before fixing them with a stern look and mustered as much authority as he was able. "Your brother cannot be moved tomorrow and maybe not for many days to come. His injury's such that he may not live even with the best care. If you move him in the morning or before I say it's safe, you'll kill him." James paused and stared directly into the eldest Harbin's eyes. "That boy will not be moved from this house. Do you understand?"

James maintained firm eye contact with the eldest until he finally nodded. James controlled his breathing so these strangers would not see his considerable relief. Entanglements of this kind had never been part of his plan for helping people when he began this journey all those years ago. It was unclear what he would have done if the eldest Harbin had refused to comply with his demands. He was beginning to wish their wagon had gone off the road in any place other than Salacoa.

CHAPTER 5

With his patients in the front room resigned to their plight and settled with quilts and pillows, James retreated to the room where Joe lay unmoving but breathing evenly. He placed two fingers against the boys' throat and checked his pulse. The rhythm beneath James's fingers was strong despite the recent trauma. He looked at Joe's eyes again and found the left pupil still responding to light which gave him hope that any bleeding might have slowed, or with great luck, had stopped. The right side of the face was swollen with the first signs of bruising and a lump was rising under the hairline. The boy would have quite a shiner and a permanent scar, but only time would tell his fate.

Sunlight streaming through the window jerked James awake. He had spent the night alternating between dozing sitting upright and monitoring his patient's progress. Joe hadn't shown any signs of significant improvement, but he hadn't gotten any worse, which was as much as could be expected at this point.

One of the Sinclair children stuck a towhead through the door and announced that breakfast would be in five minutes. James checked Joe's vital signs once more and then went over to the washstand. After pouring cold water from the pitcher into the bowl, he splashed his face several times to clear his mind. Flinging the towel back onto the crossbar above the bowl, he turned and headed for the long central hallway that ran from the front door all the way to the back porch.

He paused in the bedroom doorway at the sight of a large, framed photograph hanging on the opposite wall. A wistful smile lifted the corners of his mouth at the sight of his former benefactor, the late Mr. Sinclair. He nodded at the picture as though the old man was present instead of being a mere photograph. Mr. Sinclair had made a good choice in leaving his farm to his great-nephew, Charles. The young family was settling in to the valley well, for which James said a silent thank you to the photograph. Feeling a little foolish at such fanciful notions, he ambled toward the kitchen, beckoned by the fragrance of strong coffee and frying sausage. Halfway to the kitchen, Charles appeared, anxiety marring his normally sunny features.

He placed a hand on James's arm and spoke quietly so they would not be overheard. "Them Harbin boys are already grumbling about wanting to be gone. Do you think we can take them three in the front room home today? I'd feel a lot better with them out of the house, what with Sarah and the childern and all. You cain't believe the stories I've heard."

A sardonic smile lifted one corner of James's mouth. "I've heard the same stories. If the roads are passable, there's no reason they can't go home. Do you think Johnny would go with you? I've got to call on several patients this morning. And, I really don't think I should leave this boy for as long as it's going to take y'all to get to Pine Log Mountain and back."

Charles looked more than a little relieved. "I'm sure Johnny'll go. He's fixing their broke wheel right now. We'll get started soon's he's finished." Cocking his head at the sounds from the kitchen, Charles continued, "Sounds like they're setting the table. Breakfast must be ready. You hungry?"

Instead of answering, James hesitated. His lips twitched with what he wanted to ask, but the words would not form.

Charles frowned. "Is there something else?"

James swallowed hard. "I need a favor."

"Okay. All you need to do is ask."

"Well, you see . . ." Sudden shyness dried James's throat.

Charles's eyes narrowed. "I cain't see if you don't say. I'm hungry. Spit it out."

"Could you stop by the Campbell place and let Mrs. Campbell know I won't be able to come to supper? And please tell her the reason. I don't want her to think I'm rude."

A knowing grin spread across Charles's face. "Sure. I'll be happy to let Miss Mary Alice know why you cain't come to call."

James returned the smile. "Thanks. It means a lot."

Joe remained unconscious for two more days. On the third afternoon, his eyelashes fluttered and he slowly opened his eyes.

James gave him a moment to adjust to the unfamiliar surroundings. "Do you remember the accident? You suffered a pretty bad blow to the head when you were thrown into the creek."

Joe stared at James and then spoke through clenched teeth. "Who're you and where the hell am I?"

Clearly, Joe was on the mend. His pupils were equal in size, but his eyes flashed with distrust. So much for gratitude. James adopted a professional manner. "I'm a doctor and I've been treating you since your wagon went into the creek three nights ago. You're at Charles Sinclair's house. The Sinclairs have been kind enough to lend us their boys' bedroom."

"Where're my brothers?" Joe responded with even less graciousness than before.

"They weren't hurt as bad as you are, so Mr. Sinclair and Johnny Blalock took them home two days ago. Johnny repaired your wagon as well." James fixed Joe with a stern expression to communicate his distaste for the young man's surliness.

Joe was silent for a moment and then something in his eyes changed. It looked like relief passing across the boy's face once it registered that the rest of his family had been removed from the house.

Joe's expression softened. "Thanks, Doc, for taking care of me. And I want to thank the Sinclairs and Mr. Blalock too. When do you think I can go home? My pa's gonna be awful mad if'n I ain't there to help with the work."

James cocked his head in surprise at the depth of Joe's concern for returning to work. He looked him over carefully. "I think your pa will be happy to know you are alive and getting better. I don't think you need to worry about working just yet."

Joe attempted a smile but his features twisted into a bitter grimace instead. "You ain't never met my pa, have you? He's a hard man. I gotta get home today. I cain't be laying out of work no longer."

At that moment, James realized what he had thought was pure inbred meanness in Joe was actually fear. When the time came, he would be the one to return this boy to the bosom of his loving family. Joe would not be fit for work for some time to come. That fact must be impressed upon Pa Harbin.

A week passed before Joe showed sufficient recovery to safely take him home. As Johnny and James were loading the boy into the wagon, Charles placed a hand on James's arm and looked at him with deep concern. "You was away from the valley for too long. You don't know what you're dealing with in them Harbins. I'm sending Johnny with you and thay's a rifle under the seat, just in case."

James paused long enough to see that Charles was serious. "I appreciate your caution and the rifle, but I doubt it will come to needing it. Common sense should tell Mr. Harbin a disabled worker won't do him much good."

Charles's forehead creased. "For most men, I'd say you're right, but Joss Harbin is a different sort. Y'all just take care with him."

James climbed up beside Johnny and shook Charles's hand, then waved farewell to Sarah and the children as they came to the door.

The trip to the Harbin home on Pine Log Mountain would be a long one. The roads were in fair condition after a week of sun and dry wind, but Joe's condition was still serious and they would have to take care to go slowly and avoid as many potholes as possible. James had secured the boy's head and spine by laying him once more on the pine plank and wrapping sheets tightly around him. He took a final precaution in tying cloth strips firmly around Joe's head to stabilize it and prevent movement. It was not totally secure, but it was the best he could do.

They had been under way for about twenty minutes when the Campbell house came into view at the top of the next rise. James could see Mary Alice's youngest siblings playing in the yard. A little brother, spying James, ran to the house and called through the door. James turned to watch for a glimpse of Mary Alice. He threw up his hand when she came to the door, where she stood looking after him with a puzzled expression and then finally waved in return. He just had to see her on the return trip. He couldn't bear the thought that she might interpret his not stopping as indifference. It didn't make his mind any easier when, within a few minutes, they passed the schoolteacher headed at a considerable clip in the opposite direction toward the Campbell place.

***

Mary Alice rushed to the porch and watched the Sinclair's wagon roll by with James on the seat beside Johnny Blalock. A lump rose in her throat. It would only have taken a few minutes for him to stop and apologize in person for missing supper with her family. He couldn't avoid missing the supper. She knew that, but why couldn't he stop for a minute now? Her fists balled at her sides. Perhaps he was not as serious about their courtship as he had led her to believe.

A buggy appeared around the bend in the road. It moved at a considerable pace. Mary Alice placed her hand over her eyes to shield them from the sun. It looked like Silas Thompson coming to call. There was no way James did not see him. It would serve James right if this caused him some anxiety.

CHAPTER 6

The Harbin house proved to be nothing more than a one-room log shack with a few shed rooms attached. The yard was piled with what appeared to be years of trash and the outbuildings looked as though they were about to cave in on themselves. Whatever work the Harbin men did, it clearly had nothing to do with property upkeep.

As the wagon came to a halt beside the front steps, a woman who looked like she could be anywhere between forty and sixty appeared at the door. Her greasy salt-and-pepper hair was pulled back in a bun so tight that it gave her eyes an unnatural appearance. Her dress looked to have been pieced together from flour sacking and had clearly been patched many times over. Her tattered apron was spotted with what looked like the remains of several months' meals.

She pulled her thin shawl tighter around her shoulders and squinted anxiously at them, calling out with suspicion, "What you'uns want here?" Her snarl revealed several missing teeth. "That you, Johnny Blalock? I can make you out. No need in trying to hide yourself."

Johnny grinned as they climbed down from the wagon. "I ain't trying to hide, Azaleigh. Couldn't no ways 'cause nothing gets by any of you Harbins."

The woman's manner was odd, even for such as the Harbins were reported to be. When they were beside her on the porch, James saw that she strained to see their faces even when they were quite close. The poor woman was nearly blind. He saw no signs of cataracts, so the problem was probably glaucoma, for it was rampant in these mountains and there was no treatment.

Pity washed through James as he extended his hand. "Miz Harbin, I'm Dr. James Buchanan. I've been tending Joe at the Sinclair's since the accident. Mr. Blalock and I have brought him home to you. I'd like to speak with you and his father about the care he's going to need. Where should we take him? He needs to be kept quiet, still, and warm."

Though she ignored the offered hand, Mrs. Harbin's expression softened immediately. "You can put him on that there bedstead by the fireplace." She pointed to the far corner of the main room that served as sitting room, master bedroom, kitchen, and dining room.

As Mrs. Harbin turned to tuck an extra quilt around Joe, James noticed large purple bruises on her legs and that she moved rather stiffly. It was clear what Joe meant about his father being a hard man. Wife and child beating were considered a private matter and therefore were a blight on the social fabric of too many communities.

Without warning, the back door flew open and what could only be Joss Harbin entered the room. He was a tall, burly man with stringy ginger colored hair and a shaggy beard. Smoke-colored grime darkened his face and his mouth wore an unpleasant sneer. He didn't appear to be a regular bather for a mixture of wood smoke and body odor drifted from him.

He looked directly at James, ignoring Johnny completely, and growled, "Who're you and what the hell do you want here?"

This was apparently the standard Harbin greeting when callers appeared unexpectedly at their door. James extended his hand and again had it ignored. "I'm Dr. Buchanan and I believe you already know Mr. Blalock. We've brought your son home. Is there somewhere we can discuss his care? He's not fit to be moved again for some time. His injury is very serious, and it's a miracle he's doing well enough for us to move him at all."

Joss Harbin glared around the room until his narrowed eyes, full of suspicion, lit on Johnny. James watched from the corner of his eye as Johnny backed away quietly and slipped down the steps, coming to a stop beside the wagon. He stretched and casually rested his arm along the wagon's side, alternately shifting his gaze from the activity in the house to the rifle stored beneath the seat. He met Joss's glare with an unsmiling nod and without showing any sign of being intimidated. Joss watched for a moment more and then returned his attention to James. "Right here's as good a place as any to talk. What's he gonna need and how quick can he get back to work?"

Harbin's hardness and apparent lack of concern for his son's welfare were hardly surprising at this point, but they galled, nonetheless. James's lips thinned with the effort to hold onto his temper. His body tensed as he leaned forward ever so slightly. "Understand this. If you value your son's life, you will follow my instructions. Joe cannot be moved nor can he leave the bed until he has had time to recover from an injury that could have easily killed him. He won't be fit for work for a while longer. Is this clear?"

Joss scowled as he struggled with what must have been a battle between his overweening pride and his need for a fully useful labor force. "All right. You tell Ma here what needs doing and I'll see to it she gets it done." Mrs. Harbin seemed to cower more with each word he said. When he raised his hand like he might strike her, she shrank back. "Ma, you listen careful, now. You know how damned stupid you are." Just as suddenly as it had started, the unpleasant interview ended and Joss slammed out of the house again.

James busied himself unpacking a few medical supplies while quietly observing Mrs. Harbin. She twisted the corner of her apron with hands that seemed unable to be still. Her chest rose and fell with ragged, halting gasps. Even with her husband out of sight, the poor woman's eyes held nothing but fear. Joss Harbin was clearly an ignorant, vulgar brute who terrorized his family as much as he did his neighbors.

As James gave instructions, Mrs. Harbin trembled and continued to twist her apron until it was a balled up mess. He rolled his lower lip inward in thought. Given her emotional state, it was unclear whether she would absorb what he said. "Would it be easier for you if I wrote everything down? It will only take a minute."

She squinted up at him and shook her head. "Won't do no good. I cain't see good enough to read." She seemed to give herself a mental shake and squared her shoulders. "You just tell me what to do. I promise I'll do whatever my boy needs."

James's throat tightened. He smiled softly. "I'm sure you will. I can see you're a wonderful mother."

Pink coloring rose on the woman's cheeks. "I done my best. Warn't good enough, I'm afeared, but it was all I could do." She cast a loving look toward the bedstead by the fireplace. "He's the best of the lot. He'll make me proud someday."

James looked at Joe sleeping peacefully and nodded. "I'm sure he will." He was in no way sure Joe Harbin would ever amount to more than his father and brothers, but there was no need to inflict more pain on this poor woman. She had already suffered enough.

He and Johnny left for home only after Mrs. Harbin had repeated the instructions back to James several times and he was sure she understood completely. As the wagon turned away from the Harbin place, James's body finally relaxed. He rolled his head and flexed his shoulders. "After meeting Joss Harbin, I'll sleep better knowing several miles separate Salacoa from Pine Log. He's a brute. I felt humbled by Miz Harbin's excessive gratitude when I assured her I would call again tomorrow. I just hope I won't find a new patient when I return."

Johnny gave him a sidelong glance and grinned. "You got plenty of 'em. What difference could one more make?"

James curled his lips and waggled his brows. "None, I guess." A serious expression replaced the humor. "Did you see those bruises on her? I'd say they were fresh and made by a belt."

Johnny nodded. "Or a strop. If thay's a sorrier bastard than Joss Harbin, I don't know him, pardon my French."

James whistled softly, then fell silent for most of the trip. Thoughts of Mary Alice had him practicing what he would say to her. She was a reasonable girl, but even the most sensible females could get grumpy when they thought they were second best. Would Mary Alice understand that a doctor had no choice in putting his patients first?

When Johnny stopped the wagon alongside the Campbell's front gate, James jumped down and dashed up the front steps. He knocked and then turned back with a salute as Johnny pulled away. Across the road, the sun was dropping quickly behind Salacoa Ridge, reminding him how long this day had been. Mr. and Mrs. Campbell and the children were probably sitting down to supper just about now. This was an inappropriate time for an unannounced call, but he couldn't go another day without seeing Mary Alice.

Her eldest brother Randolph answered his knock and shouted in a teasing, singsong fashion in the direction of the kitchen at the back of the house, "Mary Alllll-ice! Dr. Buchaaaanan's here to see you!"

Mary Alice and her mother, followed by the younger Campbells, appeared in the front room. With a glance at her daughter, Mrs. Campbell asked James to sit down and then shooed the children into the kitchen, leaving the young couple alone in the front room.

Mary Alice led James to the settee, and when they were settled side by side. He took her hand, looking into her lovely eyes. "Mary Alice, I hope you got the message I sent by Charles. I'm so sorry I couldn't be here the other evening. Was your mother sorely put out?"

She smiled gently. "Charles took special care to make sure we understood you had no choice because of the accident. How are the Harbin boys?"

James gave a brief account of his patients' progress before lapsing into silence. He was suddenly exhausted and his mind refused to function clearly. He was about to excuse himself and start the walk home when Mary Alice straightened up and turned to him with a serious expression.

"I need to tell you something." She paused as if searching for the right words. A sliver of dread pierced James's exhaustion. Mary Alice cleared her throat and drew a deep breath. "Silas . . . Mr. Thompson . . . has taken a new teaching assignment over at Tate and has asked for my answer to his proposal. I've told him I would give him one by the end of the week. He leaves on Friday for the new school." She paused and shifted her position. "Before I give him my answer, I need to know if there is any reason I should decline his proposal." With that, she fell silent and looked directly up into his eyes.

If James had been befuddled by fatigue just a moment before, his attention was now completely riveted on Mary Alice. This was not how he had envisioned it, but this could well be his only opportunity. He seized the moment. "There's every reason for you to decline. I've been looking for the right time to speak to you. If it hadn't been for the Harbin boys' accident, I would have asked you this the night I was to have had supper with you and your family. I can't promise you that life with me will never again be interrupted by my patients' needs, but I can promise to love you with all my heart and to care and provide for you and our children. If you'll have me, I'll make sure you never regret your choice. Will you do me the honor of becoming my wife?"

Mary Alice looked up at James as though the sun was rising in her face and giggled. "I probably should tell you I'll think about it and make you wait, but what real purpose would it serve? Yes, a hundred times, yes."

James took her in his arms and kissed her tenderly at first and then passionately. This was the first time he had kissed her, but it would not be the last for Mary Alice answered his intensity with that of her own. He would speak to her father before he left tonight. Please Lord, let Mr. Campbell overlook the past differences between their families. If he didn't, they would elope. He was going to marry this girl, come hell or high water. He would never be happy without her.

CHAPTER 7

"Mary Alice, I want to speak to your father tonight. He may need some time to accept the idea of our getting married. Do you think he is finished with his supper?"

For Mary Alice's father, the difficult war years had left deep scars, some visible, but others hidden from view until an unwelcome event caused them to resurface. Bud Campbell rarely talked about his years as a prisoner of war at Camp Douglas on Chicago's south side. James had heard how the horrific conditions there were on a par with the infamous Andersonville camp where Union boys had suffered starvation and disease in a stockade open to the elements, dying by the thousands. Bud probably didn't talk about the war because he had made a concerted effort to put it behind him. His own father, informed by Mr. Sinclair, had told James how Bud had been very ill with dysentery for some time after he arrived home and looked for a while as though he might not survive. There was no telling how Mr. Campbell would greet the news of his proposal to Mary Alice. Hopefully, the different paths their families had taken over secession would not be thrown up as a roadblock.

Mary Alice looked up at James with an impish grin. "I know Papa can seem standoffish sometimes, but please don't mind him. It's just his way. I'm going to see if he'll come out here."

She went serenely through the kitchen door. After what felt like an eternity, Mr. Campbell accompanied her to the front room. Mary Alice smiled up at her father. "Papa, I'm just going to leave you and James to talk while I help Mama with the cleaning up."

Bud nodded to James and then gave him a stern inquiring look as Mary Alice disappeared again through the kitchen door. Since Mr. Campbell seemed determined not to be the first to speak, James plucked up his courage and launched into a speech designed to make himself appear an acceptable prospective son-in-law.

"Mr. Campbell, I think you're probably aware that my medical practice is growing and that I'm regular at Sunday meeting. I may not have as much as some, but I have enough to be able to care for a wife and children. I don't have any debts and I manage my money so I've got a little put by. I'll be able to buy a house for us with a little land around it. I don't drink, smoke, chew, or cuss. I—"

Bud cut James off with a slicing gesture. "Just get to the point, boy. I've knowed you since before you was borned. What is it you want?"

"I want to ask your permission for Mary Alice's hand in marriage. I love her and want her to be my wife."

Bud looked as though James's request came as no surprise. He paused thoughtfully and then said, "Like I told you the first time you come to the house, Mary Alice is my heart's treasure, but it looks like she's set on having you. It's hard for a man to part with his child lest he knows the man taking her is going to love her more than he loves hisself. That man would have to know he'd answer to me if'n he made her unhappy. And you might as well know I don't like your politics any more now than I ever done.

This is my child you're asking for. Harm her and you'll answer to me."

James chose his next words carefully, trying to walk the fine line between appearing a suitable husband for Mary Alice and maintaining the firmness of his convictions. "I'm not sure what I can do to convince you other than give my word that I love Mary Alice more than life itself. I could no more harm her than I could cut off my own arm. As to my politics, my family has always believed people should be free and I haven't changed my mind. Trying to dissolve the Union was a mistake and I think the outcome showed us that." James shut his mouth firmly before he totally alienated Mr. Campbell, but his gaze remained locked with the older man's.

Mr. Campbell's glare faded into resignation. After looking James up and down several times, he finally said, "Well, it don't look like it's up to me anyhows. My girl's made up her mind to have you and there's nothing else for it." His expression hardened. "But you get this straight. Don't you ever talk to me about the war again. It didn't have nothing to do with who was free or not. It was about southern states not being told what to do. I didn't own no slaves, but I was darned if I was gonna be told how to live by damned Yankees." Bud looked as if he were working up a real anger, but he suddenly stopped speaking and shook his head. "Oh hell, war's over. Cain't be changed noways. Just don't talk your politics around me. Can you live with that?"

"Yes, sir. There's nothing you've said that I can't live with. And I'll do everything in my power to do and to be what Mary Alice deserves to give her a good life."

"Well then, I reckon her mama and me cain't object." Bud turned toward the kitchen. "Guess we'd better call the womenfolk. Don't imagine they can stand waiting much longer."

Bud strolled across the room and opened the kitchen door, through which Mrs. Campbell nearly fell until she steadied herself by grabbing the doorframe. Mary Alice, who also must have had her ear glued to the door, came straight in on her mother's heels, bustling into the room while trying to close the door before her younger siblings could come tumbling behind her. Mother and daughter righted themselves and looked expectantly at the men. James fought back a grin. This was not altogether their most dignified moment.

Bud raised an eyebrow toward the ladies. "Well, Nancy, I guess you better start planning a wedding."

During the walk to his rented house, James found his fatigue seemed to have miraculously disappeared, and he whistled and laughed to himself over his good fortune. He would pay a call on his sister Lizzie before he went to check the Harbin boys in the morning. She would be very hurt if she heard the news from someone else and news traveled quickly in this tightly knit community. He thought she would probably offer to help with the wedding plans as well. James guessed a man might be more contented with his life, but he couldn't think how.

Elizabeth's joy matched his own when he shared the news the following morning. It pleased him immensely because her approval meant the world to him. He whistled a happy tune when he rode from her house headed for Pine Log Mountain and the Harbin place. As he traveled the twisting mountain road to the accompaniment of the creek's splashing laughter, the brilliant day warmed his face and filled his lungs with the sweet crisp air that had arrived with a cold front blown in on the recent thunderstorms.

Fall's vivid pallet had transformed the mountains into a multihued patchwork quilt. From the hickories' lustrous gold to the sweetgums' brilliant reds and rich burgundies, the forests were at the peak of their glory. Distant honking high overhead signaled the return of Canada geese heading for a nearby pond where they had been stopping for a respite every year for as long as anyone could remember. James's mind wandered to pleasant memories of family feasts founded on the game bagged during the fall hunts he and his father had enjoyed so much. Hunting had provided a time for the only men in the household of seven women to get away for a purely male pursuit. Hopefully, the day's beauty would not be spoiled by what he would find at the Harbin farm.

***

Mary Alice finished drying the last of the breakfast dishes then refilled her father's cup. Papa spooned sugar and poured milk into the brew then gave it a vigorous stir.

After taking a sip, he took her hand. "Sit with me for a little. I got things that need saying."

Mary Alice's heart turned over and her pulse increased. Papa was very capable of having changed his mind about permission for her marriage. She sat as asked but did not wait for him to speak. "Papa, I'm going to marry James, so don't tell me you've changed your mind. If I don't have your permission, we'll elope. I mean it."

Papa held up a hand. "Now, hold on, Missy. Thay's no need to get all huffy. Me and your ma has knowed he was your first choice for a long time now. I just want to make sure you know what you're getting yerself into."

"What do you mean, Papa?"

"I know what he says—that he'll provide for you and your childern. I believe him, but what I worry 'bout is if you understand that no matter what he says, them sick folks will always come afore you and the childern? It don't mean he don't love you, but it's the promise he tooken when he got to be a doctor. Are you ready for such?"

Mary Alice dropped her gaze and studied her hands for a moment. Was she ready to be second to his patients? She could hardly see it happening, but James *was* very dedicated. How to answer?

She blinked a couple of times then met her father's eyes. "I'm sure Mama's sister would say that she understands sick people must get cared for. I know she doesn't feel second best to her husband's patients, and I won't either."

CHAPTER 8

There were no signs of life when James turned up the steep track leading to the Harbin house. The yard was unnaturally quiet as he dismounted and tied his horse's reins to the porch rail. No chickens squawked or ran at his arrival nor did the dogs appear to warn off the intruder. James walked up the steps in some uneasiness and knocked gently. When no sounds emanated from the ramshackle cabin, he knocked harder and waited with growing concern. Finally, he gave the old wide plank door a push and it swung open onto a dismaying scene. The grime on the few small windows showed that Mrs. Harbin had never been the tidiest of housekeepers, but this was utter chaos. Furniture was overturned. Cooking pots and implements were scattered about the floor. Firewood had been knocked from its corner. The door to the back porch stood ajar. As he waited for his eyes to adjust to the semidarkness, concern for his patient grew. He had left Joe just yesterday safely ensconced in the bedstead by the fireplace. James finally made out what he sought huddled in the corner of the bed peering out at him with wild frightened eyes.

"Don't you come another step closer, Pa. I got me a log and I'll bash your skull in if'n you try to hit me again," Joe shouted as

James, backlit by the daylight pouring through the door, approached the disheveled bed.

"Joe, there's nothing to be afraid of. It's Dr. Buchanan. I've come to check on you just like I promised your mother I would. Put the log down. I'm not going to hurt you." James waited until he saw Joe throw the log to the floor before he went any closer. "Tell me what's happened here. Where's your mother?"

Joe stared into the light and sighed with relief. "Guess I must've been sort of out of it." Joe rubbed his eyes. "Pa, he ain't come in home last night and when he come in this morning, he was dead drunk. He said Ma shoulda done had his breakfirst ready and begun whipping her with his belt buckle. Ma run around trying to get away from him, but he just kept at it. He managed to hit just about everything in the room while he was swinging at her. She throwed her kitchen stuff at him to keep him off'n her, but it didn't do no good. He just kept coming. She finally got to the door and run out into the woods, I guess. Then he started in on me about not getting up to work. I picked up a log and chunked it at him and hit him in the head. He took off then and I ain't seen neither of them since."

James went to the front door and lifted the heavy hand-hewn wooden bar that was used for security against intruders. He placed it in the U-shaped brackets attached to the doorframe's sides. As he turned to speak to Joe again, a small form huddled in a dark corner behind a chifforobe caught his eye. It seemed to be shivering and looked out at him with large doe eyes.

Joe followed James's gaze. "Pearl, come out'n there. Quit your hiding. Thay's nothing to be afeared of now. This here's Doc Buchanan. The one what I tolt you about. Come on out here and say hello." Joe beckoned to the child.

Slowly, a little girl of about five years emerged from the shadows. She was small for her age, but perfectly formed in every other way. She had deep blue eyes, a pert little nose, rosebud lips, and a head full of golden curls. Under the smudges of dirt, her face was lovely. She would one day be a real beauty. That Azaleigh and Joss Harbin had managed to produce this little angel came as a shock. Sometimes a magnificent outlier appeared in the least likely of places. The child crept forward and then raced into Joe's outstretched arms.

"It's okay, little Pearlie. He ain't gonna hurt you. He's done come to help us. Now take that thumb out'n your mouth and mind your manners. Say how do."

"Hey," she said with a slight baby lisp and a shy smile.

James bent down to her level and extended his big hand in a simple calming gesture. When he spoke, it was in the gentlest of tones. "Hello, Pearl. It's very nice to meet you. Joe and I are friends and I hope you will be my friend too." Pearl thought about this for a moment and then nodded.

"I want you both to stay here while I go and look for your mother. If your father comes back, do you think you'll be able to bar the back door?"

Joe and Pearl both nodded before Joe added, "Doc, you be careful. My pa, he's a mean drunk. He'd just as soon kill you as look at you."

James went through the back door hoping he would not encounter Joss Harbin before finding Mrs. Harbin. He looked up into the woods for signs of movement and saw a thin smoke trail rising high on the ridge behind the cabin. Joss and the other boys must be at work on their chief source of income, corn liquor. Were the other Harbin brothers as in awe of their father's temper as Joe? The eldest had been very insistent about getting home the day after the accident, so they probably were.

James stood in the yard thinking about how best to go about finding Mrs. Harbin without drawing her husband's attention when she slowly emerged from the woods. She crept toward him dragging her left leg and cradling her left side with her arms. Blood streamed from her nose, which looked like it was probably broken. When her failing eyesight finally revealed a male form standing in the yard, she turned to try for escape. James rushed to her while softly calling her name and identifying himself. He reached her side as she stumbled and fell.

She raised her arms in a feeble attempt to ward off any renewed assault and began to whimper. "Joss, I ain't got no eggs nor side meat. You done ett it all two days ago. I'll fix you something quick. Just don't hit me again!"

James knelt beside her and whispered, "Miz Harbin, it's Dr. Buchanan and I want you to come with me to the house now. I'm going to check Joe like I promised and I want to see to your injuries."

Azaleigh's eyes softened with recognition. "I'll be all right directly. You just take care of my baby boy. He's the onlyest one what ain't sorry and good-for-nothing. I'll be just fine in a day or two."

James put his arm around her waist after lifting her from the ground and heard her sharp intake of breath. He dropped his arm and asked her to lean on his shoulder as he helped her into the house. After he barred the back door, James turned to inspect Joe's head wound. Despite his recent experience, he seemed none the worse and was, in fact, mending better than expected. Joe was clearly a strong young man in general good health. His mother, however, was another story.

"Miz Harbin, you need medical treatment. I'm going to get the bleeding from your nose stopped first and then I want to check your ribs and leg. I think you better remove your blouse when we get to the ribs. I want to know for sure how much damage has been done." The look of shock on Azaleigh's face made James add, "Joe will be here the whole time."

Azaleigh's eyes grew wide. "You cain't look at me like that. It ain't proper."

James shook his head. She had probably never received medical care, much less from a man whom she barely knew. "You mustn't worry. When I was in medical school, we were trained to see our patients as just that and nothing more. I promise you, it's perfectly proper for a trained medical man to treat a woman who needs help."

Reluctantly, Azaleigh allowed James to treat the injuries her husband had inflicted. Joss had broken her nose and cracked two ribs with the belt buckle. She had twisted her ankle while tripping on the overturned kitchen table trying to dodge Joss's blows. While checking her, James found evidence of previous untreated injuries. Apparently, abuse was the basis for the Harbins' relationship.

James had finished wrapping Azaleigh's ribs and was repacking his medical bag when he suddenly turned to her. "Do you have anywhere you can go to get away from your husband? I know this isn't the first time he's done this. I could tell when I examined you."

Azaleigh looked as though she had been asked to submit to torture. "I . . . I cain't go nowheres! He done said he'd come after me and kill me if'n I was to ever leave. 'Sides, my folks done died many year ago. Ain't got no place to go to."

James thought for a moment, trying to conjure a haven for this unhappy family, but each solution that presented itself was rejected because it depended on others to take on a dangerous responsibility. No one with any sense wanted to cross a man like Joss Harbin. Injury and arson usually followed in the wake of his displeasure. The tragedy was that proving his culpability had so far been out of the law's reach.

Finally, finding no alternative, James turned and looked at Joe. "If y'all ever need a refuge from him, come to my house. He won't bother you there. In the meantime, Miz Harbin, stay off that foot and keep it up as much as possible. Don't take the bandage off your nose until I return at the end of the week and keep your chest wrapped tight to keep those ribs in place. Joe, you're doing much better than I expected, but you aren't completely healed yet. Don't do more than sit up in a chair until I see you next."

Squatting down so he was eye level with the child, he continued, "Pearl, can you help your mother and Joe remember what I've told them?" Pearl nodded solemnly as she considered this new grown-up responsibility. "Good girl. I'll take my leave now. Please take care of each other." James packed his medical supplies and left the Harbins with deep concern for their safety, but without any immediate solution to their problem.

Mary Alice and his deep love for her consumed James as he rode away from the Harbin farm. Not in his wildest imaginings could he ever conceive of a situation or action that could bring him to lay a hand on her in violence. Joss Harbin's brand of patriarchy was an anomaly in James's personal experience, but he had seen its effects on a few of his childhood friends. It had been common knowledge among his early schoolmates whose daddy was a beater. Black eyes, whelps, and bruises on the children identified the abusers. What form of evil could bring a man to harm the people he was supposed to protect and love most? The sheriff must be told what James suspected when he was in town tomorrow. Surely something could be done.

***

The next morning, James made an early start for Canton, the county seat and only town of any size in Cherokee County. A large crate of supplies was due to arrive by rail. His first call was at the sheriff's office where he found both Sheriff Hamilton and his deputy sipping coffee by the potbellied stove set between the front windows.

James greeted the men as he entered the small wooden building attached to the courthouse. It contained the office and a couple of holding cells. "Morning, Ward, Bobby. I hope y'all are doing well."

"We're tolerable, Doc, just tolerable. Pull up a chair and sit by the fire a spell. It's cold this morning."

James chatted with the two lawmen for a few moments before bringing up his visit's real purpose. "Ward, do you know the Harbins—the ones over on Pine Log?"

The sheriff nodded and looked at James with a knowing grin. "Does a wild hog crap in the woods? Why do you ask?"

"I've had reason to make a call there recently and I'm concerned about what goes on in that house. Unless I've made a seriously wrong judgment, Joss Harbin beats his wife fairly often. Right now, she has a broken nose and two cracked ribs."

The sheriff's grin faded. "You're right as rain. Joss Harbin's mean as a snake. There ain't a sorrier man what ever drawed breath."

James's lips became a thin line. "Is there anything that can be done?"

Ward Hamilton let out a soft snort. "There's a law been on the Georgia books since 1857 against wife beating, but the case has still got to be proved. Last neighbor who witnessed Joss beating Azaleigh and talked about it had his barn burned for his trouble. Folks over on Pine Log are all scared to death and with good reason. If you can get Azaleigh to tell the truth about what goes on there, I'll be glad to do something about it. Until then, I ain't got no legal right to interfere."

James left the office still worried and without a solution to Azaleigh's problem. At the root of the problem? In all likelihood, she had neither the courage nor the will to report the truth about her husband. It had all been beaten out of her long ago.

CHAPTER 9

Guilt haunted James for a good while after his introduction to the Harbin clan, but ultimately, he accepted that effective change was beyond his scope. Besides, he had something happier to command his attention. He and Mary Alice were married the second Sunday in November after the regular monthly meeting.

They spent their wedding night in their own house on the small farm that became available shortly before they married. James couldn't believe his good fortune when his offer was accepted on a large clapboard family home surrounded by one hundred fifty acres of fertile bottomland. The farm's main body sat in the curve of Salacoa Road where it completed a winding path around the mountains and entered the valley proper. On one side of the large farmyard, a cart track led away from the main road and disappeared around the foot of the mountain behind their barn. The house, sitting near the main road, had a slightly elevated prospect before which the verdant valley spread her green skirts in a deep, debutant bow. The house was large by valley standards with six big rooms and a wide porch that ran around its entire perimeter. Mature oaks provided shelter during the long hot summers when fourteen-foot-high ceilings allowed the heat to rise away from the inhabitants within and tall, nine-over-nine windows caught the breezes that swept down the valley from the west. The back porch was home to a deep well where sweet, clear, cold water could be drawn in all weather without the bearer suffering the full force of the elements. Four fireplaces and a wood-burning kitchen range kept the home warm in winter. It was perfect for a big family.

As they settled into their home and James's practice began to grow, the days developed a pattern. By the time summer arrived, James often returned from his house calls to find the porch rockers filled with patients. Today was no exception.

James tied his horse's reins to a porch post and eyed the crowd gathered awaiting treatment. "I'll be with y'all soon. I need to wash up first and get a quick bite."

James mopped his face with his already sodden handkerchief and noticed the relief dawning in several faces. They must have been waiting for a good while.

In the kitchen, Maggie, the elderly midwife, was waiting for him. She was well beyond attending the long hours required for most babies to enter the world, but could still be counted on to sit for short spells with laboring mothers.

James gave her a crooked grin. "Hey, Maggie. Are you sick too? Seems like half the valley is on the porch."

Maggie eyed him as though he was still a small boy in need of correction. "I ain't sick. You can see that plain enough. Mary Alice done started her time this morning, which you'd have knowed if you paid as much attention to your own as you done to them others." Maggie was clearly in no mood for male explanations. Her vision of life's priorities never wavered and her advanced years led her to believe speaking her mind was not only her privilege, but her duty. And it didn't help that she had been present when James himself had made his entrance into the world. He took his plate of green beans and cornbread out on the porch where her critical gaze could not follow.

After he checked Mary Alice's progress, James saw to his patients' needs. Maggie was also out of sorts about having to feed that bunch on the porch. It was not unusual for Mary Alice to serve dinner to waiting patients, meaning she never knew how many would be sitting down to her table at noon. It was a blessing that the Locklins lived on the other side of the field at the base of the mountain behind the house. She and her husband Newt became James's tenants when he purchased the farm and they chose to stay on. Newt ran the farm for James and Lavinia did occasional work for Mary Alice. The arrangement worked well for both families.

In the early evening, James saw their child's head begin to crown. Maggie, who insisted on staying, held Mary Alice's hand and coaxed her through the last difficult moments while James was occupied with the business end. Once on the way, the baby demonstrated a will of its own as it appeared to push and struggle its way into the world. When tiny arms cleared the birth canal, they flailed away in what looked like an announcement that the baby would take it from here, thank you very much. His father caught him as he emitted a mighty, preemptive, red-faced bellow. He would not tolerate, nor would he need, any pops on the bottom. James placed his son in Maggie's outstretched arms.

With amusement twinkling in her eyes, she took the baby to a table where warm water and towels waited. When she had washed and wrapped the little fellow, she dried her hands and raised a brow. "You mark my words. That un's gonna be a handful. What're y'all gonna call him?"

James opened his mouth to say they were not sure yet, when Mary Alice raised herself up on an elbow. "We'll call him James for his father and Archibald for my papa." She fixed James with a firm look. Apparently, argument was fruitless. She intended to have her way in this matter.

James smiled and caressed her cheek. "And what are you planning to call him for everyday? One James per household is enough, and Archibald is a mighty big name for someone so little."

"Archie would suit just fine," she responded and then drifted into exhausted sleep.

What a blessing Mary Alice's first labor and delivery had gone well. The first was often the most difficult from what James had seen. But as they cleaned up, he noticed Maggie, who was rumored to have "the sight," snatching sidelong glances at the baby with an odd expression. The child was healthy, so what on earth could have her upset? With superstition and folk myths being rife in these mountains, there was no telling what she had gotten into her head. Better not to ask. This particular mountain tradition needed to die a quick and silent death.

Archie grew quickly and walked and talked earlier than most of his contemporaries. He delighted his namesakes as they watched his toddler antics with amused tolerance. When Archie entered the terrible twos bringing evidence of a significant temper and strong will, father and grandfather just laughed all the harder. Papa Campbell called in often, ostensibly to visit Mary Alice, but more often than not, he spent most of the time playing chase with Archie or carrying him around the yard so they could inspect bugs, anthills, and other things of interest to a small boy. This amazed the family, who had never seen Bud so animated nor take such an interest in a little one. Despite their political differences, a natural bond grew between the two men based on their mutual love of mother and child. James sought Bud's advice about running the farm and Bud could be heard speaking with quiet pride about his son-in-law, the doctor.

When Archie first began pulling himself to stand, James took the precaution of removing his medicines and other medical supplies to a small office he had built in the yard. It was just big enough for shelves, a worktable, and a clerk's desk. Its tall, narrow windows gave him a view out over Salacoa Road. There he could mix medicines and enter his patients' details in his ledgers without interruption while observing the comings and goings around him.

Early on a June morning of Archie's third year, James looked up from mixing medicine to see his father-in-law riding hard into the yard, sliding to a halt beside the office door in a cloud of red dust. Bud flung himself from the saddle and rushed in without knocking.

"James, I got bad news. I want to tell you first 'cause it'll go hard with Mary Alice, Dolph being her favorite and all. He's hurt real bad and they took him to Atlanta."

The older man sank onto the desk's high stool, looking every bit of his fifty-eight years. He bent from the waist, puffing and trying to catch his breath. James took his father-in-law's wrist while glancing at the flesh protruding over his brogans. The dropsy was getting worse.

James sat in his desk chair and looked up at Bud. "Tell me exactly what happened."

"Well, best anybody can reckon, Dolph was driving his buggy down Main Street in Canton when somebody fired off a gun. It musta been close, 'cause his horse, it rared up and bolted." Bud stopped for a moment to draw breath. "The horse run all the way to the dip in the road just before you get to the river. It was going so fast it couldn't make the turn at the bottom of the hill and the buggy turned over. Dolph was throwed clear of the wreck, but his leg was broke bad so the bone was sticking out'n his skin. Doctor said take him to Atlanta and that's what they done before we even knowed it'd happened."

Bud paused again, fear darkening his eyes. "Do you think you can see your way to go down and see how things is going? Nancy'll send one of the girls to stay with Mary Alice while you're gone."

James rubbed his chin in thought. Bud rarely showed much emotion, neither joy nor sadness, but he was very distressed over the news about Dolph. Mary Alice would be equally upset. She and Dolph were only ten months apart in age and he was her favorite brother. They played together when they were little, getting into mischief and covering for one another until marriage sent Mary Alice to her own home. Mary Alice usually bore stress with calm assurance, but she was well along in her second pregnancy and was bigger than she ought to be at this stage. She was probably carrying more than one baby. Multiples often came earlier than expected. Leaving her for the time it would take to get to Atlanta and back was not a great idea.

James sucked in his lower lip. "Do you know where they took him? There're two hospitals in Atlanta now. Old Atlanta Hospital run by the Catholic nuns and Grady Memorial, which opened about two years ago. Did they tell you where he is?" James inferred the answer from Bud's stricken expression. "Who brought you the news?"

"Johnny Blalock was sent with it. He was in town when it happened."

James and Bud walked across the yard to the house in silence. When they entered the kitchen, Mary Alice took one look at their faces and demanded, "What's wrong? Please tell me it's not Mama."

Bud slumped into a chair at the table. He leaned his head on his up-turned palms as tears coursed down his cheeks. It was clear James's father-in-law was beyond saying or doing anymore, so he told Mary Alice about Dolph as gently as he could.

She began wringing her hands. "You've got to go to Atlanta. Leave right now. You've got to find him!"

"But, Mary Alice, I don't think I should leave you so close to the time for the baby."

"Go! Now!" Mary Alice's eyes were wide and her hands were shaking. She was as close to hysterics as James ever hoped to see her.

Try as he might, James was unable to make Mary Alice see reason. It was not safe for him to leave her so close to the baby's arrival, but not knowing Dolph's condition was causing her so much distress he had no choice but to go search for his injured brother-in-law. Within the hour, he had packed enough for a couple of nights in his old black canvas grip and was headed for Canton to board a southbound train without any idea as to Dolph's exact location.

***

By the time his train arrived at the Atlanta depot, evening shadows were wrapping their gray fingers around the city's structures, creating pools of semi-darkness between the new electric streetlamps. James stepped down from the train and looked around for a hansom to take him into the city's heart where the hospitals were located. Finding none, he walked the blocks to the nearest streetcar stop and waited for a downtown bound car. Workers trying to get home for supper crowded the streetcars traveling in all directions.

James jumped onto the first available inbound car and held onto the pole on the outside platform because it was useless trying to get inside. While he rode, James planned how to proceed. Locating lodging first would provide a base of operation from which to search.

He left the streetcar when it reached the center of town. He hadn't spent a night in the city since he finished medical school, but he had kept in touch with his former landlady, Mrs. Wilkins. Reaching her front door, he knocked and waited. Presently, disgruntled mutterings emanated from the long hall as someone bustled toward him.

"Who on earth would have the temerity to be calling at this unsuitable hour, just as we are sitting down to supper?" Mrs. Wilkins opened the door and looked up accusingly for a moment before crying, "Land sakes, if it isn't young Dr. Buchanan come to call! Come in! Come in! Tell me, what brings you to Atlanta?"

Mrs. Wilkins ushered him into the hall and gave him a tight hug with her short pudgy arms. James had to bend down to return the hug and give her a peck on the cheek.

"James, have you eaten? We're just sitting down and you know I always fix enough to feed Sherman's army. Nothing's changed with these young men since you were here. They cain't be filled, no matter how much I cook. There's plenty, though. Won't you eat with us?"

"That's very kind of you, Mrs. Wilkins. I apologize for arriving unannounced, but I was called to Atlanta on urgent business and there just wasn't time to let you know. I don't want to put you out, but I'd be very grateful if you might have a place for me to stay for a couple of nights. A pallet on the floor will suit me just fine. If you don't have room, I'll certainly understand."

"I have room for you anytime you need it. You know all you have to do is ask. And there'll be no pallet on the floor, either. I've got an extra bed I set aside just for the occasional visitor. It's yours for as long as you need it. Now, come on in the kitchen and eat before supper gets cold."

Despite feeling an urgent need to be about the business of locating his brother-in-law, James lingered over the meal with Mrs. Wilkins after the current boarders had gone. He couldn't repay her kindness by rushing into the twilight without explanation. They talked briefly about mutual friends and neighbors and James shared news of Mary Alice and of Archie's latest antics before he related the true reason for his sudden trip to Atlanta. Somewhat alarmed, Mrs. Wilkins called for one her medical students to give directions to the new Grady Memorial Hospital on Butler Street. James would try Atlanta Hospital over on Baker Street first, since it was the better known and was closer to Mrs. Wilkins's.

Stars twinkled in a dusky sky by the time James was on his way to the hospital run by the Sisters of Mercy. He entered the cool, tall-ceilinged lobby and looked about, recognition sparking memories of his days as a medical student. Its walls were paneled with dark, high wainscoting, banged and nicked by many an emergency, and its graywhite-and-gray streaked marble floor was worn down in places by the passage of too many feet. He had walked through this lobby many times attending rounds with older physicians during his training. He stepped to the reception desk and hit the bell that summoned attendants when visitors wished admittance.

A young nursing sister in full nun's habit came from a room deep within the main office suite at his first ring. Her flowing black robes and veil with its stiff white wimple hid all but the small oval of her pretty face. Under normal circumstances, it would have been inappropriate for a doctor without hospital privileges to call after visiting hours, so James lost no time in explaining his purpose and waited while the nun consulted the admissions log.

When she returned, her expression revealed the answer before she spoke. "I'm very sorry, but we haven't a patient by that name."

"I see. Thank you for checking." James turned to go, but the young woman placed her hand on his arm.

"Perhaps I could say a prayer of petition for your success?"

The ward sisters had always said the rosary while they sat with patients. Although they practiced their faith very differently from what James had grown up with, he had always respected their devotion. "I'd be grateful. Thank you."

The trip to Grady Memorial on Butler Street took much longer than he anticipated. The streetcars did not run with as great a frequency at night as they did during the day. He reached the Romanesque brick and stone entrance long after the streetlamps had begun chasing the darkness from the sidewalks' brick pavers.

He pressed the bell at the front desk and waited impatiently for the night porter to answer. After two more bangs on the bell, a man finally appeared with a quizzically raised eyebrow. It was well past the time that patients should be having callers and doctors would not need to ring.

"Yeah?" The night porter's manner conveyed his desire to be of as little service as he could possibly manage.

James kept his temper under control long enough to communicate the purpose for his visit.

"Too late for callers." The orderly turned and started toward the door through which he had just come.

"Wait! Mr. Campbell is my brother-in-law. His father sent me to find him. I demand that you let me see my relative," James shouted.

The porter turned back with a scowl on his face. "Keep your shirt on. I'll see if there's a doctor still here. If he says it's okay, then you can see the patient."

After an interminable period spent shifting from one foot to the other and pacing the lobby's marble tiles, James saw an older man in a dark three-piece suit and gold-rimmed pince-nez spectacles enter through a side door. He approached and extended his hand. "I'm Doctor Fogarty. I've checked our admissions log and I'm afraid I can find no person by the name you requested. Are you quite positive he was brought here?"

James frowned in confusion. "The only information we received was that my brother-in-law was brought to Atlanta. The person who accompanied him on the train was not available to be questioned before I left, but there seemed to be only two possibilities. I've enquired at the Sisters of Mercy with the same result. I can't imagine where a man with what sounded like a compound fracture of the tibia might have been taken, if not to a hospital."

The older doctor looked sharply at James before asking, "Have you medical training, young man?"

James introduced himself in some embarrassment. "Please forgive my rudeness. My concern for my brother-in-law has made me forget my manners."

"That's quite understandable." Dr. Fogarty rubbed his chin before continuing, "You might check the private clinics around the city. There are several run by surgeons and physicians who would take such a case." Dr. Fogarty studied James for a moment. "I'm very sorry we can be of such little assistance. If you should need the hospital's services when you find him, please do not hesitate to call upon us. Tell the admissions clerk to notify me of your arrival, and I will see that you are extended every courtesy. I wish I could do more."

The older man's words trailed away into silence as James mentally prepared himself to renew the search for Dolph. First, he would go to the nearest telegraph office and fire off messages to both the doctor in Canton and the deputy who had brought Dolph to Atlanta. Surely, they would have some idea of what had happened to Mary Alice's most beloved brother.

While he was at Western Union, it occurred to him that they must have knowledge of all medical clinics in the city. His request produced a fairly short list. Unfortunately, the addresses ranged over the entire expanse of the growing metropolitan area. He scanned the list again. At least one address was within walking distance. Armed with what little information he had gleaned, he headed toward his third call of the evening. The telegraph clerk had assured him a delivery boy would bring any replies to Mrs. Wilkins's boarding house as soon as they arrived. Until then, James would make his way through his list by working in an ever-widening circle until all addresses had been visited.

At midnight, James found himself pounding on the door of a general practitioner whose home was near the new Georgia School of Technology. This final call produced nothing more than a quick rebuff from the doctor he had awakened. With a heavy heart and sudden fatigue, James returned to the boarding house. Surprisingly, Mrs. Wilkins was still up. When he was seated with her in the parlor, she poured coffee for him and pushed a plate of teacakes in his direction.

"I thought you might need a little refreshment after your wanderings tonight. Did you have any luck?"

James shook his head wearily. "I'll start on the remainder of the private clinics in the morning, but it looks like this is going to be a bigger job than I realized when I left home. If my being here becomes a burden, please let me know. I don't want to take undue advantage of our friendship and your kindness."

"Pshaw!" Mrs. Wilkins snorted. "You just let me decide who's doing the advantage taking. Give me that list. I'm going to ask the neighbor boy to help you. First thing in the morning, get enough coins to ride the streetcars for the day and a little extra for the boy. He'll be glad to get the money, and it'll help you too." With decisions made, they both went to bed.

James fell into a restless sleep filled with dreams populated by dying young men and babies arriving before they were ready to enter the world. These visions dissolved into the recurring nightmare from his medical school days. His fellow medical students appeared, but instead of imploring him to attack the immovable object of pain and suffering with them as they had in the past, they simply pointed at him. The spokesman turned and asked, "If you don't do it, who will?" The question was echoed by Mary Alice and Dolph who had inexplicably joined the others, then everyone took up the call in a chant that rang with accusation and pleading. The next morning, James woke feeling as though he had not slept at all. The bed had been much too crowded for real rest.

After breakfast, he and the neighbor boy headed in opposite directions. The calls on the city's northeastern and northwestern sides yielded no results. James returned to the boarding house late that evening hoping to find a telegram with the mystery solved. Once again, James's hopes were dashed. He was quiet during dinner and spent another restless night once again fraught with alarming dreams. He awoke early with a fuzzy mind and low spirits. He and the boy spent the day continuing the search among the addresses without any progress toward Dolph. The first break came that night when James returned to the boarding house where Mrs. Wilkins greeted him at the door, waving a scrap of yellow paper in her hand.

"James! James! It's come. He's down about Grant Park. There's a lot of new building going on there. The doctor who has him is Dr. Jeremiah Davidson. He's one of the best in the city. Even I've heard of him. The Canton doctor sent Dolph to him especially because they're friends. Isn't this wonderful news?" It never occurred to Mrs. Wilkins that telegrams were private communications intended for the addressee's eyes alone.

CHAPTER 10

Relief flooded James's tired mind and he gave Mrs. Wilkins a hug that lifted her short plump frame from the floor. With renewed hope, he grabbed the telegram and tore through the door, running for the streetcar stop. He waited some little time before a car came along that would get him headed in Grant Park's general direction and the new residential development. After three transfers and more riding, the park's gates finally came into view. James descended the streetcar steps after asking the driver for directions to the doctor's house. With high hopes and lifting spirits, he found the correct address, ran up the new stone mansion's steps, and knocked at the ornate mahogany door with its shiny brass knocker. After a few moments, a pretty young parlor maid answered. She conducted him into the library, instructing him to wait there for Doctor Davidson and then disappeared into the hall, closing the door quietly behind her.

James had never seen such luxurious appointments in a private residence. The arms and legs of the settee and chairs were highly decorated with elaborate floral carvings on their polished wood. The seats and backs were covered in expensive red velvet and the room's tall windows had long swaths of the same fabric pooling on the floor beneath them. The cavernous pink marble fireplace was dark now due to the season, but its size would surely warm the whole room when a fire roared in its expanse. The occasional tables scattered about the seating area were topped with this same gleaming pink and held lovely glass and ceramic objects beneath lamps whose elaborate stained-glass shades took on a phosphorescent, swirling glow from the electric bulbs within.

The doctor's extensive collection of leather-bound volumes was housed in mahogany shelves that stretched to the top of the sixteen-foot ceiling. The wide-planked hardwood floor was covered in a nearly room-sized colorful wool carpet in what James guessed was a foreign pattern. He had seen a picture with a pattern like it in a book called *One Hundred and One Arabian Nights.*

When the maid ushered him through the foyer, James had seen what he thought must be one of those new speaking devices that were all the rage among Atlanta's wealthy. He looked about him in some awe. Doctor Davidson must certainly be successful.

The library door's brass knob clicked and the man himself appeared. He was not particularly imposing in size or appearance, but the cut of his custom-tailored suit was expensive and he carried an air of unquestioned authority. He paused to assess his much younger visitor and then approached in a manner that could only be described as superior and condescending.

"How may I help you?"

James extended his hand and introduced himself. "I was relieved to receive a telegram from Dr. Broward telling me that I could find my brother-in-law, Randolph Campbell, in your care. He was brought to Atlanta before the family even knew he had been injured. I'd be very grateful if you would take me to him."

Dr. Davidson stepped closer and condescended to shake James's hand. "Mr. Campbell is resting quietly and I don't want him disturbed. Perhaps you could return in the morning and then we will determine whether my patient wishes to see you."

James was at first astonished and then appalled by the unmistakable, overwhelming odor of alcohol on the man's breath. James knew some people saw no harm in taking alcohol for social and even medicinal reasons, but this was beyond all bounds of what could be considered either. He had noticed a slight tremor when Dr. Davidson extended his hand and he now understood its cause. The man was intoxicated and possibly suffered tremors brought on by alcohol abuse. Dr. Davidson was a man who apparently managed to mask his condition while playing the part of a functioning physician. He apparently hid his excessive drinking from his medical colleagues, who either were very unobservant, feigned ignorance, or purposefully assisted him in denying his dependence without regard for the danger this posed to patients.

For the first time since beginning his search, fear and uncertainty about Dolph's care gripped James. "Dr. Davidson, I've traveled some distance and searched for three days to locate my brother-in-law. Would you please do me the kindness and professional courtesy of taking me to him now?"

The older man's eyes shifted, his gaze flitting about the room in search of any place to light other than James. "I don't see how waiting until my patient is well rested can possibly affect your peace of mind."

This answer to a simple request increased James's alarm. "Dr. Davidson, I insist you let me see Mr. Campbell. His father has sent me locate him and send back information to the family. Now, please, let's not waste any more time. I hope to get a telegram sent this evening before the Western Union office closes."

When the man apparently realized he could not reasonably deny access, he motioned for James to follow him. "Very well, if you will follow me. My clinic is off the main hall."

The clinic contained an office outfitted with the latest medical instruments and devices and a wall of glass-fronted cases containing medicines and their ingredients. To one side of the large room, muslin curtains sectioned off two small cubicles. In the first, James found Dolph, delirious and moaning with pain.

James did not bother with professional etiquette by asking permission to view the wound. He strode to the bed, threw back the sheet, and removed the blood-soaked bandages covering Dolph's shin. A sickening odor drifted up from the bed. Nausea washed over James. He had treated infected wounds and had even worked on one case of gangrene, but he had never thought to find such a situation here in a renowned and trusted physician's clinic. The red streaks crawling over the knee and up the thigh toward Dolph's groin heightened James's alarm. Dolph had to be gotten away from this butcher.

"Thank you for trying to help my brother-in-law. You'll be paid for your services. Now you must excuse me while I arrange for him to be moved to Grady Memorial. May I use the instrument I saw in your hall? I'll need help as I've never placed a telephone call before."

Davidson's face turned the color of his library draperies and his eyes bulged as he roared, "What impudence! How dare you come into my clinic and question my methods and treatment."

Heat crawled up James's neck and onto his face. Being several inches taller than Davidson, James stared down at the older man in disbelief. His jaw clenched. "I have not so far questioned your treatment because you have not been courteous enough to explain to me why my brother-in-law seems to have received none at all. Too much time has already been wasted. Now, may I make the call?"

Davidson's whole body shook as he shouted, "Mr. Campbell will not be removed from this house. If you attempt it, sir, I will use the instrument with which you are so unfamiliar to call for the constable and have you removed instead. You are not a member of the immediate family. If you attempt any interference with my patient, I will bring you up on charges before the medical society. Now leave my home before I have you thrown out!"

James reluctantly realized he had lost this battle, but he would not lose the war. Dolph's life could depend on the actions he took and the decisions he made within the next few hours. After catching an inbound streetcar at the Grant Park gates, he returned to the telegraph office and sent an urgent message to Bud to come to Atlanta at once. He then made his way to Grady, praying he would find Dr. Fogarty still there. For once during this nightmarish trip, luck was with him. Dr. Fogarty arrived in the lobby shortly after James's arrival.

He listened to James's story with growing dismay reflected in his eyes. "I don't know what to say about Dr. Davidson's behavior. He has no right to keep your brother-in-law in his clinic when a close family member, blood kin or otherwise, is asking for his removal. I'd heard rumors among our colleagues regarding his drinking to excess, but I've not witnessed it myself. Of course, he and I don't often cross paths professionally these days since I've come to Grady. We'll take an ambulance and a constable's deputy to Dr. Davidson's at once. Your brother-in-law will be removed from that establishment without delay. Pray we aren't too late."

Together, the two doctors jumped up onto the van and rode beside the ambulance driver, who cracked his whip over the horses' heads. The deputy followed on his own mount, which he urged to a gallop to keep up with the flying van. They raced to the Davidson mansion's front entrance and pulled to a violent halt. The horses were left stirring nervously on the brick pavement, blowing hard and sweating, as the four men ran for the steps. The deputy pounded on the door, which produced a distant light deep in the house's recesses. Presently, a manservant wearing a hurriedly thrown on dressing gown answered the noise.

"What is it y'all want? The doctor has retired for the evening and cannot be disturbed."

"It isn't the doctor we've come to see," replied Doctor Fogarty. "Show us to the clinic immediately and we may not press charges against you for aiding in holding a person against his will."

The servant's eyes widened. He ushered them into the house and down the hall toward the clinic. "I don't know what y'all're talking about. If it's the clinic you want, though, come this way." He flung open the clinic door and stepped back so the four intruders could pass.

Once inside, James found Dolph's condition had worsened. Instead of moaning, he was lying very still and taking only short gasping breaths.

The ambulance driver unrolled a stretcher he had brought with him from the van. He and James gently lifted Dolph from the bed and placed him on the stretcher while the deputy ensured the way to the door was clear. When they had Dolph loaded into the ambulance, they secured the stretcher to the floor with straps and hooks and eyes, then prepared for another flying trip through the deepening night.

The waiting horses were once again whipped up into immoderate speed. As they careened around the corner leading them away from the house, James looked back over his shoulder. A shadowy form staggered down the front steps. It appeared to be shaking a fist and shouting abuse after them before it fell on its face at the bottom of the flight. It tried raising itself, but James could watch no more. He had to turn around and hold on for dear life because they were picking up speed, bouncing over the street's cobblestones and bricks as they raced through the night.

CHAPTER 11

The ambulance screamed to a stop as the driver hauled on the reins and shoved the long wooden brake lever down on the front wheel. It came to rest with iron horseshoes and wheel rims clashing on the cobblestones, sending sparks flying beside the night entrance to Grady Memorial. Dr. Fogarty opened the door with his personal key and then conducted the driver and James, who were carrying the stretcher, to the first available bed in a ward close to the surgical theaters.

James barely registered the deputy and driver's farewells as he stood staring at Dolph's leg. He glanced over at Dr. Fogarty and saw the same anxiety in his colleague's eyes that must be reflected in his own.

Dr. Fogarty was the first to speak. "Your brother-in-law's leg is badly infected. You and I both know what must be done."

A catch rose in James's throat as he nodded. "I would like for his father to be here. How long do you think we can wait?"

Dr. Fogarty looked again at the red lines running up Dolph's leg. "Not as long as it would take for someone to arrive from Waleska."

James's heart dropped. Dr. Fogarty was right. If only his father-in-law was here to agree to what they were about to do.

Bud, Nancy, and Mary Alice would blame him and might not forgive him, even if Dolph lived. He was young with so much of his life ahead of him and was a fine figure of a man, as well.

When Dolph moved from Salacoa to Canton to work in its most successful mercantile establishment, he had found more than a job. It didn't take long for him to woo and win the owner's daughter. The menfolk had wondered what the successful merchant's beautiful daughter, who could have had her pick from among any of the town's young bucks, saw in this boy from the sticks. The women, especially the young ones, didn't even need to think about it. Dolph was that rarity among humans—an extremely handsome man who, if he was aware of his appearance, certainly did not take it seriously. There was no mystery at all in her choice, as far as the ladies were concerned.

James cast a cautious glance at the wound. Nothing had changed. In fact, the red streaks had grown. Would that beautiful girl feel the same about Dolph once the operation robbed him of his leg? If they left it intact, there was no hope. The massive infection pouring bacteria into Dolph's bloodstream was beyond curing. The decision to remove it was simple, because in realty, there was no other choice.

James stayed with Dolph to prepare his leg for amputation, carefully following the surgeon's directions. James would assist during the operation, and he hoped to gain additional insights from the older physician as he helped him and observed him work. James's training in general medicine had included only minimal experience in the operating theaters since surgery was an advanced, specialized field.

When everything was ready, James and an orderly placed Dolph on a stretcher and carried him into the operating theater where Dr. Fogarty waited, having placed a white coat over his suit. They lifted Dolph onto the operating table and placed a tourniquet around the thigh. Dr. Fogarty nodded and James placed a small wire cage over Dolph's mouth and nose. Next, he placed white gauze layers over the cage and held the apparatus firmly in place while dripping bitter liquid ether onto the gauze until it was certain the patient was in a profound state of unconsciousness.

Dr. Fogarty made quick work slicing through skin, vessels, and muscle. He tied off the main arteries and vessels and then moved to the slower process of sawing through the thick femur. The process took longer than James thought it would, and at one point, he administered additional ether when Dolph's eyelids began to flutter. It was a relief when Dr. Fogarty began the final phase by cauterizing the whole area, folding the flaps of muscle and skin over the site, and stitching everything in place. While he and an orderly carried Dolph back to the ward, James prayed they had gotten the leg off in time. He stayed with Dolph for the remainder of the night dozing upright in the straight-backed chair.

James awoke with a start. He looked up in some confusion as Bud threw back the curtain separating Dolph's bed from the others on the ward. It must already be mid-morning for Bud to have arrived by train. James followed his father-in-law's anxious gaze. Dolph's condition had not improved much. His breathing was audible and ragged. His chest rose in an uneven pattern as he struggled for air. James stood, but Bud stopped short, staring at the dip in the sheet where his son's right leg should have been.

James was mesmerized. His father-in-law seemed to visibly age before his eyes. The gray at Bud's temples spread, the lines in his face deepened, and his shoulders sagged into those of an old man, all in an instant. Or maybe it was just James's eyes playing tricks because they had not had enough rest in the last few days. Bud was, after all, almost sixty.

Bud opened his mouth, closed it, and finally opened it again. "Why did y'all have to cut off his leg? Ain't he young enough to get over it being broke? Doc Broward, he said Dolph was brung to the best thay is 'cause he asked special, him and Doc Davidson being friends and all."

James's compassion for Bud suddenly shifted to irritation. The long nights and stressful days spent looking for Dolph and then rescuing him from an alcoholic, incompetent butcher had left James with little energy to answer accusatory questions with good grace, not even from Bud.

He gained control of his rising temper, but just barely. "Bud, taking off Dolph's leg was necessary. If it had been left, he would have died from blood poisoning for sure. As it is, he has some chance of recovering. There are no guarantees, though, because that butcher Davidson was going to let him stay there in his clinic and die. He's a drunkard and should be run out of the profession. You can tell Dr. Broward that the next time you see him."

The anger in James's voice must have cut through Bud's agitation. "Oh, Son, I'm . . . .I'm sorry. I don't mean you ain't done your best. It was just the shock of seeing him like that and all. Do you think he's gonna make it okay?"

Exhaustion suddenly settled over James and he ran a hand over his eyes to clear his mind. There was also more than a little discomfort in his lower abdomen, no doubt from irregular eating. What could he say to give Bud the hope he so desperately sought? He chose the only thing that was right—the truth.

"I'm afraid Dolph's going to have a bad time. Davidson didn't clean the wound properly and he didn't take any action after that. If he had taken off Dolph's leg as soon as he arrived or tried to prevent the infection's spreading, Dolph would be in much better shape. I wish I could give you better news."

Deep remorse and guilt slithered through James as he watched the light of hope falter in the older man's eyes. The medical community knew what caused infection but had little in the way of medicines, making early treatment critical in saving lives. His anger and frustration with such senseless neglect left him drained and ashamed that his profession harbored, and even covered for, such a man as Davidson.

Toward noon, James realized he had not eaten since midday yesterday, which probably explained the gnawing ache in his stomach. During his comings and goings the last few days he had passed a small café around the corner from the hospital's entrance. He needed food. Bud could use a strong cup of coffee at the very least.

James checked Dolph's vital signs. His pulse was stronger than it had been during the night and his breathing had also become more regular. They should be safe in leaving Dolph long enough to get something to eat.

The pair walked down the hospital steps and turned toward the little café on the corner. A closed sign on the door stated that the owner was away until later in the week. James could think of no other eating establishments in the immediate vicinity so he suggested that Bud return with him to Mrs. Wilkins's. It would give him a chance to clean up a little. A change of clothes, a basin of warm water, and a little soap would be most welcome. June's warmth and his recent activity had taken a toll on his wardrobe and personal hygiene.

Mrs. Wilkins was only too happy to feed James and Bud. She even offered to put a cot in James's room. Bud had left home without a single thought about food or accommodation while in Atlanta. He didn't have the money for a hotel room and wouldn't know where to stay even if he did. After a dinner of new spring vegetables and cornbread, Mrs. Wilkins left Bud sitting in the parlor while James cleaned himself up.

The water's warmth and the soap's clean smell were a welcome relief as they washed away grime and stale sweat. Scraping away three days' growth of itchy beard was even better. A clean shirt completed his ablutions. When he returned to the parlor, James felt almost human again.

James and Bud departed for the hospital somewhat restored and in better spirits. They entered the ward cubicle to find Dr. Fogarty speaking with a very weak, but conscious, Dolph.

"Young man, taking your leg has given you a chance for life. You must use all your strength to concentrate on your recovery. There are many men who live full lives without a complete set of natural limbs. Once you've regained your strength, we'll see you're fitted with an artificial leg. The devices available today are a vast improvement over the ones we used just a few years ago. Now, my orders are that you rest and try to drink and eat normally."

Dr. Fogarty looked up and correctly guessed the new arrival's identity. With the briefest nod, he silently motioned to James to step away from the bed with him. Bud made to follow them, but James shook his head with such vehemence that Bud sat down on the chair by the bed instead while both fear and hope crossed his face.

As James and Dr. Fogarty turned to leave, Bud took Dolph's hand and whispered, "It's gonna be all right, Son. James'll see to it."

Bud's confidence would have been rewarding in other circumstances, but James feared proper treatment had come too late. When they had walked far enough along the ward to be out of earshot of Dolph's cubicle, Dr. Fogarty spoke quietly and emphatically. "There seems little improvement in your brother-in-law's condition. I know you see it also. I urge you to prepare your father-in-law."

"You're right, of course. I'll do it immediately."

James returned to the cubicle and paused by the curtain, just out of Bud and Dolph's lines of vision. He would give much to keep this pain from Mary Alice and from the others whom he had learned to love. James was not a violent man by nature, but if Davidson, whom he would never think of as doctor again, were within reach, he would kill him with his bare hands. Rage, fear, grief, despair raced through him as he prepared to speak with Bud. As much as James loved his work, this was the one thing he always dreaded. He was not a coward for himself, but inflicting pain was anathema to him as a man and as a doctor.

When he entered the cubicle, he noticed that Dolph had slipped back into a deep sleep, so he felt it safe to speak there beside the bed. "Bud, I'm afraid . . . " Deep pain reflected in the older man's eyes cut him off. Bud seemed to be reading his mind. He had limited formal education, but he was very astute where life's realities were concerned because he had seen enough horrors during battle and in the prison camp for several lifetimes.

"If you don't mind, James, I'd just as soon not hear it."

James searched his father-in-law's face and then remained silent. Bud clearly understood more about Dolph's condition than he had let on. James nodded and dropped down on the other chair near the bed. They sat in silence for the reminder of the day as Dolph slipped into ever deeper sleep. As James watched his brother-in-law, he prayed Dolph's rest was restorative rather than portending coma.

CHAPTER 12

As each day dissolved into the next, Dolph drifted between periods of wakefulness and deep sleep, rallying from time to time, but always falling back into unconsciousness. His fever waxed and waned, but never completely disappeared. A week passed with Dolph hovering between light and dark when, on the evening of the eighth day, he fell into an infection-induced coma. Despite all their efforts, they had not gotten him away from the butcher in time. The infection had already taken too great a hold by the time James located him at Davidson's clinic.

When Dolph's breathing became a shallow, ragged struggle, even Bud realized that the end was near and all hope was lost. Dolph died quietly early on the morning of the tenth day without regaining consciousness. James watched helplessly as his normally taciturn, unemotional father-in-law wept openly. It was all the more difficult to see knowing Bud had endured much in his life without uttering a sigh. For the second time, James felt a deep shame that he and the man Davidson shared the same title and profession.

Dr. Fogarty must have sensed his younger colleague's troubled thoughts for he took James aside as the orderlies were preparing Dolph's body for the mortician's van. "James, you must not reproach yourself for what has happened. You did everything in your power to save your brother-in-law. No one could have done more. As doctors, we learn to accept that we cannot save them all. It's the burden of our profession and what stirs us to greater learning. Someday, we may be able to treat disease and infection with as much ease as we remove a splinter or wrap a sprain, but that day hasn't yet arrived. Until it does, we'll continue to do what we're able. It's the best we can hope for, and it's all that can be expected."

Dr. Fogarty's words broke through the fog, but left James with little comfort. He looked at Dr. Fogarty as though he had momentarily forgotten his presence. "I know what you say is true and you're more experienced than I am, but I'll never accept what has happened. It's shameful that we . . ." James stopped himself before the rising tide of rage could take hold fully. "Please forgive me. My manners aren't usually so poor. I truly thank you for all you've done. If you hadn't been so willing to help us, Dolph would have died in far worse circumstances. If any of my patients need a skilled surgeon in the future, I hope I may refer them to you. Your kindness, help, and concern have meant more than words can adequately express. Now, if you'll excuse us, we must make arrangements for our return to Salacoa."

The sad journey home seemed to take an inordinately long time. When they pulled into the Waleska crossroads, the ever-faithful Johnny Blalock was there with his wagon to help them transport the simple pine coffin to the Campbell home, where Dolph would lie in state in the front room until the funeral two days hence.

A small army of Campbells met the wagon in the yard when it pulled up. James searched the faces for Mary Alice but did not see her. Instead, he saw Bud's and Nancy's brothers, sisters, and in-laws. Word had spread quickly among the family and they rallied in support, as they always did.

They placed Dolph on the sawhorses set up to receive his coffin and then prepared for the flood of friends and neighbors who would soon be arriving for visitation and bringing copious food offerings, as was the custom in times of tragedy or illness.

When the bustle subsided again into quiet grief, James finally was able to speak to Mary Alice's aunt. "Where is Mary Alice? Is she all right?"

"She's gonna be all right. Just having a little pain, so Nancy sent her home where she can rest. She's awful big, ain't she? Do you think she's further along than you first figgered?"

James did not stop to answer the question but sought out his mother-in-law instead. "Nancy, if you all will excuse me, I feel like I ought to go home. It's been almost two weeks since I left. It feels like two months. May I leave Archie here with you?"

Nancy looked up at him with sad eyes and smiled her consent. James bent down and placed a quick kiss on her weather-beaten cheek and departed with Johnny, who was ready to leave. James arrived home to find Lavinia Locklin sitting in his kitchen and no sign of Mary Alice.

"Lavinia, where is she?"

"She's having her a little rest. She ain't been down long, so don't you go waking her." Lavinia stood up, moving toward the door. "Well, now you're here, I'm gonna get on home myself. She been having pains on and off for most of the afternoon, but she ain't likely ready yet. Pains ain't steady enough." After giving birth to fifteen, Lavinia was about as expert as anyone in labor and delivery prognosis.

"James, is that you?" They heard Mary Alice calling from the depths of the house. James found her propped up in their bed looking small and in some discomfort.

As he entered the room, she looked up and immediately burst into tears. "Oh, James, how could anyone so young die? It was just a broken leg. What on earth happened?"

James took her in his arms and held her until her sobbing slowed and then told her all that had transpired since he left for Atlanta. She listened intently to the portion describing Davidson, looking up at James with wide horrified eyes.

"How can the man call himself a doctor? Isn't there anything that can be done about him? Shouldn't the medical society be told?"

James ran a hand over his face to clear his exhausted mind. "If I thought it would do any good, I would spend all we have trying to get this man run out of the profession, but when I said as much to Dr. Fogarty, he warned me off. He said I'm too young and unknown among the medical society in Atlanta. Davidson is well connected and he would use his influence, reputation, and wealth to ruin me instead. I don't like what he said, but I respect him and I know he's right."

Mary Alice shook her head. "But this is wrong! How can you just let it go so easily?"

"Getting myself stricken off the medical rolls won't bring Dolph back and it would mean Salacoa is without a doctor." James could hear the edge rising in his voice. "I've worked too hard to get where I am to run the risk of losing it to a man like Davidson."

Tears formed again with her next words. "But how can you not do something? He may cause more deaths if he's not stopped."

"What do you expect of me?" James snapped. He was tired beyond patience, even with Mary Alice. "I have no power to stop him. You ask too much. I'm deeply sorry about Dolph, but I will not give up my practice for something that has so little chance of succeeding."

Mary Alice turned her face from him and her next words cut to the quick. "I know you love medicine and the good you do for other people as much or more than you do anything or anyone. I have accepted it as part of what I love about you, but I never took you for a coward." She stuffed her fist in her mouth as tears steamed again. For the third time in less than two weeks, James felt deep shame.

Despite the tension between them, James knew he had to see if the pains Mary Alice felt were actual labor or just the occasional contractions that came on sometimes late in pregnancy. She was still six weeks away from a full-term delivery, but her size and the onset of pains had him worried. The longer a baby stayed in the womb, the better its chances during delivery and in the dangerous weeks following birth. There were too many tiny graves scattered throughout every cemetery and James had no intention of letting a new one belong to their child.

Mary Alice, avoiding direct eye contact, stiffly agreed she too would feel better if she knew what this baby was up to, so she did not argue when James bent to examine her. What he discovered did not make his mind rest any easier. Her cervix had fully effaced during the time he had been gone and was already dilated by a good bit. She could go into labor at any time.

"This baby may not wait for you to reach full term. I want you to stay off your feet and not get up for any reason other than what's absolutely necessary."

"But I can't do that," Mary Alice snapped. "Mama's going to need me to help with the visitations and after the funeral with the guests. I can't leave it all to her."

"Yes, you can and you will. If it makes you feel any better, I'll ask Lizzie to help your mother. I'm sure she'll offer to do it anyway. If you want a healthy baby, you'll do what I tell you."

Mary Alice's eyes flashed and she opened her mouth to spit out a retort, but James sliced the air with his hand. "Don't argue. Don't say another word. Do you hear me?"

James was about at the end of his tether. His patience was as exhausted as his body felt. It didn't help that his stomach had been giving him trouble for over a week now. He hadn't been able to keep anything down except cornmeal mush for the last two days. He would be taking his own advice when the funeral was behind them.

They buried Dolph in New Canaan cemetery on a warm, rainy afternoon. The church was at capacity despite the weather. Friends and neighbors would not let a little rain keep them from paying their respects. Mary Alice, after the initial shock, had accepted that James had done all he possibly could, and she now leaned heavily on him as the family walked up the hill to the gravesite. Once or twice, he heard her quick intake of breath and felt her shift around trying to be more comfortable. Mary Alice needed to lie down, but she wouldn't until everything had been seen to and all the social obligations fulfilled. The lying in state at home with the calls it brought at all hours was hard enough, but receiving the congregation after the funeral could go on for hours as well. There were social rules for every occasion and those surrounding death were among the strictest.

James finally got Mary Alice home just as the sun was setting. Because she was thoroughly exhausted and was in some discomfort, Lizzie had taken Archie home with her.

"Do you think you're going to have this baby tonight?" He asked in what he hoped was a lighthearted manner.

"I think I just might."

Full labor commenced around midnight. Blessedly, it was relatively short. The baby, a little girl, made her appearance about 6:00 a.m.

Mary Alice was struggling to raise herself higher to get a better look at her new daughter when James put his hand on her shoulder. "Wait. We're not finished here."

Within a few minutes, a little boy came pushing his way into the world. James drew a long breath and exhaled slowly. Three babies under the age of three on top of bereavement—Lord, help us.

CHAPTER 13

August 1895

Mary Alice dragged the back of her hand across her forehead to prevent sweat running into her eyes while she stood over the wood-burning range preparing the noon meal. Summer had arrived in early June on the updrafts of a heat wave that remained unbroken for the entire season. Morning temperatures reached the nineties earlier with each passing day and remained longer into the evening the deeper into August they got. She had just put the cornbread into the oven and stoked the flames again, when the faint, but unmistakable, acrid odor of burning green beans drifted her way. She snatched the lid up, peered into the pot, and jerked it onto a cooler part of the range, burning herself in the process. The beans needed more water and so did her stinging fingers. She turned to the water bucket in the dry sink and found it empty, which elicited a frustrated grunt as she sucked on her assaulted digits.

There was nothing for it but to go to the well again, for the third time that morning. Unfortunately, Archie and the babies, Randolph and Elizabeth, were toddling around the kitchen, underfoot and generally trying to get into everything, especially the slop bucket behind the range where the scraps for the hogs were kept. James was off again on morning house calls and the porch was full of waiting patients. She put a fist on each hip and blew at a gnat trying to get into her eye. Today was one of those days when she thought about the teacher who had once courted her. Life might have been easier with a husband less dedicated to his calling.

She lifted the heavy pine kitchen table's leg while hurriedly snatching up infant skirts. She had found that flowing baby dresses proved convenient for more than changing diapers. The long skirts made excellent tools for keeping the little ones secured and out of danger while she attended to chores that required either her absence from the room or her full attention. She placed the gathered skirts on the floor and dropped the table leg on top of them, ensuring the twins would not go near the hot range nor be able to follow her onto the high back porch where the well was located. Task accomplished, she and Archie headed for the well. He high-stepped along behind her, proud to be considered old enough to go onto the tall porch without having his hand held.

As soon as the pair was out of sight, the twins erupted in shrill cries declaiming their indignation at the circumstances in which they were left, but despite several men waiting on the porch, not one offered to help with anything other than carrying the bucket into the kitchen once she had it filled.

Mary Alice grunted and gave the man a less than gracious nod. Men! Their idea of courtesy was a peculiar thing. How they could sit there chatting and laughing, while waiting expectantly to be fed without the slightest thought as to how that meal would arrive on the table was beyond understanding. She had considered asking them to watch the twins for her, but then thought better of it. They would probably let the babies wander into the creek. Did men ever attend to anybody's wants other than their own? No, they just expected to be waited on hand and foot once they entered the house.

Her anger's depth came as a surprise. Perhaps her exasperation could be laid at the heat's door rather than an ungracious spirit. After all, James had moments when he put her desires before his, but like all men, they were fewer rather than greater in number.

A wagon's rattle announced Mr. Wilson's arrival, eliciting an inward groan. He came for medicine for his dropsy regularly and usually at dinnertime. She would need to prepare a second pone of cornbread. She felt sorry for the old man who lived alone and seemed to live to eat, but Mr. Wilson at the dinner table was a sight to behold and often left his hostess feeling as the Egyptians must have after God caused the locusts to swarm. He had never married and got by on simple food he prepared himself. Guilt over her unkind thoughts prodded Mary Alice. At least he was not a picky eater and appreciated whatever was served.

She hurried back into the house, beckoned by the crescendo erupting from her toddlers. Please let the tenor of their sobs indicate they were ready to be put down for a nap. Babies at the dinner table would perfectly round out a morning already filled with frustration. Maybe feeding them now would ensure they slept until dinner was over. They were taking shorter naps and soon they might give up daytime sleep altogether. Dread the thought. She threw together the extra pone and shoved it into the oven, before dipping up small portions of beans, squash, and carrots, which she mashed to pulp. Leftover breakfast biscuits completed the babies' meal and they were soon yawning, ready for their cots.

It was nigh on one o'clock and James still hadn't returned from his calls. Dinner could wait no longer. Mary Alice went to the porch and invited those waiting there to come in and prayed she had prepared enough. Her mother had taught her economy along with recipes and she still had difficulty knowing just how much to prepare. Of course, never knowing how many people she would be expected to feed didn't make it any easier.

The assembled group moved as a body from the porch to the dining room where the long table was laden with steaming bowls of every available garden vegetable, two pones of cornbread, and a pound cake. She fought to control an anxious gasp as Mr. Wilson selected her best but least sturdy chair, depositing his considerable bulk onto its delicately caned bottom. The chair creaked, moaned, and tilted to the left under the unexpected weight while Mary Alice held her breath and hoped for the best. The overburdened piece of furniture finally righted itself with a hard thump, settled, and looked like it might manage to hold on long enough for dinner to be eaten. She looked at the table filled with James's patients with a sigh. One crisis avoided and probably several more to go before this meal is over. She settled herself at the foot of the table nearest the kitchen door and mentally chided herself. She really was on a tear today.

To make up for her impatience and uncharitable thoughts, she asked Mr. Wilson to return thanks, which pleased him immensely. He nodded graciously and made short work of thanking the Lord for what He had provided. The heavily laden bowls then began their progress around the table and the meal was consumed with the normal flow of polite conversation. Each diner made his contribution at a socially appropriate moment with the notable exception of Mr. Wilson, who had tucked into his mounded-over plate with a will and hadn't opened his mouth for any purpose other than food since he had pronounced the blessing. Mary Alice noted with some alarm that his plate was completely empty before the others had eaten even half.

Being a gracious hostess, she marshaled her frustration and asked sweetly, "Mr. Wilson, may I pass you some beans or corn?"

"No, thankee . . . I'll just retch for them bowls," he replied with a gap-toothed grin as he reached for another helping, his words dragging over his tongue in a slow, syrupy drawl seasoned with plenty of mountain accent.

And "just retch" the table's length and breadth he did for the remainder of the meal, pausing in his inhalation of every bowl's last morsel only long enough to comment on the quality of the bread.

"This here's the bestest cornbread I done ever ett, Miz Doctor."

Mary Alice gave him a weak smile in reply. She had learned from her mother that a good hostess never comments on a guest's manners or habits, no matter how peculiar they may be, and so she was left with only one option—sigh mentally and accept the inevitable.

Now that the main body of diners had eaten their fill, they removed themselves to the porch once again and left the table clearing to Mary Alice. She was just about to ask Mr. Wilson if there was anything else she could get for him, when he rose from the chair, patted his belly and commented with deep satisfaction, "I sure enjoyed my little bite, Miz Doctor."

His description of the mountain he had eaten caught her so off guard that she started to laugh aloud. She choked back her mirth with a muffled snort, which she covered with a fake cough and a hand over her mouth.

Archie, being an observant little tike, was very attuned to adult words and reactions. This interaction had not escaped his notice and his mother was mortified to hear him chortling and saying "little bite, little bite" repeatedly as he toddled off about his own business.

Mr. Wilson heard him also and broke into a big belly laugh as he began clearing the table and carrying the empty bowls and dirty dishes into the kitchen for Mary Alice. Mr. Wilson's unassuming good humor and thoughtfulness went a long way toward easing her irritation with the fact that "the bestest cornbread he'd done ever ett" was in reality half of her pound cake.

James arrived home in the middle of the afternoon and immediately began seeing the waiting patients. When the porch was finally empty, he came into the kitchen, whistling and appearing very pleased with himself. Mary Alice's lips thinned as she watched him from beneath her lashes. He absentmindedly patted her shoulder while inspecting the pots on the stove. Apparently satisfied with what he saw, he began rummaging through the pie safe. His eyes widened when he lifted the cover on the cake tin. With a shrug, he cut himself a sliver of pound cake and shoved it in his mouth. Mary Alice plopped down at the table, grabbed Archie's pants, and began stabbing needle and thread through a tear.

James planted a cakey kiss atop her head. "You'll never guess what good luck I've had." Without waiting for her to look up, he rushed on. "You know the old Babcock farm? It came up for sale a couple of weeks ago and I put in a bid. I didn't really think they would accept it, but seems no one else bid, so the farm is mine."

James stood expectantly, grinning from ear to ear, apparently waiting for Mary Alice's exclamations of delight and praise. When she didn't respond, he continued, "I've already talked to Newt about what we're going to plant. He's ready to hire a day hand to help him now with this addition. I think we're going to put most of the cleared acres in cotton. Prices are predicted to rise, and we think that'll do well."

Mary Alice put her mending aside and looked up through narrowed eyes. "Is that where you've been all day?"

James ignored her tone and raced on. "Yeah, I had to go into Canton to the lawyers to sign the papers and finish up the loan from the bank. I thought Newt might like a trip into town, so he went too. Newt and I had a real good dinner in town at the café. They have the best lemon chess pie. You haven't fixed one in a while now."

On his best days, James was an observant, perceptive man. Today was not one of those days. Mary Alice's breathing increased as she replied through clenched teeth, "I see you're enjoying the pound cake, even though it's not chess pie."

"Uh-huh. It's good. Y'all sure did eat a lot of it at dinner. Who all was here?"

"Did you see everyone on the porch when you arrived this afternoon?" The edge in her voice should have been a warning.

"Yeah."

"Well, all those people were here from about nine o'clock this morning." At her tone and volume, he finally met her eyes. Heat crawled from Mary Alice's throat onto her cheeks. "You can thank Mr. Wilson for half the cake being gone and the whole bunch for me having to prepare more vegetables for supper, instead of having something left from dinner. And now you waltz in and announce that you've spent what little money we have on another farm. Just when are you going to get a water pump installed in the sink for me? You promised over six months ago to get it done. The kitchen table isn't going to keep Randolph and Elizabeth tied down much longer. They are getting so that they can drag it along a little more every day. But I guess since you don't have to worry about them, you just don't ever think about it, do you? Well, do you?"

"Of course, I . . ."

"No, you don't or it would already have been done!"

In the time-honored tradition of men who suddenly and inexplicably find themselves on the wrong side of an argument with a woman, James prepared to beat a hasty retreat. "I've got to finish up the journal entries out in the office. I guess supper'll be soon?"

Mary Alice did not deign to look at him and simply nodded, her displeasure seething and pouring through her at such a pace she began to feel lightheaded and headachy. Well, that would just be the living end. All she needed was to get sick right now.

Supper was a stressful affair, with Mary Alice eating in stiff silence. Archie must have sensed things weren't right between his parents, which made him disagreeable and cross. The babies picked up his distress and became fretful and whiny. When she could stand no more, Mary Alice shoved her chair back with a jerk, barked that she was going for a walk and felt sure Papa would be happy to watch the children for a while. James nodded and stared at this stranger who used to be his loving Mary Alice. No one offered to go with her.

The screened door slammed shut. Mary Alice stomped down the back steps and stormed off down the path through the field. While she marched among the cotton rows, her anger began to subside somewhat, but her disappointment that James had once again failed to take care of her kitchen water problem did not abate. She stalked along deep in thought without mind to where she was going when a loud friendly shout made her jump.

Lavinia Locklin waved from her front porch. "Hey, Miss Mary Alice! Come on up and set a spell. I seen you coming down the path and hoped you'd come this far."

Mary Alice sighed at the unwelcome intrusion, but good manners dictated no choice other than to join Lavinia on the porch. She turned, threw up a hand in greeting, and hoped her ungracious attitude didn't give itself away. She trudged up to Lavinia's porch with a drag in her step and a forced smile on her face.

Lavinia studied Mary Alice with a practiced maternal eye but asked no questions about what had sent her neighbor fleeing from her home. Instead, she offered a cup of sweet, fresh sassafras tea. Lavinia believed sassafras tea could cure any ailment, whether of the body or the spirit.

Mary Alice accepted the tea, even though she had just left her own supper table. Lavinia probably knew full well where James and Newt had been today and what their business was. She also knew Mary Alice desperately wanted and needed some improvements around the house.

The two women rocked in silence, sipping the sweet, rose-tinted brew, giving its woodsy, slightly spicy flavor a chance to bring its calming effect.

Without warning, Mary Alice felt tears streaming down her cheeks. Lavinia looked away long enough for courtesy and then placed her sun-darkened, work-calloused hand over Mary Alice's and gave a gentle little pat.

Mary Alice looked up at Lavinia and smiled weakly through the tears. "I'm sorry to come visiting and then sit here blubbering like a baby. I don't know what's gotten into me lately."

"Wyy, you just work yourself night and day. A body cain't work like you do and have babies close together and not get a little tired sometime. You just sit and drink that tea. Don't you fret none 'bout what's just twix you and me. I done had them feelings myself sometimes."

The two women sat in the evening, sipping, rocking, and talking until they noticed a strange figure that appeared to have enormous arms and an unusually shaped tail striding with a purpose from the direction of Mary Alice's house.

She frowned and sighed. "Oh, Lord. What's happened now."

James set the twins down, detached Archie from his leg, and placed his hand on the porch rail. "Evening, Lavinia. Mary Alice, Joe Harbin's come with word that his little sister is real sick with her stomach. I've got to gather supplies and then be on my way."

Mary Alice looked at him in surprise. "I thought Joss Harbin didn't want you there. Are you sure you should go?"

James answered rather more sharply than he usually spoke. "I can't refuse to treat a sick child just because she has a criminal for a father. Now, come back to the house because I've got to go."

Mary Alice got up, thanked Lavinia for the tea, picked up Randolph, and followed her husband and the other children. She lagged a few steps behind. She wasn't ready to talk with him yet. She was just so tired these days, and she had begun to suspect the reason. When they reached the house, James didn't even stop to kiss her before he rushed toward the yard. She swiped at renewed tears as she watched her husband's receding back.

CHAPTER 14

James went to the office and mixed small quantities of mineral salts and sugar, which he poured into small glass vials closed with cork stoppers. He next grabbed his supply of laudanum. All of this was placed in the holding straps inside his black leather medical bag. The disease, probably dysentery, would have to run its course since there were no actual cures, but restoring body fluids early on was the key in preserving life. Identifying and eliminating the source of the infection would keep the rest of the family from coming down with the illness.

As he rode through the valley, Mary Alice's question haunted him. It swirled through his mind in a constant circle. Would he live to regret coming to the Harbins' aid again? He had snapped at Mary Alice for voicing what he himself was thinking, but he couldn't justify refusing someone in need. It was against his physician's oath and his promise to help the mountain people. It had never occurred to him, however, that his resolve would be tested by the likes of Joss Harbin. During the years since the Harbin boys' wagon accident, James had heard nothing directly from them, only rumors of their nefarious activities. The situation must be dire for Joss Harbin to have allowed him to be summoned.

He arrived at the Harbin place after dark. As he mounted the steps, the sackcloth curtains over the front window twitched a little. Azaleigh cracked open the door before he could raise his hand to knock.

"Evening, Miz Harbin. Joe brought word that your daughter's very ill."

Azaleigh looked past James into the darkness as if she was trying to see some unnamed evil lurking in the woods surrounding the house. Satisfied that nothing was there, she opened the door just wide enough for James to squeeze through, allowing as little light to escape as possible. James had long ago ceased to be surprised by anything the Harbins might do, but this excessive caution and Azaleigh's almost palpable fear were making him very uneasy. James turned sideways and eased into the room. It was in much better order than when he last visited, although no cleaner.

Joe sat on the floor next to the fireplace. On a pallet in the corner lay a small form with sunken, feverish eyes and damp golden ringlets. Joe was bathing Pearl's forehead with a wet cloth and murmuring softly to her.

"Now, you just lay still, little Pearlie. Ain't nothing gonna hurt you with your Joe here. Doc Buchanan done come. He's the bestest doctor thay is. He's gonna make it all better."

While James appreciated Joe's confidence, the girl's wasted appearance was alarming. He strode quickly to the pallet. "How long has she been sick?"

Joe looked up with unhappy eyes. "She started about a week ago, but she's only been down for a couple of days. She just got beyond going. I'da come for you before now, 'cept Pa, he said he ain't gonna have you on the place. He ain't never forgive the way you talked to him when I was hurt. He even made the other boys stay up in the woods whilst you was here last time. Said they'd heal okay without that meddling, jumped-up medical man.

Course, Jeb's arm ain't never been the same. Pa, he's just hard-down sorry mean."

Joe's words did not reassure. James peered through the open back door. "Where's your dad? He has no idea I'm here, does he?"

"Oh, you ain't got no need to worry. Him and the boys done gone up to Ellijay. They ain't gonna be back for two, three days."

Azaleigh spoke for the first time since James's arrival. "Law, Joe, you know you cain't never depend on what your pa says. He might come through the door any minute. Dr. Buchanan, you best get on with it."

More than ever, James wished he had never met this bunch, but he put those thoughts aside. "Joe, bring that kerosene lamp over here." He then turned to the little form on the pallet. "Pearl, don't be afraid. I'm just going to pick you up and put you on the bed."

When he lifted her, the child weighed no more than a feather pillow and her cheeks were only dark hollows in her little face. Her lips were beginning to crack from dehydration. The wasted week could well be the death knell for this pretty, pitiful child. He called for extra sacking to be placed on the bed before he gently placed the trembling little body on it.

"Miz Harbin, I think you must know how ill Pearl is. I'm going to start treatment now, but I'm not leaving until I believe she's well on the way to mending. Joe, please ride to my home and tell Miz Buchanan what the situation is. If you don't mind, I'd also appreciate it if you'd stop by my father-in-law's and ask him to send one of my wife's sisters over to stay with her while I'm gone. She's got her hands full right now."

Joe looked between James and Pearl for a moment before placing a quick kiss on the little girl's cheek. He whispered reassurances to his mother and then was gone, taking James's horse since it was still saddled.

When James and Azaleigh were alone, he turned to her. "I'm going to need water that has boiled for ten minutes and then allowed to stand covered until it is cool enough to drink and a sterilized cup."

After Azaleigh brought the requested items, James set about preparing the solution with which he would treat Pearl's condition. He took a small vial from his bag and emptied its contents into the cup. To this, he added sterilized water until the cup was almost full and then a drop of the laudanum to ease pain. He gave the solution a quick stir and lifted Pearl's head high enough for her to be able to drink. His heart ached as Pearl looked up at him with complete trust and a wan smile.

"You gonna make me better, ain'tcha?" she whispered hoarsely.

James glanced at Azaleigh, who returned his gaze with wide-eyed anxiety, before replying, "I'm sure going to do everything in my power. Right now, I want you to drink what's in this cup. It's got medicine in it and some sugar to make it taste sweet. You need to drink all of it. Are you ready to try?"

She nodded and began slowly, choking and sputtering with the first sips. The sugar didn't totally mask the medicine's bitter taste, but Pearl did not whimper or complain. As the mixture lubricated her parched throat, she began to take larger sips until she gulped the last from the cup. Almost as quickly as the last swallow went down, her eyes widened and her little face crumpled in despair. She began to cry softly as her bowels betrayed her once again.

As James looked up to ask Azaleigh for help with the cleaning up, he was momentarily struck by Pearl's strong resemblance to her mother. The girl's lovely features flickered briefly across her mother's face in the shadowy glow cast by the kerosene lamp, and then were gone just as quickly when Azaleigh moved to do as requested. In her girlhood, Azaleigh had been judged one of the prettiest and most capable girls in the community. She had made an impression on teachers and classmates alike during her few brief years at the local school before she had been forced to quit to help out at home. What possessed her to marry Joss Harbin was beyond understanding, unless you believed the gossip that he had once been the handsomest boy to ever pass through Pine Log School. The years of hard living had erased from his face any trace of physical beauty.

Whatever her reasons for joining forces with Joss, the years of abuse and privation had taken a severe toll on Azaleigh's looks and mental health. If she had ever possessed above average intelligence, she gave no sign of it now. Her mind and body had been shattered by the violence in which she had lived since her marriage. Looking at Pearl's emerging blond beauty and Joe's dark good looks, James found it easier to see what their parents might once have been. If he had ever needed proof that evil existed in the world, he needed to look no further than Joss Harbin's life. It was hard to imagine what else could bring a man to such a low state of lawlessness and cruelty.

James and Azaleigh nursed Pearl through the night with frequent attempts at re-hydrating her delicate little body with the salts mixture and boiled water. Finally, toward daylight, the flux seemed to be slowing enough for Pearl to finally drift off into an exhausted, but peaceful sleep.

When her breathing slowed into an easy rhythm, James turned to her mother. "Has anyone else in the family been ill? Have y'all had any visitors who were sick?"

"Wyy, nobody but Pearl's been down with any kind of complaint this whole spring. Joss, he ain't never sick. Boys mighta had colds, but that's all. We don't never have no visitors."

James thought for a moment. "Has anything changed here on the farm? Where does Pearl play?"

Azaleigh looked at James in wonder. "She don't play much. None of the childern has never done no playing. Joss, he won't allow it. Says they's gotta work to earn they keep. But being a girl, she stays here in the house with me and I let her go down to the creek where she cain't be seen to do a little playing when her pa ain't about. I cain't think of no changes on the place except Joss, he moved the hog lot couple of months ago. He put it so's the fence run right down next to the creek. The hogs stick they heads under the bottom of the fence and can drink. That way he ain't gotta haul water to them."

James was beginning to understand the possible source of Pearl's illness. When it was full light, he asked Azaleigh to show him the new hog lot.

It sat on a low rise that sloped gently down to the creek. The shed, which sheltered the animals, sat on the highest point and he could see the tracks left by the hogs as they went up and down the small hill to and from their drinking water. Like all hog lots, this one was probably its inhabitants' whole world. They were born and died without ever leaving its confines. All their life functions were performed there, including ridding themselves of bodily wastes. James shook his head in dismay. It didn't take a medical degree to figure out what happened to the wastes when it rained even a little.

"Where exactly does Pearl play when she comes to the creek?"

Azaleigh lifted her arm and pointed downstream. "She plays behind them bushes down there so's as Joss and the boys cain't see her if'n they was to come to the house unexpected. Joss, he's easier on her cause she's a girl, but he still don't like her to be away from the house. Says she's old enough to haul water for me and the like. She's little for her age and she ain't big enough to lug a heavy bucket loaded with water, so I send her out to play when the men folkses has left for good for the day."

James walked to the spot Azaleigh had indicated. He would have missed it if she hadn't told him exactly where to duck under the bush just beyond a pile of rocks by a big oak. The place was shady and noticeably cooler than the sunny path he had just left. It was no wonder a child would find this an intriguing playhouse and hideaway, especially when there was so much need for secrecy.

As his eyes adjusted to the dimmer light in Pearl's little glade, he saw her few pitiful playthings tucked into a dugout under a small rock shelf in the hill that rose toward the house. The ground under the trees and near the creek had been worn bare and smooth by little feet. If it hadn't been for the danger that James suspected lurked in every drop of the crystal-clear creek water, this would be a perfect place for the little girl to dream her dreams and play her games.

He stooped down to inspect the creek bank and the flowing water. He searched for just a few seconds before he saw what he was looking for. Caught in the undergrowth and tangle of weeds trailing in the water's edge were signs of waste that surely must have been washed from the hog lot just upstream. James took a water sample, which he planned to examine under the small microscope he had packed with his medical supplies in his saddlebags. Joe had been thoughtful enough to bring the bags into the house when he had returned late last night, but he had disappeared from the house before dawn. There was no telling where Joe had gone or what he was doing. Probably, it was in pursuit of Joss's usual business interests.

CHAPTER 15

James returned to the house and immediately examined the water sample for signs of bacteria. He peered into his simple microscope's eyepiece for only a few seconds before he saw multiple organisms swimming vigorously in the water droplet. Clearly Pearl had been playing in and probably drinking the infectious water. He knew the Harbins must be drawing their household water from somewhere above the hog lot or perhaps from a well, since no one else in the family had been sick. Several families downstream depended on this creek as their sole water supply. Not everyone felt the need to dig a well when a dependable water supply ran close by. The thought of confronting Joss Harbin again sent a chill through James, but the hog lot would have to be removed to its original location or, at least, to a place away from the creek.

Toward late afternoon on the second day, Pearl began to show significant improvement, so much so, that James thought he could safely return to Salacoa and spend the night at home. There were still no signs of any male Harbins, so James left several vials of medicine and instructions for its administration with Azaleigh and headed for home. Maybe Mary Alice would be more herself.

When he rode into the yard, the western sun was backlighting the house and bathing the valley beyond in a golden glow particular to lingering summer evenings. The giant oaks were casting long cool shadows, a welcome relief after the day's intense heat. There was a general feeling of calm, quiet, and peace about the place that had been decidedly absent when he left. Although he had gazed over this same scene more times than he could count, he was struck afresh by all for which he and Mary Alice had to be grateful and paused to simply enjoy the moment.

It wasn't clear why he should be awed by all that was so familiar. Perhaps close observation of the Harbins had made a greater impression than he wanted to acknowledge. It took self-assurance and determination to face down death and disease everyday with so few tools at his disposal, and he sometimes forgot his work was not his alone. It affected his wife and children too. It was his calling, but it was their burden. Being with Joe's family reminded him to be grateful for the one he and Mary Alice had created and the home they had built.

He found Mary Alice alone on the back porch. At the sound of his step, she turned and came toward him. She was smiling and the expression in her eyes contained more than a hint of relief.

"I'm so glad you're home. I was afraid you'd be gone much longer. You just missed Sister and Papa. They left after supper. The children are all asleep. Have you eaten?"

She gave him a hug and then propelled him into the kitchen. Food was the first, but not the last, warm homecoming delight Mary Alice bestowed on him that night. As he drifted off to sleep, James wondered if it were possible to love a woman more than he did Mary Alice.

With peace restored on the home front and Newt commissioned to install a new water pump and sink in Mary Alice's kitchen, James could not put off going back to the Harbins' any longer. He dreaded the interview he knew would have to take place with Joss. He had never been particularly brave when it came to confronting physical aggression, and he wasn't sure how Joss would react to his words. He left after dinner the next day and arrived by midafternoon in the depressingly littered Harbin yard. James looked around for any sign that Joss was about the place and seeing none, walked to the front door where Joe admitted him with a welcoming grin and handshake.

"Afternoon, Joe, Miz Harbin. How's our girl?"

Joe grinned as he gave the child an affectionate wink. "She's asking to get up and go play, so I guess she's done got lots better."

"Well, that's a good sign." James spoke with as hearty a tone as he could manage. He dreaded asking for Joss, but he could not leave today without discussing the issue of the creek and the damage being done to it by the hog lot's proximity. He assessed Pearl's progress by palpating her abdomen and checking her temperature. She was clearly on the mend.

Since the topic could no longer be avoided, James asked quietly, "Joe, where's your father? I know the source of Pearl's infection. I need to speak with him about how to prevent the problem in the future."

Joe cocked his head to one side, his eyes screwed up in a speculative squint. "You sure you want to do that? He ain't gonna take kindly to anything you got to say. I'm dreadful sorry to have to say this, but it's best if'n you just stay out of his way. He done said again he ain't gonna have no truck with you. I ain't told him you been here for Pearl. He thinks she just done got better on her own."

James drew a deep breath and fixed Joe with a determined expression. "The hog lot's got to be moved away from the creek. The runoff from it is poisoning the water downstream. Please get your dad to the house."

Joe gave James a searching look and then quickly turned and left by the backdoor. James would know within the next fifteen minutes what effect his request would produce in Joss.

Waiting for Joe's return left James alone with Pearl and her mother and little to talk about. Over the last few days, Azaleigh had shown herself uncomfortable with small talk. She rarely initiated conversation and answered questions with as few words as possible. Perhaps practical help might be welcome, so he gathered plates and crockery and carried them to the sink.

Azaleigh's eyes widened. "Doctor, what you doing? I'll get to them dishes directly. You don't need to be bothering yourself with woman's work." Both shock and amazement played across her face.

James took off his coat and rolled up his sleeves. "It won't be any trouble. I'll get some boiling water so we can get these plates good and clean."

When Azaleigh hesitated, he continued more firmly. "These need to be washed really well because I'm sure you don't want anyone else to get what Pearl has. Besides, I do dishes at home all the time." James wasn't sure whether she believed the lie, but Azaleigh shrugged and joined him at the sink.

With some shame, James pumped the handle at the sink. Even the Harbins had an indoor water pump, indicating a well somewhere near the house, which probably explained further why the other family members had escaped illness from the polluted water. This would probably make it even more difficult to convince Joss to move the lot. The danger it posed to the neighbors downstream should be sufficient persuasion, but experience and common sense predicted this was a foolhardy expectation.

James was drying the last of the dishes when the backdoor flew open and Joss Harbin's ursine form filled the opening, blocking out most of the daylight. The echoing crash of wood on wood caused James to jump and his heart to thump hard. Appalled at the slight tremble in his hands, he prayed Joss wouldn't see it as well. Even with his face in shadow, it was clear Joss was in high temper. Joe was nowhere to be seen.

"Well, lookie here! If'n it ain't that jumped-up medical man hisself. And doing up the dishes, just like a girl. Who the hell said you could be here? Was it you, Ma? Goddamnit, I told you, woman, not to have him here. Someday you're gonna push me too far and I'll take care of you for good. I told you Pearl'd be all right and, by God, look if'n it ain't so. Wyy, she done got up and is playing over there by the fire. I told you, ditten I? Well, ditten I?"

With each "ditten," Azaleigh took a step backward and Joss took one toward her. He raised his fist as if to strike her, but James stepped between them before Joss could launch a blow. Joss was so startled by what must be the novel experience of someone thwarting him, he momentarily stopped in his tracks. This gave James enough time to move out of reach, taking Azaleigh by the arm and pulling her with him.

James's face flamed and his heart pounded as an ungoverned fury replaced his fear. His words came as though they had a will of their own and he momentarily lapsed into childhood speech patterns, something he had left behind in college. "Miz Harbin ain't at fault. She didn't send for me, but you can be sure Pearl wouldn't have got no better without treatment, whether from me or some other doctor."

By now, Joss had recovered from the surprise of being challenged. He moved to within a few inches of James's face and growled in the most offensive manner possible without resorting to physical assault. "What my goddamn woman does or don't do ain't none of your fucking business. She was told. They was all told. You ain't allowed on the place."

Something was holding Joss back. It was unclear, but James was grateful for it, whatever the reason. Joss could take him in a fight any day of the week and twice on Sunday, but showing fear at this time could give Joss the excuse he was probably looking for to beat James to a bloody pulp, so he stood his ground and did not let his gaze waver. It was anathema to James why a father would resent treatment for a child who had been so ill, but confronting

Joss with his shortcomings would simply make Azaleigh's situation worse.

James took a firm grip on his temper and fear. "Mr. Harbin, Pearl was severely dehydrated, which can be as fatal as any disease. The medicine I gave her helped her get better. I'm sure you want her to continue to recover and to not get sick again."

Above his beard, a deep red burned in Joss's face. "My family ain't your damned concern. They all do what I say or else." His shout echoed in the exposed rafters.

James glared while words flew from his mouth as though he was simply a conduit through which they poured. "A man ought to take care of his family instead of beating them and making them afraid of him. It's your hog lot that's at fault. Anybody knows better than to put an animal lot or outhouse so close to a water source. Pearl got sick from the creek water that was fouled by your hogs."

James regretted his words as soon as they escaped his mouth. He had intended to try and reason with Joss, but instead he had let his anger overcome his common sense. His jaw clenched as he once again fought to control his emotions.

James stared Joss down while a venomous tirade began. Joss was so angry that his first words spluttered and saliva flew from the snaggletoothed opening in his unkempt beard. "You . . . you . . . goddamn uppity jackass! You go to hell. I'll put my fucking hog lot anywheres I take a mind to. And I can promise you this—you'uns are gonna be sorry for interfering. Now get out of my house, and keep your sorry ass away from here."

Now, it would probably take involving the law to get the hog lot moved. As much as he had intended to do good for the unfortunate Harbins caught in the web of Joss's cruelty and domination, he had probably simply made things worse for them.

This time, James took a firm grip on his temper. Reacting to Joss's threats would be counterproductive and meaningless. He chose his next words with great care, maintaining a deadly calm, speaking in a voice so quiet that Joss had to remain silent to hear what his self-selected enemy had to say. Surprisingly, James's voice sounded authoritative and confident. "Mr. Harbin, I have no desire to be in conflict with you. For everyone's sake, I'm asking you to move the hog lot away from the creek by the end of the week. I don't want to involve the sheriff, but if you don't move the lot, you'll give me no choice. Since there's nothing more you and I have to discuss, I'll be taking my leave."

Joss raised his fist as if to strike James, but then dropped it. Once again, he seemed to be holding back. Instead, he growled, "You might want to think real hard before you go getting the law over here. Now get out."

James nodded to Azaleigh and gathered his supplies, turned his back on Joss, and walked through the door. It was difficult to know what had kept Joss from physically attacking him. Maybe Joss still had a little respect for, more likely fear of, the law remaining in his sorry soul. Bullies were often cowards when they met a superior force.

As James started the long ride home, he mentally reviewed what had just transpired. What kind of trouble he had stirred up? A shiver went down his spine and he startled when his horse's hoof kicked a stone. Joss's words had accomplished their intended goal. It was beyond comprehension how people could live as the Harbins did—common sense, reason, and decency played absolutely no part in their lives. With a sinking heart, James knew it would probably take the intervention from the law to get the blasted hog lot moved.

This was not how he had envisioned his work in the community all those years ago when he felt he was destined for medicine. He hadn't in his wildest dreams thought he would be contacting the law to ensure public health and safety, but then he had never known anyone quite like Joss Harbin.

A sudden movement in the woods caused his horse to prick its ears and dance sideways. James's heart pounded and he searched for what caused the bushes to rustle, ready to kick his horse into a gallop. Joe stepped out of the shadows with a deep frown etched into his handsome features and waving his arms, flagging James to a halt.

"Doc, wait up. I gotta tell you something. You best watch your back. Pa, he's saying how's he's gonna get even with you for how you talked to him. I don't know what he's got a mind for, but you need to be careful. He ain't likely to let this thing go, 'specially if you get the law on him."

James eyed Joe for a moment and then replied, "Your pa will leave me no choice if he doesn't move that hog lot. I don't want a fight with him, but he can't keep contaminating the drinking water for several families. Do what you can to convince him to do what's right."

James wasn't in the mood to spend any more time on Pine Log Mountain than he had to. He gave his hat brim a sharp tug and kicked his horse into a canter. He felt nothing but disgust for all the Harbins now and wanted nothing more than to be home where life made sense and was lived by a code he understood.

While he rode over the five miles of rough tracks that passed for roads, he had an inescapable prickling sensation that raised the hair on the back of his neck. He looked back over his shoulder every so often. It felt like someone was following him, but he couldn't see anyone on the road behind him. Once or twice, he thought he saw an unusual or out-of-place movement in the forest's undergrowth, but nothing he was sure of. He shook his head to clear his thinking. Maybe he was becoming as fanciful as Maggie, the midwife.

CHAPTER 16

James unsaddled his horse and gave its sweat-glossed back and withers a vigorous rubdown, something the animal usually enjoyed, but this evening it must have wondered whether its master was attending to its grooming needs or exorcising his demons on its innocent hide. James brushed and scrubbed with such force that the poor animal flinched and glanced over its shoulder at him in wall-eyed displeasure. A particularly energetic stroke elicited an unhappy squeal, bringing James up short and slowing his ministrations to a more acceptable pace. When he finally put the animal in its stall, his arms ached, but his mind was cleared of the turmoil the interview with Joss Harbin had roiled up.

James crossed the distance from the barn, which sat in the pasture between his house and the Locklins' and loped up his own back steps. It was good to be among normal people again.

Mary Alice greeted him with a quizzical smile. "How did things go at Harbins'?"

As James described the confrontation with Joss, her expression slipped from concern to fear. "James, please leave those people alone. They're dangerous. Joss Harbin usually makes good on his threats from what I hear. We don't need their kind of trouble."

The peace of moments ago melted. James's mouth thinned. "I have no choice. He has no right to poison the creek that his neighbors depend on for water."

Mary Alice appeared displeased with his response, but she said no more. As she began to prepare a supper plate of vegetables for him, James stopped her. "Just fix me some cornmeal mush, if you don't mind. My stomach isn't feeling up to anything more. Little touch of flu, I guess. After I eat, I think I'm going to turn in. It's been a long day."

Shortly after midnight, frantic pounding on the backdoor awakened James and Mary Alice. "James, get up! The barn's on fire."

James jumped into his pants and rushed onto the porch where Newt waited, Mary Alice and Archie close on his heels. What he saw made his heart stop. A bright orange inferno roared where the barn was supposed to be. Flames, which had completely engulfed the barn, were setting the sky ablaze in a red and yellow display that threatened to catch the whole mountainside if it was not contained. James shouted for Mary Alice and Archie to stay in the house and then ran with Newt to face down the raging fire.

As they passed through the pasture gate, he looked all around for his saddle horse and milk cow among the plow mules, which were not put up at night, shouting to Newt over the flames' roar, "Where're the rest of the animals?"

Newt just shook his head as the acrid stench of burning flesh drifted by on the growing breeze.

By the time James and Newt crossed the pasture, the barn was starting to cave in on itself with no hope of saving anything it contained. The best they could do was wet the ground around the flaming mass of timbers so the mountain rising behind them wouldn't catch fire as well. Lavinia had already arrived with buckets and her eldest boys. They all set to work with a will, drawing water from the trough beside the barn. They worked in a bucket brigade, wetting the ground around the barn and throwing water onto the pasture grass as it was set by sparks drifting on wind blown from a fiery mouth. At times, the heat from the flames was so intense they had to back off and let the fire simply burn before they could approach the area around the barn again.

James insisted they all wet themselves so the heat and sparks wouldn't catch their hair and clothing even though the water supply was dwindling. More quickly than anyone could believe, the fire began to burn itself out and the only choice that remained was to simply stand and watch.

As the flames reduced themselves to a pile of smoldering embers, Newt looked at James and spoke the words both were thinking, "Thay's no way the barn just up and caught fire by itself. Thay ain't a cloud in the sky so it wat'n lightning, and we don't keep no lanterns nor such in a barn. Somebody done set it. Got any idea who?"

James's voice was near a whisper. "Yes, but I doubt if I can prove it." He went on to describe what had transpired during his last visit to the Harbin farm. "I'm going to the sheriff tomorrow. If you'll go with me, I'll ask Charles to keep an eye on the place when we're not around. We'll stop and ask Bud to come to the house on our way to town."

James and Newt worked for much of what was left of the night to ensure the fire did not flame up again. When Newt finally went home, James stood alone looking over the ruins and breathing in air heavy with the stench of his destroyed animals. In the initial crisis, he had not had time for the arson's full implications to sink in. Now, they hit a blow to the gut and he found his hands trembling when he lifted them to wipe the sweat from his eyes. He wasn't sure whether it was the fear or the rage that was more responsible for his churning stomach and his pounding heart, but he was confident of one thing. He could have lost more than his barn and his saddle horse tonight. Tomorrow before they could leave for town and the sheriff, he and Newt would have the gruesome task of burying the carcasses outlined in the ashes where the stalls had been. His gaze lingered on those two sad mounds while visions of a burned house and very different bodies tumbled through his tired mind. With the waking nightmare of Mary Alice and the children replacing his horse and milk cow, he leaned over and vomited, the sour taste of bile replacing that of ashes.

No one in either family got much sleep that night, most of it spent fighting the fire and worry consuming what little dark remained. It seemed as though he had just drifted off when James jerked awake to the sound of retching coming from the side porch. In her haste to get outside, she had left the door connecting their bedroom to the porch open. James inwardly sighed because he knew what early morning illness probably meant. Mary Alice was young and strong, but too many babies too close together could damage her health and weaken her system. He made a mental note to ask Lavinia about providing daily help with whatever Mary Alice needed most and to see a widow woman in the community who might be willing to do the laundry. Mary Alice was getting thinner by the day, which wasn't good for her or the new baby she was probably carrying.

James and Newt left for Canton shortly after breakfast. They found the sheriff in his small office enjoying his first cup of morning coffee. "Well, what brings you boys out so early? Thay's plenty of coffee in the pot. Grab a cup and pour yourself some."

Ward Hamilton had served Cherokee County for much of his adult life, beginning as a deputy and working his way up to the elected position of sheriff. James had heard the story from his own father, from Bud, and from Mr. Sinclair, all of whom had voted for Ward in every sheriff's election. Even though Ward was a Democrat, James liked and supported him too.

The tale was that after the war, Ward came home to find his parents dead and their small tenant farm in ruins. Without a home, he took the only job offered him and worked hard to adjust to civilian life again. To everyone's surprise, he found law enforcement to his liking and his war experiences as a Confederate intelligence officer were believed to aid him in successfully carrying out his duties. He was judged by all to be a fair, honest man who knew the law as well as most judges.

The walrus mustache on his upper lip and his hair were mostly gray now and he walked with a rolling gait due to arthritis in his hips. People had begun to speculate on how much longer he would be able to stand up to the job's physical requirements. Ward probably knew what some people thought, but James had told his friend he had a few good years left in him. The deputy would just have to wait his turn.

James accepted the offer of coffee gladly and poured for himself and Newt before he began. He described his most recent interaction with the Harbins and Joss's final words.

The sheriff looked thoughtful for a moment. "Newt, y'all live closest to the barn, don't you? Did y'all see anything to tie this to Joss?"

Newt shook his head. "We was all asleep. First I knowed was when one of the boys yelled out that the whole world was on fire."

Sheriff Hamilton emitted a frustrated sigh. "I'd give a whole lot to be able to pin something on Joss Harbin and make it stick. He's a mean, sorry bastard, but until we get some real proof or an eyewitness, which ain't likely, thay ain't much I can do. All the same, Bobby and me'll ride over to Pine Log and remind Joss we got our eye on him. He'll come to a understanding nothing else unfortunate better happen at Buchanan's and it's in his best interest to move that hog lot."

For the next two months, James and Newt made sure one of them was always on the place. The eldest Locklin boys were also put on alert to keep an eye open for anything unusual. James had no choice but to ride a plow mule to his calls, which placed a burden on the farm with harvest time coming on, so in early September, he returned to Canton.

He rode his mule through the little crossroads just above the Etowah River and turned southwest, trotting uphill to the crest of the low mountain where Gus Coggin's Crescent Farm and Race Barns sat. Gus was a noted breeder of harness racers and occasionally sold retired trotters he did not want to use for breeding stock. Perhaps Gus could be persuaded to part with one that would make a good saddle horse.

When James arrived in the yard, Gus was welcoming several sulkies back from their early morning training run around the track located in the meadow below the barns. Gus motioned to one of the drivers who wheeled about and rolled to a stop beside his boss. The sulky was pulled by a pretty little bay mare, which snorted and blew as she slowed her pace. As she came up to Gus, she stretched her head out, clearly expecting some affection from her owner, who absentmindedly gave her the nose rub she sought and a bite of the apple he had been eating. Gus and the driver began a deep consultation as James approached, so he stopped and waited at a polite distance until they finished their conversation.

"Good morning, Gus. How've you been?"

"Morning, Doc. We've been tolerable, about tolerable. And how're you and yours this beautiful day?"

"Can't complain. We're doing about as well as could be hoped. Mary Alice and the children are all healthy and the kids are growing like weeds. Last time I was in town, though, was to see Ward Hamilton about some trouble we had on the farm. I need a good saddle horse, and I'm hoping you might have something for sale that would suit."

Gus nodded. "Yeah, I heard from Ward about what happened. It's a shame about your horse. He was a fine little gelding with a right smooth trot, as I recall. Something's got to be done about that Harbin clan. They been barn burning and scaring folks for too long now." Gus paused and shook his head in disgust. "Well, nothing to be done right now. Why don't we take a walk through the barns and see what we can find. I've got a couple you might be interested in."

Gus saw that his barns' interiors were as clean as most people's homes, cleaner than some. As they entered the dimness of the first barn, James paused, allowing his eyes to adjust and breathing in the sweet fresh scents of hay and wood shavings. He had not lost his childhood love for animals, especially horses, and had to control his desire to stop at each stall and stroke the occupant's outstretched head. Gus's trotters were famous for their speed, skill, and beauty, and his breeding program had produced several regional and national champions.

They strolled along until they came abreast the little bay mare's stall, where Gus stopped and gazed at the horse for a moment. "This little mare's done pretty good on the track, but she don't have the conformation nor breeding I want to keep in my blood stock. She'll do tolerably well under saddle with some training, but she's ready to pull a buggy right now. Have you thought about a buggy horse and a saddle horse? As much wear as you put on your mount, you really need both. Let's bring her out and I'll have one of the boys track her for you."

The groom walked and trotted the mare up and down the long hallway. She moved with a fluid athleticism. The groom brought the horse to James so he could look her over at close range. She was curious, a sign of intelligence, and she liked attention.

James asked, "Gus, can we put her in harness and let me try her out?"

It took only a couple of circuits of the track to seal James's bond with the little mare. She moved out willingly when asked and responded to his every request with quiet confidence. When he pulled up beside Gus, James grinned. "You know what you're doing with breeding and selling. She's perfect, but can I afford her?"

Gus scratched his head as he gazed off into the distance. "I'm right attached to this little mare, but I can't keep them all. They gotta pay their way and she ain't doing that. I'd rather see her go to someone who'll take good care of her than make a bundle of money on her. How much can you pay?"

James made what he hoped was a fair offer. Gus looked from James to the mare and back. "Well, that ought to do." Relief flooded through James.

Gus glanced toward a stall at the stable's far end. "You still need a saddle horse, don't you? Have you ever been on a Plantation Walker?"

James shook his head, puzzled by how Gus had come to be in possession of a horse of that breed.

Gus rubbed his chin. "I got a nice gelding in the next barn. Man from Chattanooga traded him and some cash for one of my trotters. Thought I might keep him for myself, but what do I need with two saddle horses? Would you like to look at him?"

Gus had a groom saddle the big chestnut gelding and ride him into the ring behind the barns. The groom first urged the horse into the flat foot walk and then opened him up into the famous running walk. James watched in fascination as the horse moved out, placing each rear hoof directly ahead of its corresponding fore hoof's print in a fluidity that was the very definition of grace. The glossy red coat rippled as powerful muscles moved beneath it. Could there possibly be a more beautiful sight in the equine world? The groom brought the gelding to a halt beside his boss and dismounted. James was probably courting another contentious scene at home, but he needed a strong saddle horse to carry him on his far-flung rounds and to get him home fast, if trouble should mysteriously arise there again.

All doubt about the big gelding's future melted within the first few minutes of James experiencing the famously smooth ride. Guiltily, he totaled the potential cost for both horses and compared it with his checking account balance in the new Bank of

Canton. If he planned carefully and if the price of cotton didn't fall, he should be able to cover the amount.

Gus grinned knowingly as James dismounted. "What do you think?"

James responded with the repeated question, "Can I afford him?"

Gus stated a price that surprisingly fell within James's budget and the deal was struck. James envisioned himself speeding to his patients and happily began writing the check, but the subliminal fear that lurked these days pushed to the surface. He said a silent prayer he would never need to urge the Walker to maximum speed because of a new crisis at home.

James mounted the gelding, leading the mule and mare, and turned toward the road. In an effort to focus on more pleasant things, he called back over his shoulder, "Do these horses already have names?"

Gus yelled in reply, "The Walker is Searchlight and the mare is called Elizabeth."

CHAPTER 17

"You told James 'bout being in the fambly way again?" Lavinia eyed Mary Alice.

Mary Alice replied through a strained smile. "I think he probably knows already. I've been really sick with this one every morning since it began. First time for everything, I guess. The sight of food just turns my stomach until about 11:00. I wonder why some babies bring on the sickness and others don't."

"I ain't sure neither, but always seemed I's sickest when I needed most not to be. I hope them boys'll have the new barn finished 'fore Christmas. It won't do to have it dragging on for the rest of the month." Lavinia stopped speaking for a moment and pulled her shawl tighter about her shoulders, tying it in a firm knot over her ample bosom. "This here's been a cold winter already. Only get worser after New Year's. We gonna have ice this year. I can feel it in my bones."

Mary Alice sighed. Lavinia's bones were as good a forecaster as anything could be. They were usually pretty accurate with their predictions of bad weather and other misfortunes befalling the community. With Maggie's death earlier in the month, Lavinia was coming into her own as the local prognosticator. Pray she had missed it this time because icy weather meant Archie would be cooped up in the house for long periods. At age four, he was a whirlwind of activity and mischief, with the twins shadowing his every step. Dealing with them and everything else required left Mary Alice exhausted. Another baby was just going to add to her already heavy workload.

Lavinia looked through the kitchen window to the where hired men were working on the new barn across the road from the house. "You 'bout ready for me to call them boys in for dinner?"

"Might as well. No need waiting for James." Mary Alice winced and placed her hand on her lower back as she turned toward the range.

Lavinia cast a speculative eye on Mary Alice. "That man just about always makes his own time, don't he?"

Mary Alice did not trust herself to answer. Dissolving in tears would serve no purpose.

***

On Christmas morning, James watched five-year-old Archie's excitement when he found a brightly painted stick horse beside the fireplace in the front room. He promptly named it Searchlight and began riding through the house at breakneck speed, ignoring his mother's pleas that he slow down and lower his volume.

"Archie, do as your mother asks," James shouted, "or Searchlight will be given to another, more deserving little boy! And change into decent clothes. We're due at your grandmother's in less than an hour. The rest of the family won't take kindly to being kept waiting for their Christmas dinner."

Archie was taken so off guard by this uncharacteristic display of temper from his usually overly indulgent father that he responded immediately and remained subdued for the rest of the morning. By the time they arrived at Papa and Mama Campbell's front steps, however, Archie had regained his normally high spirits and bounded through the door ahead of the rest of his family to traditional greetings of "Christmas Gift." He was brought up short by his least favorite relative's frowning visage.

Great-uncle Moses, Bud's youngest brother, had come from Cartersville to spend the holiday with his brother and sister-in-law in the house where he had been born. Although his hair was still dark, he resembled Bud in most other ways including the solid features and dark blue eyes. Unlike the family's other men, he had left the valley shortly after the war ended, a decision that had never been adequately explained and had caused his mother considerable distress.

A crusty bachelor, Moses had no patience for children and shouted at them with the least provocation. Moses was never short of opinions and evaluations of others, but most family members tolerated his outspokenness with humor. When he blared out at someone for some perceived slight or act of stupidity, the older Campbells would simply smile and say, "Now don't you mind Moses. He don't mean no harm. It's just his way."

After dinner, Moses waited impatiently in the yard with his shotgun's breech broken over his arm. When James and Bud ambled onto the porch, they were greeted with a snarl. "Day's a-wasting. Cain't hunt quail in the dark. What took you so long?"

Bud's face split with a knowing grin and he winked at James. "And Merry Christmas to you too, Moses. Nothing ever changes with you, does it? It's beyond me how the youngest of us always acts like he's got one foot in the grave. Well, I'm ready when y'all are."

The trio set off across the fields, following the creek behind Bud's barn, and over the course of the afternoon bagged enough birds to share with the whole extended family.

Late in the afternoon, they surprised a buck that had come to the creek for a drink. Bud, being fond of venison, cracked open his shotgun's breach and quietly replaced his birdshot with heavier buckshot. He raised the shotgun to his shoulder, fired, and hit the deer, but did not kill it. The panic-stricken animal fled back up the ridge from which it had come and the men had no choice but to follow. The blood trail and broken undergrowth led them higher and higher until they were on a narrow path lying just under Salacoa Ridge's lip. James and Moses searched the surrounding undergrowth while Bud climbed on toward the ridge's edge.

He whistled softly and pointed. The wounded buck stood on top of the ridge, panting and in plain sight. He turned his head in Bud's direction, his nose twitching, scenting the air for signs of his pursuers. His eyes widened and he began staggering away from his enemies. With his next step he turned sideways to find an easier escape route. Bud took aim and fired a second time directly into the deer's chest in the area over the heart. This time there was a resounding thwack as the buckshot hit its mark. When they approached the fallen animal, the buck appeared to be in an almost impossible attitude. His middle section seemed to be rising and attempting to lift the rest of his body with it. His hind legs were pointing as if directing attention to the nearest treetop. Moses approached the deer and then stopped suddenly, an odd expression on his face.

James drew up beside him. "Look at the way the ground rises up in those two humps. If I didn't know better, I'd say the buck is lying across a couple of graves."

Bud shook his head. "Thay ain't nobody buried up here. Why would anybody want their folks in such a place?"

Moses looked quietly at his brother and nephew-in-law. "Maybe 'cause somebody don't want folks knowing they's up here."

Bud glanced at his youngest brother. "And just who might that be?"

Moses didn't answer for a moment as he looked intently at James. "I guess y'all can be trusted, even if James's family was on t'other side. It was me and Grandpa what didn't want nobody knowing. It was while you was away in the war. Grandpa and me agreed not to talk 'bout it after we killt them."

Bud stared at Moses. "But you was just a boy during the war."

Moses's eyes reflected something close to anger. "Don't mean we didn't have our own set of troubles around here."

Everyone knew things had been bad everywhere in Georgia once Sherman invaded from Chattanooga, but none of them had ever heard of fighting in Salacoa.

"What kind of troubles you talking about?"

"Them're the graves of a couple of Yankee soldiers who tried to steal our mules back in '64. They come on foot from Pickens County right before the battle over at Dalton. We reckoned they'd been talking to the Union folks over about Jasper and were headed back to Sherman. They stopped here and asked for Grandpa to sell them our mules, but he wouldn't 'cause they was all we had to keep the planting going. They pretended to leave, but Grandpa, he thought they might come back to steal the mules that night. Grandpa had me take the mules over the mountain and hide them in Uncle Jacob's barn."

Moses paused and his face took on a distant expression. His next words sounded like someone describing an event he had just witnessed, not one that had occurred almost thirty years ago. "Me and Grandpa was hiding behind the water trough in the mule lot waiting with our rifles in case of trouble. Sure enough, them blue bellies come up the driveway toward the barn not long after the house went dark. When they couldn't find them mules, they decided to burn us out. We had no choice but to kill 'em." Moses stopped speaking and looked away toward the mountains in the distance across the valley. "Always worried 'bout the families that never knowed what happened to them boys. Them was bad times . . . plenty bad."

For the first time, James had some insight into why the family said Moses was so changed after the war. Bud had told James that when he returned from the prisoner of war camp, he found a little brother who had experienced an almost complete change in personality. Before the war, Moses had been the somewhat spoiled baby of the family with a sunny outgoing disposition. Afterward, Bud had found a quiet and sullen boy who seemed only to want his own company. Bud once asked Moses what was troubling him, but the boy rebuffed him so gruffly Bud gave up and waited for a better time. A better time never came and Moses drifted into a troubled, solitary adulthood away from Salacoa.

James had heard or read somewhere that Sherman was quoted as having said "war is hell." From what little Bud had described, James certainly agreed. Over the ensuing years, he had come to understand that those not directly involved in fighting could be left deeply scarred by it as well.

James had remained quietly observant during the brothers' conversation. He felt accepted, even loved, by his in-laws, and he knew Bud was proud of his reputation in the community as an excellent doctor. What he was never quite sure of was how his Confederate in-laws felt knowing the pro-Union stance his own family had taken during the hellish war years, not so long over that the various factions were willing to forgive and forget.

James's father's youngest brother, Uncle Hiram, had even scouted for Sherman and eventually joined the Georgia First (USA). Many in the county still harbored deep resentment, even hatred, toward the opposing side, especially the northern carpetbaggers of the federal occupation, and would probably do so until old age or death finally erased all memory. He and Bud had only spoken about the war once and James had never asked because he feared opening a wound that he sensed was covered by only the thinnest scar.

Bud remained silent for some few minutes after Moses' revelation. When he finally spoke, it was to James. "I think we best keep this to ourselves, don't you? Even with Yankees gone from the state, it might go hard if'n this was to get out. I done had me enough of Yankees to last me forever. Don't need them plundering about looking 'round here for long-gone soldiers."

James searched Bud's face before he finally answered, "Nothing can be done to change the past. Moses and Grandpa Campbell did the best they could in a bad situation."

Moses gave James an evaluative glance. "You look to be just what Bud's always said—a good man who loves family and can be counted on when there's need."

James's throat tightened. Trust was something Bud was cautious about giving and James now knew just how close they had become. This was a secret he would take with him to his grave rather than cause trouble for those he held so dear.

As they prepared the deer for transport home, it suddenly hit James that he might have found himself in a similar situation with Joss Harbin. If he had suspected Joss would burn his barn, would he have taken the same course as Moses and Grandpa Campbell? James puzzled over the question for the remainder of the trip back to the house. He never came up with a completely satisfactory answer, but since he never expected to see or hear from the Harbins again, he forgot all about it when he caught sight of Mary Alice through the front window. She was laughing at some unseen amusement's source. She looked like a young girl. His breath caught for a moment, but then the spell was broken. Mary Alice frowned and began rubbing her back.

CHAPTER 18

May 1896

Lavinia had made up her mind. She was making it her mission to arrive before James left for his rounds. Plain speaking was what was needed. She marched toward the Buchanan's back porch with the confidence of assured righteousness. She would have her say and out of earshot of Mary Alice, as well.

She mumbled to herself as she mounted the back steps. "That girl don't need no more worry than she already got."

Rather than calling out and entering the kitchen as she usually did, she quietly sat down in a rocker to lie in wait for her quarry. Stealth and cunning came naturally to one who had reared fifteen children. She didn't have to wait long, for in a moment James dashed out the door shouting a final farewell to his family as he crammed his hat on his head. In his haste, he failed to see Lavinia and nearly tripped over her feet.

"Well, good morning, Lavinia," he said after he righted himself. "How are you? Why don't you go on into the house and have coffee with Mary Alice? She's mighty glad you're coming to do for her today."

Something in Lavinia's expression must have caught his attention, because he paused and took a harder look at her. "Is everything all right?"

This gave Lavinia just the opening she wanted. She drew a long breath and fixed James with a determined glare. "James! Mary Alice's 'bout to have this here baby." Her voice was short and authoritative as though she spoke to an unruly child. "You ain't give this no thought as usual, have you? That girl's 'bout dead on her feet, but for all you knowed, she's living like one of them there Vandibelts or Rockifellers. Now you mind what I'm 'bout to say. I cain't help her with the birthing, watch after your childern, and do for y'all in the house all by myself. You mind you stay close to home from now on. Them patients can just get theysleves over here if'n they need something. You hear me?"

James stood in stunned silence for a moment and then replied in an injured tone, "Lavinia, I assure you I've every intention of being here when the baby's born, and I'm going to ask my sister, Liz, to take the children for a few days after it comes. Now, I must be on my way. My patients really do need to be seen and most of them don't need to get out of bed to bring themselves over here. Please excuse me." He turned and walked to the office.

"She's gonna have that baby soon and you best be here," Lavinia shouted as she watched James's retreating back.

***

James saw Lavinia's concern was not misplaced because Mary Alice went into labor that evening. She had a long and difficult delivery that left her exhausted and showing less than her usual enthusiasm for her new offspring. James watched Mary Alice as she looked at the little bundles he had just placed in her arms. She did not show the pride and excitement she had with the births of Archie and the twins, Randolph and Elizabeth. She had just given birth to a second set of twins. What were the odds of two sets of twins coming one right after the other? He shook his head at the very thought. Lavinia was right. Mary Alice needed help.

The baby boy let out a fretful cry. James took the baby and stroked his cheek while swaying like he had seen so many mothers do. Mary Alice yawned and her eyes grew droopy. Before she drifted off, there were two important questions that needed asking. James put the baby boy in a cradle, sat on the edge of the bed, and took Mary Alice's hand. "Have you settled on names? We didn't really talk too much about them. I realize I've been gone too much. Forgive me?"

Mary Alice handed him the baby girl. "I think Hiram, since it's a traditional name in your family, and Nancy Alice for my mother."

James smiled and stroked her hair. "Those are perfect. We're keeping a good balance with the family names. I loved my uncle Hiram. Thank you for thinking of him, and your mother deserves to be honored with a grandchild for a namesake."

Mary Alice shifted around trying to find a more comfortable position in the bed while James hesitated on the next topic. He had given Lavinia's accusation a lot of thought while they were waiting for the new twins to enter the world. She was right and he must make amends now that there were five little ones.

"What would you say to us hiring Lavinia to come in every day but Sunday? I think she might say yes if you ask her. She's not too pleased with me right now."

Mary Alice settled and closed her eyes. Before she drifted off, she mumbled, "No need to ask. She's already said yes."

CHAPTER 19

May 1898

James looked up from his account books as twilight was blanketing the valley in purple shadow and the evening star was coyly calling attention to herself in a cloudless sky. Stealthy footsteps were beating a path to the office door, making James sigh in resignation since he rarely had patients call this late in the day unless there was real trouble. He put down his pencil and waited for the knock on the door. It came presently, sounding more like a hammer pounding than a social call's light rap. He went to the door and opened it, expecting a community member bearing news of an impending birth or an accident victim who needed his help. Instead, he found a man standing in the shadows who seemed reluctant to make himself known.

"May I help you?"

"Dr. Buchanan, are you alone?"

"You can see that I am, but I warn you my shotgun's here behind the door. Show yourself and state your business."

From out of the shadows stepped a young man, filthy with what appeared to be at least a week's grime and sporting a black eye and busted lip. The bruising around the eye was beginning to change from the purple black of recent injury to yellow green. The lip was no longer swollen but had an ugly gash. He looked at James with wild, haunted eyes and appeared unsure of what he wanted or why he had come.

James studied the young man then light dawned. "Joe Harbin! It's been some time since I saw you. Come in and tell me how you and your family have been." James extended his hand in welcome. Despite his differences with the young man's father, James genuinely liked Joe. The boy had somehow managed to survive with his ability to love and to show compassion intact in a family of cruel louts.

It must have been James's warm welcome, for the tension radiating from Joe's every pore dissolved and he did as he was bidden. Once he was inside the office, he slid behind the door. "Can you cover the winders? I think I mighta been follered, and I don't want to bring trouble down on you'uns."

James, remembering only too well how the Harbins defined trouble, reached for the lamp. "Why don't I just put out the light and then we can go up to the house and have a bite of supper. You look like you could do with a good meal."

They walked the short distance to the house while darkness enveloped the valley. James decided to delay questions until the younger man was filled with Mary Alice's good supper, and Joe offered no explanation for his sudden unsettling appearance.

When they were inside the brightly lit kitchen, James cleared his throat. "Mary Alice, could you set another place at the table? We have a guest for supper."

Mary Alice looked up in surprise, for she had expected only her husband to come through the door, but she recovered her manners quickly. "Well, of course. Supper'll be in just a minute. Why don't you two wash up?" She surveyed at the stranger. "It's Joe Harbin, isn't it?"

"Yes, ma'am, Miz Buchanan. I apologize for coming in on you like this. If'n it's too much trouble, just give me a chunk of bread and I'll make do on the porch."

"Don't be silly. There's always room for one more at this table. Now, get those hands washed. James, will you see that the children wash also?"

Supper was eaten at the normal Buchanan pace, frantic spooning of food into the babies' mouths while an eye was kept on the older children to prevent poking, giggling, kicking, and other forms of mischief. Archie and Randy were clearly fascinated by Joe and stole surreptitious glances at him whenever their parents were distracted. They knew better than to openly stare, but they had never seen anyone sit down to their mother's table in such dirty clothes and with the marks of a fight so obvious on his face.

Randy watched Joe with burning curiosity and then looked down the table to his mother. "Why can he come to the table in dirty clothes and we cain't, Mama?" This overt rudeness set Archie off into a fit of giggles. Lizzie simply stared at her brothers and then at Joe.

"Boys, mind your manners. Mr. Harbin is a guest in our home and at our table." James gave his sons a corrective look as well, but Joe just laughed.

"Well, I guess I'm probably the dirtiest feller what's ever put feet under your mama's table, ain't I?" Joe's eyes held a mischievous gleam.

Archie, Randy, and Lizzie all nodded in wide-eyed agreement despite the thunderous glares cast in their direction by their parents.

To distract her children from the object of their fascination, Mary Alice commented, "We received a letter from Cousin Mary Ellen today. She's getting married to the young man she brought with her on her last visit. What do you think we should send for a wedding present?"

Lizzie cocked her head to one side. "Why do people get presents when they get married?"

Mary Alice shot her daughter an encouraging smile. "Because they are just starting out and need help with things to set up housekeeping."

The child's nose wrinkled in thought. "Do they get lots of presents?"

"They do if they have lots of friends with the money to buy them something."

Lizzie took a sip of milk before declaring, "I think I'm going to get married lots. I like presents."

"I think you will be excused from the table and say goodnight to our guest," James interrupted.

When James and Mary Alice had gotten the children settled for the night, they returned to the kitchen to find Joe washing the dishes. Coffee cups were still on the table since the promised cake was yet to be served.

Mary Alice went to the sink. "Joe, the girl who gets you will be mighty lucky. I appreciate the help, but you really don't have to do that."

"It's the leastest I can do for barging in the way I done."

"Well, let's have dessert while the fire in the range is still hot enough to give us a good cup of coffee."

As they were settling themselves around the table again, James cleared his throat and cast a quick glance at Joe. "I was surprised to see you at the door tonight. Please don't think me ungracious, but it's been several years since we last met. What brings you to us? Are you in some kind of trouble?"

"You might say I am. About a week ago, me and Pa, we had us a fist fight. He was on at Ma again about how she don't never do nothing right, and I couldn't take it no more. She does the bestest she can, what with her eyesight and all. Now, you know ain't nobody goes agint Pa without paying the price, and he run me off the place and told me never to come back . . . ever . . . so I took off for Canton."

Joe stopped speaking and appeared to be fighting some strong emotion. "You remember my little sister, Pearl?" James and Mary Alice nodded in unison. "She don't ever say nothing when Pa gets his temper up, but when I was leaving, she set up to squalling and begging me to take her with me. I told her I couldn't, but that I'd sneak back and visit her when I could. I left her crying and it 'bout broke my heart. Yesterday when I saw Pa leave in the wagon, I went to see Ma and Pearl. I been living in the woods not too far from the house since I got back from town. I snuck down after the wagon was gone and asked Ma how Pearl is. She started in crying and saying that Pearl, she done been gone for nigh on the whole week and nobody ain't got no idea where she's at. Ma said she just run off in the middle of the night. I been looking for her ever since, and I got to thinking how she talked a lot 'bout you and the time you made her well and I was hoping she mighta turned up here."

James and Mary Alice looked at one another with raised brows as James shook his head. "I'm afraid we haven't seen her. I doubt she would know the way over here even if she thought to come to us. Do you know why she begged to go with you and leave her mother?"

Joe shrugged. "She's afraid of Pa, I guess. Everbody is. I got enough of him for good. Reason I went to town was to join up with the army. They been calling for men to train up and go fight Spain down in Cuber, wherever that is. I'm leaving for training camp in the morning and I thought to check in here 'fore I went."

"So you're going to be a soldier." James looked at Joe and smiled. "Well, I know you'll be a good one. Cuba, by the way, is about ninety miles south of Key West, Florida. Do you know what type of soldiering they have planned for you?"

"No. I guess they'll figger it out when we get to Camp Griffin on t'other side of Atlanta in Chamblee. You know, I ain't never been anywheres out of the county 'cept Jasper or Fairmount and now I'm going to another country where they don't even speak our language. It's a wonder, ain't it?"

Mary Alice cast a maternal eye on Joe. "Yes, it is. And if you're going into the army in the morning, you'll need a good night's sleep. Take the extra bed in Archie and Randy's room. It's the side room across the porch from the main bedroom."

The next morning, Joe was off before dawn. He didn't even wait for Mary Alice to get breakfast on the table but took cold biscuits left over from supper and slipped away before the family awakened. Archie and Randy were disappointed to see that their intriguing guest was no longer with them when they awoke, finding only an empty bed instead of the thrilling ruffian.

After Joe's departure, there was no more news of any of the Harbins. James and Mary Alice searched the newspaper every week for news of the army units from Georgia and their progress toward deployment to Cuba. They had no idea which battalion Joe was assigned to but were relieved that none of the boys from Georgia were seeing combat. The men provided by the state were all still in training camps or on deployment within the United States. Teddy Roosevelt's Rough Riders included no one from Georgia.

When the struggle in Cuba concluded after only a summer's skirmishing, James scanned the newspaper every day, but the New Year came and went without word of Joe's return. A brief news item in February noted that a few Third Georgia Infantry companies were deployed in Cuba as part of the occupation force.

James held up the newspaper for Mary Alice to see across the breakfast table. "This article lists local boys who were among the occupation forces. Joe's name is on it. He must have made a fair soldier because he was not mustered out like the majority." James passed the paper to Mary Alice. "Joe must be finding military life to his liking. He's certainly had enough experience with following orders without question."

"Yes, he certainly has." Mary Alice's voice was tinged with irony. "You know, Joe might even have some leadership skills hidden under the years of abuse meted out by Joss." She scanned the article James had already read aloud. "I suspect there's more to that boy than anyone has ever given credit."

CHAPTER 20

On a dusty afternoon in late July, a vaguely familiar figure strode into the Buchanan yard and headed for the backdoor. Mary Alice saw a handsome, clean-cut young army corporal in an immaculate uniform standing on her porch and answered his knock.

She smiled inquiringly. "May I help you? Are you lost?"

"No, ma'am." The young man laughed quietly. "I guess I can understand why you don't recognize me, Miz Buchanan. I've changed a lot, even by my own lights, since I left Cherokee for Cuba."

Mary Alice looked hard at the young man before replying, "Well, I'll be. Joe Harbin! I must confess I wouldn't have known you if I'd met you on the road. You look wonderful. Come in and have a glass of tea. I've just taken teacakes out of the oven. Let's have some before the children get at them."

When Joe had followed her into the kitchen, she turned and briefly enfolded him in maternal arms, causing surprise and then pleasure to cross his handsome face. "My, it's good to see you home safe and sound. James is at the barn with Newt. I'll send Archie for him."

Joe and Mary Alice were settled at the kitchen table enjoying the refreshments when the screened door opened. Joe jumped to his feet and stood at formal attention as James entered. "Dr. Buchanan, I'm heartily glad to see you, sir, and hope you've been well since we last met."

***

James grasped Joe's outstretched hand. "How are you? Army life seems to have suited you quite well. Sit and tell us all about it."

Joe described what the training camps and occupation duty had been like. After regaling James and Mary Alice with several humorous tales of army life, his gaze drifted to the window looking out to the road. He was quiet for a moment while his expression became serious. "I guess I like army life as good as I ever hoped to like anything. The army's been good to me, and my commanding officer says I can have a career if I want it. Whoever thought a Harbin would have a career? I jumped at the chance to stay in and got a little leave before I'm shipped out to the Philippines. I've only got a four-day furlough, but I was hoping to hear word of Pearl. I ain't been home yet and probably won't try to go there. Pa ain't the forgiving kind and I don't have time to truck with him and his temper." Joe met James's eyes. "Have you heard anything about her?"

James shook his head. "Sorry, but no, I haven't. I did talk to the sheriff right after you left and he said he would keep an eye out in case she turned up in Canton. I check with him every so often, but no one's seen or heard anything of Pearl since she left home. When I was on Pine Log making a call last week, I did hear that your mother is expecting another baby, which was a surprise considering her age. They said the baby is due sometime next spring. If you want to see your mother, we can ask Newt and Johnny Blalock to ride over with you. I'd offer to go myself, but I have to return to a patient who is probably going to deliver tonight. I just came home to get more supplies."

The crease between Joe's eyes deepened. "I cain't believe nobody's heard from Pearl in all this time. It just don't make sense that a young girl would leave home on her own and not come back." Joe paused and his eyes became troubled. "It's just as well you don't go near Pa ever again. Last thing I ever heard him say about you was that he'd kill you if he ever set eyes on you again. It's on account of you interfering with the way he done things and the way you talked to him. I still laugh when I remember his face the first time I saw you tell him how it was going to be."

Joe stopped speaking while disgust, longing, and regret passed across his face. He sighed heavily and continued, "You stay away from him. He's just mean enough to do what he says. Thank you for telling me about Mama. I was going to be mighty sorry to come this close without seeing her. Pa probably won't come off the mountain if he thinks he's outnumbered." Joe pushed a spoon around his cup and looked beyond Mary Alice's shoulder to the mountain visible through the window over the sink. "I guess you heard my two oldest brothers are serving time. They got caught setting a barn. I heard this from the sheriff himself when I stopped by his office today to ask about Pearl. It only leaves Pa and the one next to me in age. I think that evens the odds pretty good."

Mary Alice cast a quick glance at James. "Joe, it's far too late to start to Pine Log this afternoon. Stay here tonight and then y'all can have a good trip tomorrow. In fact, I want you to think about what I'm going to propose. I know you love your mother and sister a lot, and I don't want you to take this the wrong way. I would never want you to think we are trying to take their place, but you need somewhere safe to stay when you come back to Cherokee. I . . . we would be very happy if you would think of this as your home and come to us when you have need."

James and Joe both shot startled glances at Mary Alice who simply smiled and rose to call the children in since suppertime was drawing nigh. After he recovered, Joe responded, "That's the kindest thing anyone's ever said to me. I appreciate it more than I can say, but I would never want to put you out or be a bother."

Mary Alice gave James a piercing look, prompting him to add, "Joe, you won't be a bother. Mary Alice is right. You need a place to stay when you come back here. We'd be very pleased for you to come to us."

James wasn't so sure it was a good idea, but he couldn't fault Mary Alice's desire to help. Only time would tell whether her kind heart had led her common sense astray.

Fortunately, Joe's trip to Pine Log passed without incident. James and Mary Alice went to Canton to see him off when his furlough was over.

As they waited for the train, Joe seemed reluctant to leave his new adoptive family. "I'm sure grateful for all y'all have done for me. I never expected to find such kindness from people who don't owe me anything. Fact is, I owe y'all more than I can ever repay. I hate to ask for more, but I'd be very grateful if you could let me know any news of my mother or if anyone ever hears from Pearl. This is the only address I can give, but I guess any letters will eventually catch up with me."

James took the scrap of paper with Fort McPherson, East Point, Georgia, scrawled across it. "We'll be only too happy to let you know anything we hear about your family. I have a few patients over on Pine Log, so I'm sure I'll be able to pick up news. And don't you give another thought to owing us anything. It's our pleasure. No one gets along in life without help. I certainly had help from an older man when I was your age. Let's just count this as my repaying his kindness to me. Take care of yourself and let us hear from you when you're able."

Joe shook James's hand and hugged Mary Alice as the train whistle blew. He boarded the train and was gone again, headed for yet another war-torn part of the world. James and Mary Alice really had no expectation of hearing from Joe for some time to come and certainly not before he left for the Philippines, but a dutiful note arrived before the summer was out telling them that Joe was due to ship out in October and that he had been promoted to sergeant.

James was pleasantly surprised to find the writing was actually decipherable and showed a concerted effort at using correct spelling and grammar. The Army looked to be the making of this young man who had started life with so many strikes against him. In some ways, James saw so much of himself in Joe and he determined to do whatever he could to support the boy, including providing help to his mother whenever possible.

***

The fall of 1899 passed as any other with the days drifting from warm to cool and finally slipping to cold, the first frost appearing shortly before Thanksgiving. James and Mary Alice did not hear from Joe again before he shipped out and could only hope he was safe and doing well. Good to his word, James kept an eye on Azaleigh, albeit from a safe distance. When he went to Pine Log to see the small number of patients he had there, he inquired after her and asked if anyone had seen or heard from Pearl, always with the same answers. Nothing ever changed at the Harbin house and her neighbors remarked on the black eyes and bruises that were a constant in Azaleigh's life.

The families in Salacoa were planning their annual hog killing the Friday after Thanksgiving and James decided to have a word with Newt. "Do you think we could kill an extra hog this year?"

Newt scratched his head. "I reckon we can get by with killing one more than usual, but why do you want to? There's hardly room in the smokehouse for more meat."

"I was over on Pine Log this week and the neighbors hinted that food is becoming a problem for Joe's mother. Joss apparently spends what little money they have on the still and in gambling.

They say a continuous poker game has started up in the Pine Log feed store's backroom."

Newt gave James a piercing look. "I thought you was done with going to them sorry folkses' place."

James shrugged. "She needs the food, Newt. It's an act of Christian charity."

"Well, the big sow over yonder by the shed usually has a big litter, so we can spare the extra hog. I'll see to it that we have enough meat to take some to Miz Harbin after the New Year. But I'll ask Johnny Blalock to go with me. For some reason, Joss don't seem to give him as much trouble as he done others."

When January arrived and it was time to deliver the hams, side meat, canned spareribs and such, James watched from the kitchen window as the wagon was loaded.

He put an arm around Mary Alice and kissed her temple. "This isn't right. It's my idea, so I'm responsible. I can't just send the meat with Johnny and Newt. I've got to go with them."

When the last of the load was in place, Mary Alice followed James into the yard. She grabbed his hand. "Please don't go over there. You're not wanted and you know what Joe said about his father threatening to kill you if you ever came around again. How can you put yourself in such danger?"

James gave her a hug and tried to laugh, but the sound he emitted was nearer a growl. "I'll be just fine. I've got Johnny and Newt with me. Besides, I can't ask them to do something I'm not willing to do myself. What kind of man would I be?"

Johnny turned away from the tie-down he was working on. "Miss Mary Alice, I can come and go to the Harbins' whenever I want and nothing bad don't never happen."

James nodded as he swung up into the saddle. "For a reason no one can discern, Joss tolerates Johnny better than he does most men." He grinned and tipped his hat to his friend. "It's probably because when they were children, Johnny regularly punched

Joss's lights out. Of course, it's hard to visualize Joss Harbin as a child, but he must have been one."

Johnny grinned as he pressed tobacco into his corncob pipe. "Oh, he was a kid all right and as sorry and mean then as he is now."

As they pulled into the Harbin yard, James looked around uneasily, checking for signs of Joss and his remaining son, but they never materialized. The only movement around the place was a twitch of the window curtain and a quickly opened door. James hardly recognized Azaleigh when she stepped out onto the porch. Her face was gaunt and her much patched dress hung on her like the flour sacks it had once been. It was a miracle this last pregnancy, coupled with an inadequate diet and her age, had not ended her life, but Azaleigh greeted them with a chubby baby girl in her arms. The baby had downy golden ringlets and big blue eyes, the very image of the missing Pearl. Her mother said she was called Ruby.

CHAPTER 21

January 1903

Mary Alice placed her hand to the small of her back and massaged her aching muscles as she gazed through the bedroom window's frosty panes. Warmer weather could not come too soon so the children could play outside again. Even with their walking the two miles to and from school each day, they still felt cooped up when cold weather and early dark kept them inside. As usual, James was away on calls and wouldn't be in until dark because whooping cough was running rampant through Salacoa Community School, affecting the younger children in greater numbers, including their youngest son, Hiram. He was ensconced in a cot near the fireplace in his parents' bedroom where a boiling pot created enough steam to help ease his ragged breathing. This usual dynamo of perpetual motion lay quiet, lifting his head only when the racking coughing fits were upon him. His fever still had not broken.

The other children were required to cover their mouths and noses with cloth strips just to pass through the room. James also insisted upon the frequent application of hot water and soap, leading the children to complain they would soon have no skin left on their hands and arms. These complaints fell on deaf ears. Mary Alice did not escape her husband's demands and inspections either. His continual questions about the quality and frequency of her personal cleanliness and that of her kitchen, while well intentioned, were beginning to wear more than a little thin.

James was so busy with the valley's sick children that he sent for Dr. Thornton from Waleska to see to his own son and the Locklin's youngest child. Mary Alice glanced expectantly through the window toward the road once more. Still no sign of the doctor.

Mary Alice went to Hiram and placed a hand against his forehead. His temperature was down a little due to the cool bath she had just given him. He had fussed and squirmed when the tepid water touched his feverish skin, but the water had done some good and he was resting a little easier now. He had asked several times why his papa wasn't taking care of him instead of going to see other children. Mary Alice did the best she could to explain, but Hiram was skeptical of each reason she offered. Hooves clattering on the frozen ground brought her to the window again. Sighing with relief, she went to the backdoor to admit James's colleague and friend.

"Hello, Dr. Thornton. Thank you for coming. Let me get you some coffee to warm you up on this cold day."

"Coffee'd be mighty welcome. I don't believe it's going to get much above freezing today. If you'll direct me to the patient, I'll see to him while you're pouring."

Dr. Thornton went to the bedroom and Mary Alice followed shortly. After listening to Hiram's chest and taking his temperature, the doctor turned to Mary Alice. "I'm going to leave this medicine and I want you to give him a teaspoon every four hours. It'll help ease the coughing and his sore throat. I'll take that coffee now and then be on my way to your neighbor."

After the doctor left, Mary Alice pulled the stopper from the bottle and poured a dose. She lifted the spoon to Hiram's mouth and waited. Hiram's mouth stayed resolutely shut.

"Son, open up and take this medicine. It'll make you feel a whole lot better."

Hiram's response was a feeble shake of his head.

"Now Hiram, you want to feel better, don't you?"

A small nod was his reply.

"All right now, open your mouth."

Hiram just stared at his mother.

What had gotten into him? The first hints of exasperation stirred. She tried once more to induce her truculent son to open his mouth. Her efforts bore fruit in a view of the back of his head. "Hiram, why won't you take this medicine? Dr. Thornton rode all the way from Waleska in freezing weather just to help you feel better."

His face still turned to the wall, Hiram finally deigned to suffer his mother a hoarse reply, "Ain't no good. Want my papa's medicine."

Mary Alice choked back a chuckle at the side view of Hiram's protruding lower lip. "Hiram, this medicine is the same thing Papa would give you if he was here."

"It'n." The muffled reply came from beneath the quilt Hiram had pulled over his head.

Mary Alice sat back and looked at the small stubborn form on the cot. With a sigh, she rose. "I guess your papa's medicine might be better. Let me see if he didn't leave some in the kitchen just in case Dr. Thornton wasn't able to come today."

Mary Alice waited until she closed the bedroom door before hugging herself with quietly controlled laughter. She counted to twenty and re-entered the room. "Well, guess what I found. Your papa did leave a bottle of his medicine. Now let's get it into you so you'll feel better soon."

Hiram's mouth popped open immediately to receive the now acceptable medicine. He slept peacefully for the remainder of the afternoon, which was a godsend. The ache in her lower back had little to do with bending and lifting and a great deal to do with a baby wanting to make its entrance into the world. She winced as a particularly sharp pain stabbed. Maybe Hiram was right. Perhaps James should be here with them instead seeing to other families' needs. When a tapping on the roof began, she looked out the window and her spirits fell. If it continued, sleet would soon have the world covered in ice.

***

James's clothing was frozen to his saddle by the time he returned home from house calls. Riding Searchlight onto the porch, he rapped on the kitchen window. "Archie, bring a bucket of hot water and a rag out here."

James watched the boy dip water from the reservoir in the wood stove and struggle to get the bucket through the back door without a spill.

Archie raised the bucket to stirrup height. "Here you go, Papa."

James took the rag, wet it, and began detaching his clothing from the leather. Once free, he dismounted and took the shivering animal to his stall with a bucket of oats. Searchlight cared for, James walked into the kitchen just as Lavinia was setting out supper for the children.

Randy greeted his father with a shrill cry. "Mama's gonna have the baby tonight and Archie was going to help if you didn't get home in time."

James raised an eyebrow at Lavinia, who just smiled at the boy. "Archie, he woulda been mighty good help if'n you hadn't made it in time. Mary Alice's up in the front room. I'll take the children home with me now you're here." She eyed his dripping pants. "You best get out of them wet things."

After changing into dry clothes, James went in search of his patients. He found Hiram sleeping soundly beside a gentle fire. He then went to the front bedroom where Mary Alice was pacing and rubbing her lower back.

After checking her and listening to the sounds emanating from her huge abdomen, James hung his stethoscope around his neck. "I believe I can hear two fetal heartbeats which would explain why this baby is on its way earlier than we thought."

Mary Alice looked at her husband in resignation. "I figured as much by the amount of kicking and squirming. It feels like it did with Randy and Lizzie and Hiram and Nancy. Why on earth can't we have them one at a time like other people?"

James smiled and searched for a suitable reply. "I think it's because you're a better mother than most and so they're sent two at a time. You rest easy while I get a bite to eat. Do you need water or some hot tea? It won't be long now."

But James was wrong. Unlike her previous deliveries, these babies were taking their time, causing their mother a get deal of pain and their father a great deal of worry. By the second afternoon, the babies still had not made their way into the world and James was becoming increasingly distressed. Mary Alice had been in labor for almost forty-eight hours and had made little progress since initial dilatation. She was exhausted and James felt ffuzzy-headed from lack of sleep.

He reached a decision. "Mary Alice, I'm going to send for Dr. Thornton. He's the closest and he's good with difficult deliveries. I should have sent for him yesterday."

Archie was dispatched to fetch Newt with instructions to stop only long enough to inform Bud and Nancy before traveling on to Waleska and Dr. Thornton. Mary Alice's parents arrived not long after Newt left.

After a seemingly interminable wait, they heard hooves clattering in the now darkened yard. Instead of the anticipated help, Newt alone burst through the door. "Doc Thornton, he cain't come. He's got a bad sick feller he cain't leave up to Pleasant Hill. Miz Thornton says she'd give him the message if'n he was to come home anytime soon, but she don't think he'll be in 'fore morning."

The blood drained from James's face. He had delivered many babies, including all his own up to this point, but it was clear that Mary Alice was in real trouble and he had desperately hoped for a more detached judgment to be involved in making the most difficult decisions. He briefly considered sending to Canton but rejected the idea quickly because those babies had to be born for their sake as well as their mother's. Mary Alice was so exhausted by the long painful hours of labor that she had gone somewhere deep within herself and seemed barely aware of her surroundings.

The first problem he faced was delivering the larger baby whose head had finally crowned a few minutes earlier, but in the posterior position. James disliked forceps deliveries because of the danger to the child, but he knew he had no choice.

He glanced over at Bud. The older man's hands were trembling, the color drained from his face. James needed a calm atmosphere, not another patient. "Bud, could you go to the kitchen and make sure water is kept boiling?"

Bud left the room quickly and James turned to his mother-in-law. "Nancy, I'm going to need your help. Mary Alice is in trouble and she can't wait any longer. I have no choice but to pull the baby out and I need for you to be ready to catch it. Grab one of those clean towels and let's get started."

Nancy stood quietly rooted in place without acknowledging his request, her face ashen. Both must master their fear if his wife and unborn children were to have any chance at all.

He marshaled his own emotions and spoke quietly. "Nancy, it's going to be all right. You can do this. You gave birth to seven. You know what to do, and we can't do this without you."

Nancy looked miserable. "It's just so much harder when it's your child what's in danger. You just wait and see if it ain't so once yours is older."

"I'm sure you're right, Nancy. Now let's see if we can help these two get born so they'll have a chance to get older."

Nancy nodded and they began the procedure with the first baby. As he worked, Mary Alice cried out. James's focus intensified as he saw that the baby's big head was causing deep tearing. Mary Alice moaned again with the force of an intense pull on the forceps, but this time they yielded the desired result. The baby's head cleared the cervix in an instant and its wet little body soon slid with a plop into its grandmother's waiting arms. The baby, not at all pleased to be yanked into the world so unceremoniously, wailed with indignation.

Nancy held the little bundle close to keep it warm. "It's a girl. Mary Alice's girls just do come out first."

James wanted to check his new daughter's health, but there was no time to stop. While Nancy cleaned her granddaughter, James palpated Mary Alice's abdomen to ascertain the second child's position. It was breech. Being as gentle as he was able, James turned the baby so that it was head down and then they waited. Mary Alice had mercifully passed out when he first began the procedure.

They waited for what seemed an eternity until the baby finally began engaging the cervix. What James saw made him draw a long anxious breath. The baby, though tiny, had turned itself back in the breech position with its feet, not its head, protruding from the cervix.

James called to Nancy. "I'm going to need your help. This baby has got to be turned, and I can't use the forceps this time."

Nancy put the baby girl down and rushed to James's side as he reached deep within, placing his thumbs on the baby's hips and turning it face down. With gentle constant pulling, the small form was eased into the world, but it emerged pale and seemingly lifeless. James placed the baby on the towel Nancy held and then immediately took it from her. He gently cleared the baby's airway while massaging its tiny chest, but the baby did not respond.

Nancy's brow creased. "What you doing? I ain't never heared of rubbing helping."

James answered honestly. "I read a report of a doctor reviving a patient using this method back in '91, and I don't know what else to do."

He was desperate for anything that might save this child. As he continued the procedure, each passing moment brought greater fear that this baby would not live, and he was on the verge of despair when he felt a tiny shudder beneath his fingers. With another shudder, the little mouth opened and a weak mewing escaped the bluish lips. More massaging brought a noisy intake of air, producing a pinkish stain in the face. Once the baby began to breathe normally, James wrapped it in the towel and held it close for warmth.

Nancy had watched in fascination. "Is it a boy or another girl?"

James gave her a tired smile. "I have no idea. Let's take a look." He opened the towel just enough so they could see what they were looking for. "Looks like we've continued the pattern. A girl and a boy each time. Do you think you can tie off the cords? Mary Alice needs attention."

Mary Alice had recovered enough to ask in a weak voice, "Are the babies all right?"

James leaned over and kissed her forehead. "They're like all of your babies. They're perfect and beautiful." There was no need to tell her the total truth. Only time would tell whether the boy would live despite his initial recovery. The baby was underweight and weak, unlike his larger, more robust sister. The difficult births had taken a toll on Mary Alice. It was possible they would have a long-term effect on her health. As with the baby boy, only time would reveal the extent of the damage that had been done. After doing what he could for his wife, James sat on the chair by the bed and immediately fell into a deep sleep.

***

Keeping the boy twin alive and overseeing Mary Alice's recovery consumed much of James's time for the next few months and even Lavinia, for once, could find no fault with the attention he showed his own family. The baby required frequent medical attention, suffering severe bouts of colic and chest congestion. He didn't seem at first to have the ability to thrive on his own that the other children had as infants, but as winter faded into spring and spring warmed into summer, both mother and child showed improvement. At age six months, the boy was almost as big as his sister and crawled before she did.

To everyone's surprise the babies were a constant source of amusement to Archie, who teased and played with them and they laughed whenever he came near. Zackary and Mary Catherine were the names given the twins by their parents, but no one called them anything other than Archie's pet names for them. He had taken one look at the babies and said they were too little for such grand names. Tot and Buster fit them so much better.

CHAPTER 22

Over the next two and a half years, life in the valley and with its families drifted along as it always had. The crops were planted and harvested, the young were born, the elderly went to their reward, Sunday Meeting days came and went, nothing much exciting happened at all. So little happened that the young people could be overheard complaining about never having anything new to do or places to go or anything to even talk about.

Life in the valley seemed much too sedate for Archie, who was now a tall, gangly adolescent. When he and his crowd of young rowdies weren't at school or working in the fields, they ran the countryside seeking thrills, usually of the self-made and dangerous kind. When they were around the adults, they chafed under the strict dictum that children were to be seen and not heard. Nowhere was this more sternly enforced than at school, so Archie and his friends rejoiced when they heard the schoolmaster had taken a better paying job in another county and a new man had been hired for the fall term.

On a golden afternoon in October, James spied Archie and his brother Randy sitting on the back porch steps discussing their new teacher, Mr. Butts, a name destined to cause great amusement among his students. Something in the boys' manner made James stop just out of sight. Furtive and secretive best described their tilted heads and quiet voices.

Archie slung an arm around his brother and nudged him in the ribs. "Mr. Butts, he sure does like his food, yes he does. How much would you say he weighs? I'm guessing it must be at least three hundred pounds. Do you remember when Mama had him to supper when he first came? He ate a whole chicken almost by himself. Butts sure is the right name. Mr. Butts' butt oughta be hanging in the smoke house!" Archie and Randy dissolved into howls of laughter accompanied by streaming tears.

Randy wiped his eyes and offered his thoughts. "He's so fat he cain't even get up from his desk chair. Wyy, today, when we was all running around the schoolroom and throwing stuff, he just sat there yelling at us to stop. I thought sure he was going to get the cane out and come after us, but he never done a thing. Bobby Locklin jumped out the window and ran into the woods and hid after he shook his own butt at Mr. Butts. I sthure do like it now that Mr. Butths hasth come. Squool isth weel fun." Randy's imitation of Mr. Butts's unfortunate speech impediment was dead on, sending both boys into renewed giddiness.

"Is that so, boys?" Their father's voice came from behind them in the vicinity of the well.

Sobriety descended immediately. Archie looked at Randy, signaling to follow his lead and then both boys jumped to their feet. "Hello, Papa. It sure is nice to have you home earlier than you said. Are your patients better? We finished our homework and helped Newt stack the hay in the back field. We're having fried pork loin for supper. It smells real good, don't it? Mama fixes the best—"

James silenced his son's verbal barrage with a look. "Archie, did I understand Randy to say that you boys were running around the schoolroom instead of doing lessons today?"

"Oh, no, Papa. You must have misheard what we was talking about. One of the eighth graders, he jumped up and ran out of the room after he threw a slate at a girl. I bet he'll be in lots of trouble tomorrow."

James fixed the boys with raised brows and a firm mouth. "I see. Well, you two and your brother and sisters need to behave yourselves in school. Now let's get washed up and you boys ask if your mother needs any help."

After supper, James looked over the children's schoolwork, then set up the carrom board for their nightly game of skill and wits. While their father used a short cue stick, the children simply used their fingers to thump the striker against the rings sending them into one of the small board's four corner pockets. When the girls came in from helping their mother with cleaning the kitchen, play commenced.

"Nancy, that was a good shot." James kept his voice intentionally casual. "Tell me girls, did anything unusual happen at school today?"

Both girls gave Archie and Randy sidelong glances, glued their gazes to the game board, and answered in tight little voices. "No, Papa. Nothing at all unusual. Just school as normal."

James suspected dishonesty in his children's report, but he didn't pursue it until they were in bed. "Have you heard anything about how well Mr. Butts keeps order at the school?"

Mary Alice looked up from her mending with raised brows. "No, I haven't been to the school since the first day and everything seemed fine then. Why do you ask?"

"Just something the boys said. It may be nothing, but I've got a feeling they didn't give me the whole story when I asked how their day had been. I doubt they would lie outright, but it felt like their account, while perhaps accurate, was incomplete."

A few days later, James had to visit a patient who lived on a road that would take him near the school, so he made an investigatory detour on his way home. As he turned up the lane leading to the schoolhouse, a strange buzzing sound floated toward him from the top of the hill on which the school sat. It increased in volume until it became a raucous roar as he rode into the schoolyard.

What he saw was as amazing as it was disheartening. It appeared most of the boys, led by Archie and including Randy and Hiram, were making a circuit from inside to out and back again without using any portal other than the large open windows. Those who were not traveling about in this manner were standing on the tops of the desks throwing paper, books, and any other item that could be used as a missile. It seemed war had broken out in Salacoa Community School.

James looked about for Mr. Butts. Surely the man must be deathly ill and in the outhouse. No teacher, sane or otherwise, would tolerate this behavior. He narrowed his eyes against the bright sunlight for a better look and continued to search for the teacher. His gaze finally fell upon the unfortunate Mr. Butts. He was standing with his back to the wall behind his desk, flapping his arms, and apparently adding his own voice to the general uproar, but it was hard to tell whether he was calling for order or crying out in fright.

James held Searchlight very still for some time in dumbfounded fascination, wondering just how long this would go on. He was rewarded with a seemingly impossible increase in the cacophony. It might have gone on unabated if Archie and Mr. Butts had not simultaneously caught sight of Dr. Buchanan observing the mêlée. Archie stopped his progress through a window so suddenly that the force of his comrades crashing into him from behind sent him flying to the ground below. Mr. Butts ran from the building, using the door.

Red-faced and eyes bulging, the teacher stumbled to a halt by Searchlight's flanks and spluttered, "I mutht thaye, Dr. Buchanan, your thuns are a dithwuption and a bad example to the other childwen. Will you pleathe sthee to it that they sthop this outwageous behaviowr at oneth!"

James sucked in his cheeks and pursed his lips while he eyed Mr. Butts. With a smack, he gave his answer. "I'll be only too happy to deal with them, and I assure you they will not behave in this manner again. I cannot, however, make that promise for the other children."

It seemed unlikely that the man's eyes could bugle anymore or his face turn any redder, but he managed these changes in appearance as he spluttered, "Now, you sthee here. If it were not for Awchie, there would be no pwoblem. I know my job and how to do it."

Not wanting to have an open argument with Mr. Butts before the now silent student body, James kept his reply short. "I see. Yes, well, you can rest assured the Buchanan children will cause you no further distress. I would like a word with my boys before I go."

A subdued Archie, Randy, and Hiram marched from the schoolhouse and came to rest at Searchlight's feet. The two younger boys nodded agreement as they were told how it would be from now on, but Archie wore a sullen expression and only grudgingly answered when his father asked, "Do you understand what is expected?"

James made a mental note to deal more firmly with Archie later, but at the moment, he was already overdue at an impending birth. Disciplining Archie would have to wait.

James's next unannounced pass by the schoolhouse showed that his words had produced improved behavior among all his offspring except one, leaving James to regret having forgotten the talk with Archie. He could see Archie's upper half in the open window through which the boy's voice floated. "Mr. Butth, Jamestown was founded in 1607, not 1609. Evewybody knowth that."

This imitation of their teacher's speech impediment reduced the older boys to a guffawing gang on the verge of complete insurrection. Archie's chest puffed out and his smile widened as he surveyed the pandemonium he had created. Most of the girls and the younger children were sitting obediently doing lessons, so Mr. Butts had apparently managed to gain some semblance of order since James's last visit. Rather than attempt any further intervention, James turned for home. He wasn't sure where the money would come from, but there seemed no alternative.

He walked through his own back door and announced without preamble, "Mary Alice, Archie can't stay at the school. He creates nothing but chaos."

Mary Alice, who was rocking Buster, looked up in surprise. "What do you mean chaos? I thought you talked to the boys the last time you went by the school."

"I did and our younger children are behaving, but Archie's completely out of control. I'm going to Waleska today to see what we need to do to get him registered there."

Within the week, Archie was enrolled in Reinhardt Academy, the small secondary school and two-year college established at the Waleska crossroads by Captain A.M. Reinhardt and Col. John J. A. Sharp in 1883 and governed by the North Georgia Methodist Conference. He would board with a family across the road from the college until the Salacoa School situation was resolved. Perhaps the academy's required daily chapel attendance might also instill in Archie a new sense of responsibility and desire to behave.

When James next visited Salacoa School, he was disheartened to see that removing Archie had not helped as much as he had hoped. Another boy had simply taken up where his son left off.

CHAPTER 23

The unproductive '05/'06 school year drew to a premature conclusion with Mr. Butts's stormy departure. He announced on a Monday morning in April that he was leaving. He shouted it was now clear that bookkeeping was much more to his liking than teaching backwoods yokels' wretched offspring and then simply walked out the door.

Archie was brought home from Reinhardt Academy and life in Salacoa returned to its expected rhythms for the next three or four years with little of any significance occurring. The only change of any import was the addition of a second teacher and three more grades to Salacoa School, which meant families no longer needed to send their children away from home to get a high school diploma.

When Archie graduated from eleventh grade at the end of the decade, he elected to go on to Reinhardt for college. It was easier than staying home where his only option was to help Newt with running the farms, a dismal prospect since Archie had little talent for or inclination toward agriculture. He found campus life exhilarating after the valley's dullness, joining a social club, the glee club, and the men's debate team. He excelled at everything social, becoming a popular, well-known figure around the campus and the object of female attention. The only fly in this rich and stimulating ointment was the onerous requirement that he attend class in order to remain a bona fide student, a task he avoided as often as possible with great skill and finesse. There were too many far more intriguing activities to be enjoyed in Waleska's backstreets and in isolated shacks hidden in the surrounding hills, if one only knew where to look.

Many students were locals so there was a never-ending river of companions to assist Archie in finding the entertainments that so consumed his waking hours. It was a testament to his intellectual ability that he managed to maintain the gentleman's C required to stay in school and still run the mountain roads at all hours any day of the week. Archie Buchanan was becoming known in certain circles throughout the county's northwest end as a young man on the lookout for a good time, especially any game of chance. His favorite pastime was high stakes poker and it was assumed he had the money to play since his father owned several farms and was a well-known physician with an extensive medical practice.

It was in pursuit of his greatest pleasure that Archie became a regular at the weekly game in the backroom of a feed store located at Pine Log Mountain's base. The store's owner lived in Waleska and was never on the premises after closing time, leaving his hired help, who lived on the mountain, to lock up each night. This employee, eye ever on the main chance, took the opportunity his situation presented to provide the local riffraff with the things they craved most—booze, women, and poker—in a discrete environment with guaranteed security.

***

On a sultry night in late summer 1910, Archie encountered a new face at the poker table—one who was older than him by about fifteen years but who seemed to take an immediate liking to him.

The stranger made a great impression because he was wearing a dark suit of fine linen, the one Archie had seen displayed in a Canton store window. Archie would have dearly loved to buy the suit, but it was priced far beyond anything he could afford.

The newcomer looked up from the table and smiled. "Name's Jeb. Glad you decided to join us. This chair here by me has been empty all night. What's your pleasure?"

Archie sat down at the large round oak table that must have once served as a family dinner table. Jeb seemed to be running the game tonight and Archie was surprised, but pleased, when he was asked to name the game they would play. He chose straight poker, at which he considered himself expert.

As they played, Jeb asked Archie about his family and what he was studying in school. Jeb seemed interested in anything Archie had to say, lavishing him with attention and congratulations as his pile of winnings grew. Jeb even made sure Archie's glass was seldom empty, filling it from bottles that seemed to magically appear at Jeb's elbow.

When his companions were merely blurred images in a slightly tilting room, Archie asked, "What do I owe for the liquor? I've had about all I need."

Jeb's face seemed oddly smeared, seen as it was through a haze of alcohol, but his grin was friendly. "What's an empty bottle between friends? Forget about it. You bring the booze next week."

When the game broke up well past midnight, Archie's new friend sauntered out to his conveyance and called, "You staying on Salacoa tonight?"

Archie nodded.

"How about me giving you a ride home? You can leave the nag in the store's shed and get it in the morning."

Archie, having consumed enough white lighting to cloud several men's minds, was only too happy to abandon the aging Elizabeth to the feed store shed. He staggered over and swung himself up onto the seat beside his new friend, slamming the Ford

Model T's shiny black door. He had only ridden in an automobile a few times, and it was still thrilling to be transported behind something other than a horse's rump. He took any ride offered to him, regardless of the situation.

Elizabeth didn't take kindly to being unceremoniously shoved into an unfamiliar shed with no food or water and whinnied disconsolately as the Ford spluttered, backfired loudly, and finally roared to life. The auto gathered speed as they wound around the mountain curves until it was going its maximum forty miles per hour. They almost missed the Buchanan driveway, turning in on two wheels. They careened into the yard and screeched to a halt just short of the porch where Archie's mother waited.

"Archie, where've you been? Where's the horse? Has there been an accident?"

Archie shook his head to clear his vision and laughed, "Hey, Mama. What you doing up thish late?"

Archie staggered from the Ford and planted an alcohol-laden kiss on his appalled mother's cheek. "Elizabeth's just fine. She's in the shed at the feed store. I'll get her in the morning. That's my friend's new car. Ain't it a beauty?" Archie threw his hand up as the Ford roared away from the yard.

"Who is he and why were you riding with him, Archie?"

"I told you. He's my new friend, Jeb."

"And does this Jeb have a last name?" His father's voice came from the darkness near the well.

"I . . . I . . . Well, I guessh he does, but I don't know it. Forgot to ask." Archie flopped down on the edge of the porch and collapsed in a heap of giggles.

Mary Alice bent toward him. "Come on in the house, Son, and go to bed."

As she tried to lift him, James called to her. "Leave him. It's a warm night and he can sleep it off on the porch as well as in the room with the boys. They don't need to see him in this condition."

***

While Mary Alice cried herself to sleep, James tossed and turned. Sleep was becoming an elusive mistress, which he sought, but could not locate.

The mood around the breakfast table the next morning was subdued. Even Tot and Buster sensed things were somehow not right and whined about wanting anything other than what they were offered until their mother spoke so sharply to them that they fell silent and remained so for the rest of the meal.

As the plates were being cleared, James fixed Archie with a stern expression. "When is your tuition due for the fall term?"

Archie, his eyes bloodshot and his features appearing bleary, had the good grace to look sheepish. "Papa, I don't think I'm going back to school in the fall. I've been offered a job in the general store in Waleska, and I can make more in a week working there than I have all summer here on the farm. I want to buy me one of those new Fords like my friend Jeb has. He went to Atlanta to buy his, and he has connections with a man there who will give me a really good deal."

James slammed his hand against the table, causing the coffee mugs to clatter. "Archie, that's the most foolish thing I've ever heard. If you think I'm going to support this life you've chosen, you're sadly mistaken. And if you are ever in the condition you were in last night, do not bother to come home. Do you have any idea how much an automobile costs?"

"Well, not exactly, but Jeb said I could get one real soon with what I'll be making at the store."

Mary Alice turned from the sink, wiping her hands on her apron. "Your father has paid out good money for your education. How can you just give it up?"

"Aw, Mama, you don't need college to make money. I want to get started on something that pays and I want to have my own place. I'm too old to be living here with my parents."

Dismay spread over Mary Alice's face. "Archie, please don't do this. Surely having a car can wait until you've finished school."

Against his parents' wishes, Archie took the job as clerk, living above the store, and not long afterward, drove a new Ford into the yard. He got out and posed for effect with one foot on the running board and his arm cocked up on the open door. His self-satisfied grin broadened as his mother and younger brothers and sisters poured into the yard for a better look. Tot and Buster ran from their play to admire the new wonder and beg a ride. They pulled on his coat pockets looking for the treats he always had for them when he came from the store, shrieking with laughter as he tickled and teased them. He was their favorite brother and they adored him.

"Mama, I'm going to town to get a haircut, and I'm gonna take Tot and Buster with me," Archie called as he boosted the twins up and over the running board into the front seat.

Mary Alice ran from the porch. "Those children are filthy. You can't take them to town. They look like ragamuffins."

Archie ignored his mother's pleas and called over his shoulder as he turned the car around and aimed it toward the road, "Tot and Buster'll just sit in the car and eat their ice cream while I'm in the barber shop." The Ford stirred up a cloud of red dust as the three rode away with their mother calling after them to not let those dirty children within sight of anyone she knew.

Shortly before Christmas, Archie again roared into the yard and called to his baby brother and sister, "Tot, Buster, come see what I've brought you."

As they ran to leap into his arms, they were pulled up short by the sight of a fuzzy bottom with a stubby tail wiggling from under Archie's coat.

Tot's eyes grew big. "What's that? Is it a puppy?"

"It sure is. He's a bulldog puppy and his name is Rawl."

As the children played with their puppy, Archie sauntered into the kitchen, gave his mother a peck on the cheek, and straddled a chair. "When's Papa due home?"

"He's here now, son. He's up at the hog lot with Newt seeing to one of the sows. Have some coffee while you wait. Supper won't be long, so don't spoil it by eating anything. By the way, I wish you'd asked before you brought a puppy home."

***

When supper was over one evening not long after the dog's arrival, Archie asked to speak with James privately, so they went out onto the porch. "Papa, I need to ask a favor. I need a loan. Just for a little while and I'll pay you back. It's just a little help until I get things straightened out."

James didn't like Archie's oily tone. It smacked of desperation. "How much do you need and why do you need it?"

"I just need a hundred dollars. I'll pay you back real soon. I promise."

James's eyes narrowed. "You haven't answered my other question. Why do you need so much?"

"I've got an opportunity to buy into the store, but I've got to let them know what I'm going to do before the end of the year."

"It doesn't seem a hundred dollars would hardly be enough to buy an interest in a prosperous place like that."

Archie scuffed at a floorboard with the toe of his boot. "It's just a down payment. I'll work off the rest as I can. It's a real opportunity to get ahead, Papa. I thought you of all people would understand that a fellow sometimes needs a little help to get started. After all, if it hadn't been for the loan from old man Sinclair, you would never have gone to medical school. Come on Papa, it's just for a little while."

Despite the whine in Archie's voice, his argument hit home. James placed a hand on his son's shoulder and nodded. "Well, if it's for your future, I guess a hundred-dollar loan is the least I can do for you. Come on in the house and I'll write you a check."

The look of relief in Archie's eyes was unmistakable, making James hesitate. He searched Archie for signs of deception but found none. The boy's relief was probably owing to a deep desire to buy into the lucrative store and get a start on something permanent in his life.

Time passed quietly for two more summers and James's concerns for Archie's wild behavior subsided as the boy seemed to be progressing in his chosen career as part owner in the successful general store on Waleska's Main Street. He wasn't living up to his potential, but at least he wasn't running the roads and coming home drunk anymore.

***

In July 1912, a letter with a military postmark caused excitement around the supper table as James read it aloud to the family

> *Dear Dr. James, Miss Mary Alice, and Children,*
> *I am very pleased to let you know I should be home by September as I have been posted to Fort McPherson, just south of Atlanta. I have been promoted to master sergeant and I will be a training instructor at Fort Mac, as the locals call it. I cannot tell you enough how much your letters have been appreciated and I look forward to seeing you soon. I will write again when I know more.*
> *Your friend,*
> *Joe Harbin*

James folded and returned the letter to its envelope. "It'll be good to have Joe so close in the future. From what I hear about Pine Log, things have calmed down up at the Harbins'. They say

Joss has let up on some of his worst activities and they haven't seen Azaleigh with a black eye or such in quite some time. I haven't heard of any mysterious burnings lately either. Maybe a leopard can change his spots after all. I know Azaleigh'll be glad to have Joe home. He was always her favorite, you know. Maybe he'll be able to visit her in the open now."

Mary Alice looked thoughtful. "It's hard to believe a man like Joss Harbin can change after a lifetime of wickedness. He may have slowed down, but it would be a miracle if he'd stopped altogether."

"I suppose you're right. Maybe he just keeps his activities quieter these days."

As the time for Joe's return to Georgia drew near, anticipation grew at the Buchanan house. He had written that he would be very glad to accept their invitation to spend some of his leave with them and the children were looking forward to hearing his stories. The two older sets of twins remembered him as being a handsome young man in uniform, but little else. They knew him best from his letters and knew the story of how Joe had become so closely acquainted with their family. Randy and Hiram hoped to hear stories of army life and Lizzie and Nancy giggled over the photograph showing a very handsome man in an immaculate uniform. Tot and Buster were somewhat perplexed because everyone else seemed to be so looking forward to a visit from this stranger, who was talked about almost like another brother by their parents, but who couldn't possibly be as wonderful as Archie, so they took a rather blasé attitude toward the whole affair.

Finally, the long-awaited day arrived. Johnny Blalock was dispatched to fetch Joe from the Waleska rail stop, and he returned with a master sergeant decked out in a new uniform with bright new stripes and insignia. When they pulled to a stop in the yard just before supper, Joe jumped down and started toward the porch where the whole Buchanan family waited to greet him like a long lost relative instead of the son of a man who had once threatened James's life. As he approached, James noticed new lines around Joe's eyes and the touch of silver at his temples that had not been there when he was last in Salacoa. Joe now had the bearing of a leader of men, which he wore well.

Joe was halfway across the yard when he stopped abruptly and stared at a spot on top of the mountain rising behind the house. His eyes scanned the crest with a sweeping motion in the practiced manner of a soldier seeking an enemy hidden behind trees and brush. Shaking his head and twisting his mouth into a lopsided grin, Joe went to the porch and embraced Mary Alice, but James had caught the look of fear in Joe's eyes. As the others went into the house, James placed his hand on Joe's arm and held him back.

"It's good to have you home."

"It's good to be here, sir."

"Do you mind telling me what you were looking for on the mountain?"

"I guess I've been in combat areas too long. I can't stop myself looking for the enemy when there is unusual movement nearby. It was nothing, I'm sure. Probably just a deer or something. I thought I saw movement. That's all."

"Well, let's get inside and put our feet under Mary Alice's table. She's gone to special effort to cook everything she thought you'd like, so be ready to eat heartily."

"I assure you that won't be a problem. Miss Mary Alice is the best cook I've ever known. She could make a sow's ear taste like the finest prime roast."

As they laughed and headed for the kitchen's warm glow, James looked back over his shoulder toward the mountain. Nothing moved other than the breeze through the trees. Perhaps Joe had seen too much action.

CHAPTER 24

The Saturday afternoon before Joe was to leave for Atlanta, he rode over to pay his respects to Charles and Sarah Sinclair. He had never forgotten their kindness all those years ago when he and his brothers ran off into the creek during a heavy storm.

Joe tied the reins of his borrowed mount to a porch post, ran up the front steps, and knocked. While he waited for Sarah to come to the door, he turned toward the valley and the mountains on its far side, taking in the view and the changes that Charles had made to the farm since his last visit. He had always loved this place and how it sat higher than the surrounding valley, providing anyone who chose to sit in its high-backed porch rockers with a serene vista. Although the placement reminded him somewhat of his former home over on Pine Log Mountain, the differences between the families inhabiting each place were so stark that he couldn't prevent the touch of sadness and regret the beautiful view elicited. One day, maybe, he might have a home like this, but for the time being, the army was his home and he was grateful for the life it had given him.

The screened door behind him scraped and he turned toward the sound. Surprise and something more caused his breath to catch in his throat. His knock was answered not by Sarah, but by a pretty stranger whose eyes had the sparkle and color of fine emeralds.

Joe snatched off his cap and stared for a moment before stuttering, "Is Charles, I mean, Mr. Sinclair at home?"

The girl looked a little flustered as she replied, "I'm afraid he's out in the far field, but would you like to see Mrs. Sinclair?"

A faint "yes, please" was all Joe managed before being shown into the front room where he was asked to wait.

As she left the room, the girl looked back over her shoulder and smiled. "Mrs. Sinclair will be right in. Please be seated and make yourself comfortable. May I bring you a glass of tea?"

Joe grinned and nodded, thinking he must look rather foolish, as he seemed to have lost his tongue. The girl smiled again in response, but this time with a charming flutter of her lashes as they dropped, brushing her cheeks, and then she hurried from the room.

He felt an uncharacteristic desire to rush after the girl and demand her name. Although he had traveled across the world and experienced a lifetime of adventures since joining the army, he had never felt the urge to settle down or even walk out with a girl for more than a few months. He certainly had many opportunities and was the object of female attention wherever he went owing to his own dark beauty, but no girl or woman had ever held his attention long enough to form any permanent attachments. Joe was considered something of a ladies' man among his comrades, who envied the ease with which he wooed the females and was wooed by them in return. What had just transpired in the Sinclairs' front room was a totally new experience.

After what seemed an eternity, but was really only a few minutes, the girl returned bearing a tray with Sarah close on her heals. As the ladies were being seated, an amused expression lit Sarah's face. "Joe, I don't think you've met our friend and the new teacher at the school, Sally Ann Morgan. Sally, this is Joe Harbin, a friend of the Buchanans' and ours." Sarah looked from Joe to Sally and back. Her smile became broader, as though she smothered a laugh. "Since our boys married, we have the extra room, so Sally boards with us during the school year. She's such a pleasure to have here."

Dimples formed in Sally's peaches-and-cream cheeks. "I'm so lucky to have found friends like Sarah and Charles. I didn't know anyone when I came here, and they have made me feel like a member of the family."

Sarah patted Sally's hand. "I wanted a daughter, but wasn't blessed with one, so I guess Sally has been drafted to fill the vacancy."

Joe was in no doubt that having Sally near must be one of life's greatest pleasures. As the visit progressed, he found himself having difficulty concentrating on the casual pleasantries of the small talk required in such social situations. His attention kept wandering to the questions he really wanted to ask. Does Miss Morgan have a serious gentleman caller? Would Miss Morgan consider Mr. Harbin's request to call upon her in a more personal manner in the very near future, like tomorrow? What is Miss Morgan planning to do for the rest of her life?

The time for the visit to end came all too soon. As he shook hands, Joe found he was unable to make himself release Miss Morgan's hand until she laughed softly in embarrassment. "It was nice meeting you, Mr. Harbin. How long are you planning to be in the valley?"

Joe drew a deep breath. "Only until Monday. My leave was for just a short time." He paused, looking into her lovely emerald eyes and could not stop himself. "I hope you won't be offended by what I'm about to ask, but you see my time here is so short, and I'd so much like to make your better acquaintance. May I call on you tomorrow?"

It was now Joe's turn to be embarrassed. Sally looked so surprised that he was ready to make a hasty exit before he made any further blunders. As he was turning to leave, she spluttered, "That would be very nice. Would three o'clock be suitable?"

"It would work just fine. In fact, it would be wonderful."

***

Although Joe rarely attended church, he was up and ready the next morning before Mary Alice had even opened her eyes. She was surprised by Joe's sudden interest in attending Sunday Meeting, but she and James made no comment and introduced him to the members of the congregation with such pleasure and enthusiasm it was assumed this handsome military man must be from another Harbin family, not the notorious clan over on Pine Log. Mary Alice made no effort to disabuse them.

Mary Alice discovered the reason for Joe's sudden enthusiasm for church when she saw him approaching the Sinclairs and their boarder, Miss Sally Morgan. She couldn't help but notice the pretty flush in Sally's cheeks and how Joe's dark eyes had a new light in them that had not been there the moment before. Mary Alice decided the relationship needed all the help it could get since Joe was leaving for Atlanta tomorrow at dawn, so she joined the conversation by inviting the Sinclairs and Sally to dinner in honor of Joe's military service and recent promotion. Having put it that way, it was unlikely Sarah Sinclair would mention the dinner she had ready for her family's return from church. Well, they could eat it for supper just as well as dinner. Joe was with them only until tomorrow and he needed her help.

As the group sat around the long dining room table, the conversation turned to Joe's military experiences. Admiration, and something more, glowed in Sally's eyes as he talked about the moments of intense danger followed by long periods of boredom. Randy and Hiram hung on his every word.

"Did you bring any war trophies back?" Hiram's eyes were big with excitement.

"No, we didn't have time for that, but . . ."

Tot wasn't at all impressed with this intruder of whom she had no memory. "Our brother Archie would've brought back stuff."

Mary Alice looked at her youngest with a pained expression. "Tot, mind your manners."

"But he would—"

James shot the twins a withering look. "That's enough. You heard your mother."

To ease the tension, Joe turned to his dinner partner. "Miss Sally, how did you decide you wanted to be a teacher?"

Sally gave him a conspiratorial smile and told a story of which Mary Alice was only slightly aware. "I grew up in an orphanage in Gainesville because my parents died when I was little and I had no other family. I had a teacher there who took a special interest in me and showed me that a woman could have a sense of purpose." She stopped for a moment and appeared to search Joe's face for his reaction. "I knew teaching was what I wanted because of her, so I made up my mind to work my way through Reinhardt. And the rest, as they say, is history."

If Sally was afraid her answer might have made Joe less interested, she found how wrong she was when he suddenly asked, "May I ask you to take a turn down to the baptizing hole with me? I hear it's a pretty walk."

Though Sally looked only too pleased with the suggestion, Mary Alice couldn't resist offering a little more help. "Joe, take the buggy. It's too hot to walk that far along this road. You'll both come back coated in red dust from head to toe."

As the pair drove off, James grinned. "Are you trying to play matchmaker?"

"Joe doesn't need me to tell him who to court, but every suitor needs a little help. I just think they'd be perfect for each other, and I want them to be happy. They both deserve someone special and I think they've found what they need."

"Well, time will tell if you're right."

The afternoon was well gone before the buggy appeared again. As Joe helped Sally step down, the group on the porch heard him say, "Miss Sally, once I'm settled on base, I'll have most of my weekends free. I'm planning on coming home a lot more in the future. Do I have your permission to write to you and call on you when I'm in the valley?"

Sally looked up at him with shining eyes. "That would be wonderful."

Mary Alice glanced over at her husband, cocked her head, and smiled like the cat who had just caught the canary.

The next morning, as Joe was saying his goodbyes and putting his gear into the wagon, he stopped suddenly and peered at the mountain behind the house, a perplexed expression furrowing his handsome brow.

James noticed. "What do you see, Joe? You've been right jumpy since you've been home."

Joe shook his head. "I just can't shake the feeling someone's on the mountain watching us. I've had the feeling all week. I guess I just haven't gotten used to peace time soldiering."

CHAPTER 25

James did not see Joe off at the station with Newt because he had an appointment with a man who was coming to buy Searchlight. The Plantation Walker was getting up there in age and having difficulty with the demands of a far-flung practice, but he still had years of easy pleasure riding ahead of him. James spent a productive hour in the office working on his account books and inventorying his supplies as he waited for the man to arrive.

He had already spoken with Gus Coggins about a new saddle horse, and Gus had promised him several to look at later in the week. James planned to use the generous price offered by his potential buyer to purchase the best mount Gus had.

The clatter of a horse and buggy pulling into the driveway drew James to the door. After the usual pleasantries, the two men walked across the road to the barn where James brought Searchlight out for inspection.

They hadn't been in the barn's yard for more than a few minutes when pounding feet tore across the road accompanied by soprano shrieking. Lizzie, Nancy, and Tot tumbled to a halt beside their father. They stood shuffling their feet until Nancy poked Tot in the ribs as a reminder of their mission.

"What you doing with Searchlight, Papa? You just showing him off cause he's such a good horse, ain'tcha?"

"Let's mind our manners and say hello to our guest before we burst into a string of questions." James raised a corrective brow toward the children, then turned to the buyer. "These are my girls."

After the introductions, Tot tugged on James's sleeve. "Why're you showing him Searchlight, Papa?"

James didn't even look at Tot as he answered. If he had, he might have been more cautious with his explanation. "Well, he's getting a little old to be doing the constant going that I do day and night. I need a younger horse and this gentleman needs a good saddle horse, so I'm selling him Searchlight."

If a death in the family had just been announced it could not possibly have been met with more tears.

"Sell Searchlight? Papa, you can't mean it." Lizzie's wail filled the barn.

"He's been with us all our lives. He's a member of the family." Nancy's whine followed.

Tot took command of the situation. "It's like you're gonna sell Archie or Randy or Buster or something. How can you?"

"Please don't sell Searchlight." Three young voices trembled while tears rolled.

Both men looked at the girls in consternation. The visitor's mouth thinned with irritation. James looked at his daughters as copious tears streamed down their faces. He looked at his buyer with the generous offer, his cash already in his hand. He looked again at his girls, whose shoulders were now heaving. He looked once more at the man and his money, sighing in resignation. "Sir, I'm sorry you've come all this way for nothing, but I just can't sell this horse with these girls so upset. They're far more attached to the animal than I realized. May we offer you some refreshments? I believe my wife made teacakes this morning."

The man refused the offer of hospitality and could be heard muttering over the slap of reins on his buggy horse's rump something about a man being master of his own home, especially where his children were concerned. James smiled as he thought about the considerable sum he had just turned down simply because his children couldn't bear to part with an animal they didn't tend and rode infrequently. Well, that was about to change. They wanted Searchlight, so they were going to take over his care. But that could wait until later. Mary Alice had fried a chicken for dinner.

Later in the week, James went to Coggins Sale Barn and selected a good-looking bay Thoroughbred mare with an eye to possibly breeding her to Charles Sinclair's stallion at some point in the future.

"Gus, she's a fine little horse. I have to go to the bank this morning anyway, so I'll withdraw enough cash to pay you for the mare. I'll be back after I grab a bite at the cafe."

"She'll be here waiting for you. Have some chess pie for me."

James entered the bank's marble lobby where mahogany furnishings and brass fittings gleamed from frequent polishing. He approached an available teller and presented his withdrawal slip.

"Dr. Buchanan, it's good to see you, sir." The teller looked up at James and smiled. "We haven't seen you in town in a good while now. Those patients in Salacoa must be keeping you pretty busy."

"It's good to see you again too. I'm staying busy enough to keep me away from town, that's for sure. It seems we have more sickness each year or maybe it's just more people in the valley."

"If you'll excuse me for a moment, I'll be right back. This is a larger sum than we keep in the tills, and I need approval for the amount."

James leaned on the mahogany counter as he waited for the teller to return. His stomach growled with hunger. What could be taking the man such a long time? He was on the verge of asking another teller to see what was going on, when the first teller returned with the bank manager in tow.

The manager looked embarrassed. "Dr. Buchanan, could you please come to my office? I have something I must discuss with you."

James gave a puzzled nod and followed the manager into his bright, well-appointed office at the back of the building.

After offering James a chair opposite his own, the manager took his seat behind his desk. He made a temple with his fingers and peered over them as though he was reluctant to speak.

James's felt the first twinges of uneasiness. "Is something amiss?"

The manager's face glowed a bright pink. "Dr. Buchanan, I'm sure this is just an oversight on your part. I know how busy you must be with your patients and that it's very easy to forget things under those circumstances, but the fact is your account is overdrawn by five hundred dollars. Now I know this is a larger sum than you usually spend all at once, but you see the checks all came in relatively quickly, one upon the next, and the overdraft occurred before we were able to get in touch with you, the mail service being what it is, you know."

James was stunned. "What do you mean the account is overdrawn by five hundred dollars? There must be some mistake. I have nearly nine hundred dollars in the account. I haven't written a check on it in over two weeks. Please check your records again."

The manger's voice dropped and took on a solicitous tone. "Dr. Buchanan, there is no mistake. We've checked the records several times while trying to decide how best to proceed with this matter, you being such a respected citizen of the county and a professional man and all. I assure you, there is no error on the bank's part. I can get the cancelled checks for you, if you wish to see them."

James leaned forward and placed his hands on the desk's edge. "I most certainly do wish to see them."

The manager went in search of the evidence, leaving James to mentally search for any possible explanation for so much missing money. When he returned, the manager placed a small mountain of cancelled checks before James, all bearing his signature.

James stared at them in disbelief and then at the manager. "I don't know what to say. They all look like they were signed in my hand, but I know I haven't written any of these checks. How on earth could this have happened?"

"Well, I could not venture a speculation regarding who, but is there any possibility someone could have gotten your checks and copied your signature? We do verify the signatures before we honor checks, but as you can see, this looks as though you yourself signed each and every one."

The manager was clearly distressed, and James was feeling something he had not in many years. Not since the awful train ride to Atlanta, racing against time to find Mary Alice's brother. He hadn't made it in time to save Dolph and he had a terrible premonition he would fail again in some awful, yet unknown way. As it had over the years, his old stomach ailment reared its head just when he needed to be at his strongest and most clear.

James massaged his midsection as he rose. "I assure you the situation will be rectified. Now, if you'll excuse me, I must get to the bottom of this mystery." What he did not add was that a possible explanation had begun to take shape.

CHAPTER 26

Without a thought to Gus or the mare, James kicked Searchlight into a gallop that did not end until they had traveled the six miles to Waleska. James pulled the lathered animal to a stop in front of the general store, leaving him blowing hard and tied to the porch post as he went in search of the one person whose signature so resembled his own.

"I'm looking for my son. Is he in the back?"

The clerk behind the counter looked surprised. "Archie ain't been in all week, Dr. Buchanan. He said he needed some time off cause his mother was real sick."

James left before the clerk could inquire after Mary Alice's health and looked up and down the road in a cloud of indecision. While he was trying to make up his mind where to look next, one of the elderly men who spent much of their time watching the world go by from chairs on the store's porch tugged at James's sleeve and nodded toward the side of the building. He then got up and motioned for James to follow him.

Once he was out of sight of the road, the old man's eyes filled with pity. "I didn't want to say this where nobody mighta heared it, but I'd look over to that red barn at the foot of Pine Log if'n I's you. That's most likely where you'll find your boy. But don'tcha go telling nobody where you heared it. I ain't got no notion to have my barn burnt."

With a gnawing fear, James once again kicked Searchlight into a gallop. Although James did not drink alcohol or gamble himself, he was worldly enough to know what kind of place he sought. If Archie had fallen in with that crowd, then God help him, for they were about as a low a form of humanity as there was.

James reached Pine Log and went directly to the feed store. He had heard about the games that took place there after hours and suspected the clerk there would know where to find the barn. The store was nothing more than a shack with sheds attached and bordered on three sides by the pine forest from which the mountain rising behind took its name. It was a cheerless place around which the idle and shiftless loitered during the day and in which they gambled after dark. Why the owner had never caught on to how his premises were being used was a mystery because it was certainly common knowledge in Salacoa. Perhaps the man turned a blind eye so that he could share in the illegal profits the clerk was rumored to be raking in from the games and the other illicit activities he provided.

When James entered through the store's front door, he saw the clerk lugging a sack of grain into the main room from a storage shed at the back of the store. The man dropped his burden on the stack already in place and looked at James with a knowing expression.

"I'm looking for my son, Archie Buchanan. I was told I would find him at a barn somewhere nearby. Will you direct me there, please?"

James didn't like the smirk adorning the clerk's mouth. His uneasiness increased when the man replied, "Well, well. You ain't never been in here, have you? Archie, he's been in here lots of times. If you want him right now, you might oughta be looking down that first track to the left. Go on down 'til it ends. You'll most likely find him there, but I'd be careful if I's you. They don't take kindly to strangers down there."

James followed the man's directions and found what looked like a ramshackle barn that must have been a bright red long ago. He left his horse tied to a tree on the edge of the clearing and approached the structure. It appeared deserted. No horses, wagons, autos, or any other form of conveyance stood in the yard.

As he lifted his hand to the barn door, a shotgun barrel appeared through a crack and a gruff bass voice demanded, "Who're you and what you want here?"

"I'm looking for my son, Archie Buchanan."

A derisive chuckle emanated from the barn's dark interior, sending alarm crawling through James. He itched to yank the door open to reveal the man within, but he had little choice other than to wait for his inquisitor to finish laughing at the private joke. "He ain't here. What you want with him anyhow?"

"We have a family emergency. It's extremely important that I see him."

"You can leave a note and I'll see he gets it if he happens by."

The same anger and frustration rose in James as when he had spent three days searching for Dolph all those years ago. His heart lurched, and he had an uneasy feeling that things were not going to turn out much better with this search. He hurriedly found a scrap of paper in his medical packs and scribbled a plea for Archie to come home at the earliest possible moment. As he handed the note through the crack in the door, he caught sight of a hairy well-muscled arm that hadn't seen soap in some time, then the door slammed in his face and all was silent.

What could Archie be thinking by associating himself with people like this? As James rode home, he ruminated on what Archie could be doing in such a place. None of the options that came to mind were in the least reassuring and all of them involved illegal activity in some form or another. He decided to keep all he had learned or suspected to himself for the time being.

There was no need in worrying Mary Alice until he knew the complete truth of what their eldest child was up to.

James, still deep in thought when he walked into the kitchen, planted an absent-minded kiss on his wife's cheek.

As they sat down to supper, Mary Alice looked at him for several seconds before asking, "What has you so lost in thought? You haven't said two words since you got home. Is something wrong?"

James adopted what he hoped was a neutral expression. "I'm sorry, my love. I've just got a difficult case that has me stumped. I can't figure out what to do next."

The explanation, which was at least partially true, would have to do for now. There was always someone over whose treatment he had concerns. He begged off going to bed at the time she did with an excuse about reading up on a possible treatment. He intended to wait up for Archie and confront him. Hopefully, Archie would read his note and come home quickly, but James had no idea whether it would be given to his son by the hairy arm or if the boy would even go by the barn. James sat at the kitchen table, ostensibly reading a medical book, until his head dropped onto its pages.

At about one a.m., feet scuffling on the porch woke James. He raised up on an elbow, bleary-eyed and fuzzy-headed, to a loud thump against the kitchen's exterior wall and then what sounded like a sack of potatoes hitting the porch floorboards. James hurried outside in time to see an automobile roaring from the yard, but he was unable to see who drove it or how many people it contained. What he saw next made his heart stop. A crumpled form on the porch floor wore Archie's coat. The form groaned and began moving, trying to raise itself to a sitting position.

James leapt to its side and found to his horror a vaguely familiar face, but he had trouble making the battered features organize themselves into Archie's. He called Archie's name once and the head turned to face him. It was Archie, all right, but he had received a tremendous beating. His eyes were mere slits, his face was deeply bruised, and blood ran from his mouth, trickling down his chin and staining his white shirtfront.

James could hardly speak. His voice came in a strangled whisper. "Son, what's happened to you? Who would want to hurt you so?"

As James helped his battered son into the kitchen, he couldn't help looking over his shoulder to the mountain rising behind the house. He saw nothing out of the ordinary, but he still could not shake the feeling that something or someone malevolent watched them from the shadows. He really must get some sleep tonight. His imagination became too active when he went too long without adequate rest.

James treated the cuts and abrasions covering Archie's face. Fortunately, none of the damage appeared to be permanent in nature, although the cracked ribs would cause him some discomfort for a while in the future. There was no sense to be gotten from the boy tonight so he put him to bed on a pallet in the front room. James didn't want the other boys to wake to the sight of Archie's swollen, damaged face nor did he want their mother to find him when she went in to wake the children.

Instead of getting the rest he needed, James spent the remainder of the night tossing and turning, unable to sleep. As he struggled to understand Archie's latest trouble, a distant memory came unbidden. Maggie's strange expression and comment moments after Archie's birth rose like a specter. James had no belief whatsoever in "the sight," but Maggie had called it true where Archie was concerned, special powers or no. He dreaded the coming conversation with his son about how he had been living, which was so obviously contrary to what they had been led to believe. What depths of misadventure would be revealed?

CHAPTER 27

Dawn broke on what should have been an ordinary day. On any other fall morning, Randy would be heading to his job in the store recently opened on Salacoa Road by Charles Sinclair. Lizzie would be helping her mother with the daily chores. Hiram, Nancy, Tot, and Buster would be gathering their books and lunch pails in preparation for the walk to school. James and Mary Alice would be following their normal routines. This was not, however, an ordinary day.

James stuck his head through the door separating the kitchen from the dining room. "Can you come in here? I need to tell you something."

Mary Alice breezed into the room, looking unsuspecting and happy. "What is it? I've got a lot to do today."

"I need for you to get the children out of the house without their going into the front room. Archie's up there and it isn't a pretty sight. I'm not sure what happened, but someone has beaten him badly. I don't want the other children to see him."

Mary Alice's placidly distracted expression changed immediately. "He hasn't said a word about having trouble with anyone. Who could have done such a thing?"

After she had seen Archie and dealt with the shock, she dispatched Lizzie to the Locklins with an excuse about having promised Lavinia some of her jelly for breakfast this morning. Mary Alice also instructed her daughter to stay and help Lavinia with the ironing that was waiting to be done. After the others left for school and work, James assisted Archie to the breakfast table where he ate his eggs in silence and with some difficulty. The tension in the room was palpable. Archie avoided his parents' eyes, keeping his own glued to his plate. When the food was eaten, the inevitable confrontation could wait no longer.

"Archie," James said quietly, "what is the explanation for your condition? Could it have anything to do with the overdrawn checks you forged on my account?"

Archie looked at his father through his eyes' swollen slits and had the good grace to at least appear ashamed. He nodded slightly but did not open his mouth to speak.

James's pulse pounded against his ear drums. Fury beyond anything he had ever imagined brought bile up into his throat. He had to force himself not to reach across the table and add to the injuries his son had already suffered. "Don't sit there like a child and just nod your head. Tell me exactly what has been going on and do not spare me any of the details."

Slowly and with painful difficulty, Archie began his story. "I guess it really started when I was in school at Reinhardt. I ran short of money and decided to go with the boys to a poker game that's run by a man in Waleska. I got pretty good at the game. Just seemed to be a natural born gambler. After a while, the fun just wasn't the same because I was so much better than the other players, so I asked one of the boys if he knew about a bigger game with higher stakes and he said his older brother could probably get me into the game at Pine Log, which he did." Misery played across Archie's damaged face as he stopped speaking. After a moment's hesitation, he continued, "That's where I met Jeb and I got to playing there regularly. At first, I did real well, but after a while, I just started losing and couldn't ever make up the losses. Finally, I owed so much that I started writing checks on your account, which I'm not proud of, but I felt like I didn't have a choice. Yesterday, the bank bounced five hundred dollars in checks." Archie stopped for a moment and nervously fingered the fabric of his pant leg.

James noticed the boy was wearing what looked like new pants. The fabric was finer than anything he would have been able to afford. His eyes narrowed. "What were the checks to Jones's Mercantile for?"

Archie looked up with a pained expression. "I admit that over the last few months I wrote some checks to Jones's for new clothes. A fellow has to keep up appearances, but now the store manager says he was gonna call the sheriff. Of course, the store ain't got nothing to do with this." He pointed to his battered face. "What happened to me last night is because I can't pay off the guys holding my gambling debts."

Archie finally met his father's eyes. Desperation shone in the sweat on his forehead and in the tears rolling down his face. "They said if I didn't pay up by the end of next week, I'd get more than just a beating. I think they mean to kill me, Papa. I just got to have your help. I'm sorry for lying to you and writing bad checks, but I just didn't know what else to do."

James was appalled by Archie's revelations, but the thing that disturbed him most was the ease with which Archie had been lying all these years and that he now expected his parents to risk the family's financial security to pay his debts to such lowlifes. Archie had stolen nearly fourteen hundred dollars from them. Even if he had the money, James would be loath to contribute to such vultures' ill-gotten profits. As it was, Archie had stolen everything they had and still owed five hundred dollars. No doubt these men would follow through on their threats to harm Archie further or even kill him if he didn't come up with the money.

James rolled his lips inward as he thought. Finally, he withdrew a pencil and note pad from his suit coat pocket. "Your part in the Waleska store should be worth something. Do you think these men would wait until you found a buyer for your share?"

Archie looked startled and then the blood drained from his face. He was quiet for so long that James asked the question a second time. "What about selling your share in the store to raise the money?"

Archie's gaze dropped. He signed heavily and mumbled, "There isn't any share in the store."

James's head jerked back and he blinked. "What did you say?"

Returning color flooded Archie's face in a rush as he stood up on wobbly legs and screamed, "There isn't any share in the goddamned store. I spent the money on poker. There isn't any store share. There isn't any money. And if you don't pay them off, they're gonna kill me. You've gotta pay them."

At first James couldn't speak and when he finally found his voice, it came in a low growl from somewhere about the level of his belly. "First, let's be very clear. I don't have to do anything. You have lied and stolen and forged checks and broken the law. You . . . and only you. You have endangered yourself, and possibly this family, all for so fleeting a moment's pleasure that you have absolutely nothing to show for it except trouble. You're a liar, a cheat, and a thief. Explain to me exactly why you believe you deserve any help."

Archie had the good grace to drop his gaze to the floor. "Because I'm your son and you love me."

James aged ten years as he sat thinking about what Archie had said. The unhappy realization dawned that there were only two possible outcomes from this mess Archie had created—prison for forgery or being killed by the criminals the boy had fallen in with.

As much as it would grieve them, the family would survive the shame of prison, but James wouldn't sit by and see Archie killed regardless of what he had done. He shook his head. There was no way out of this dilemma save one.

He looked at Archie through eyes filled with tears as he spoke with an eerie calm. "You're right. We do love you despite everything you've done, but the truth is I couldn't pay your debts to these people even if I wanted to. You've stolen every extra dollar I have. All I have is fifty dollars in my pocket. It's everything I have left. Take it and use it to buy a train ticket to a destination as far from Cherokee County as it will take you. Make it a one-way ticket and don't plan on coming back here until you've made right all the wrong you've done. This is all I can or will do. I have six other children to consider and they deserve better than this. Randy wants to quit at the store and read the law with your mother's uncle, the judge. Hiram and Nancy have college fees due next year. Lizzie looks like she's going to marry that boy who's been coming around for so long now, and she deserves a nice wedding. Tot and Buster need to have their educations looked after. I'm not sure how I'm going to pay for it, but I'll manage somehow for their sakes."

James's eyes hardened and he glared at Archie. His jaw clenched as he spoke again. "But you have stolen everything from me you will ever get. Do not think you will be left anything in my will. You've already stolen more than your share. In the morning, Newt and I will take you to Canton and see that you get on the train."

Mary Alice cried out, "Oh, James, you can't mean that. Please don't . . ."

James's hand sliced the air as he continued through clenched teeth, "Do not tell the other children what you've done. I don't want them influenced by your behavior. And above all, don't you dare tell Tot and Buster that you aren't coming back. They idolize you. At least leave them with some illusions."

Archie nodded silently and left the room as his mother sobbed and his father stared through the window at some distant point on the horizon.

The next morning, the three men left for the station before first light. Archie had been as good as his word and had said nothing to the other children about where he was going or why. They stopped only once, in Waleska, to collect those possessions that Archie could carry in two grips. They paid thirty dollars for a ticket to California, leaving Archie twenty dollars for meals. At nine a.m., James said goodbye to his firstborn for what might be forever.

Just before he boarded the train, Archie began talking about a new life in California. As the train chugged away from the station, he didn't even bother to look back to where his grief-stricken father stood watching him disappear into an uncertain future.

James had Newt drop him by the backdoor and he walked through it slowly, wondering what he would find. Mary Alice's back greeted him as she slumped over the kitchen table, her head propped up by her arms. Her shoulders shook and she pulled away without speaking when he placed a solicitous hand on her arm.

Two weeks to the day after Archie's departure, James looked up from mixing medicines to see the unusual sight of an automobile pulling into the yard. A dark-haired man emerged from the vehicle and limped to the office door. He had a vague familiarity about him, but James couldn't place him.

As he invited the man into the office, he asked, "How may I help you? You seem to have injured your leg."

"You're right about that, Doc. I think I mighta cracked something when I fell off'n my mule yesterday."

"Why don't you sit and let me take a look at it? Please remove your shoe and sock."

James felt the leg and ankle. "Well, nothing's broken, but you need to stay off the foot for several days. You've sprained it fairly seriously. I'm going to wrap it and then help you to your vehicle. Can you drive with your foot in this condition?"

"I made it over here, so I'll make it home."

When James had gotten the man into his auto, he asked, "May I know who it is I've treated? I feel as though we've met before."

The man's lips curved up in a grin. "You sure will want to know who I am, and I got a message for you from somebody you know purtty well. In fact, you been interfering with this man's way of doing things for a long time now. My name's Jeb Harbin and my pa said to tell you since you tooken his son, he tooken your'un." Jeb paused long enough to enjoy the effect his words had on James. "Pa, he's the one who runs the gambling on this end of the county and he can make a feller win or lose, if he takes a mind to. You see, he follered Joe here ever time he been home and Pa, he seen how you and yours took him in and turnt him agint his own family. So's I guess what goes around, comes around, don't it? Well, good day to you, Doc. Don't guess we'll be seeing each other again. Oh, and thanks for setting my arm all them years ago." With an ironic salute, Jeb Harbin roared from the yard.

James stared at the road long after Jeb's automobile disappeared. All he had ever wanted to do was help people with his medical skill. If he hadn't treated those Harbin boys all those years ago, if he hadn't insisted on going with Johnny to take Joe home after the accident, if he had refused to go where he wasn't wanted to treat Pearl, if he had been firmer with Archie as he was growing up, if, if, if . . .

Agonies of self-doubt descended for the first time since he had begun this journey in medicine. Had he put his oath and calling ahead of his own family's needs and best interests? James sought the answer in the beauty of the surrounding valley and mountains, but he found no comfort in the golden afternoon or the rushing sounds of the cold clear creek. His peace and contentment with life were going to be disturbed for a long time to come, maybe forever.

CHAPTER 28

August 1914

Mary Alice lifted the paper funnel and looked wistfully though Sarah Sinclair's kitchen window. A summer wedding was something Mary Alice had always dreamed of for Archie and some pretty local girl. She had looked forward to being mother of the groom to her eldest as he took a bride in New Canaan Baptist Church. How handsome he would have looked dressed in a new suit, but she would never see that lovely event now with Archie being forced to leave home. He had been gone for two years and there was never a day that went by that she didn't think about him and grieve over how things had turned out. They occasionally received a letter with a distant West Coast postmark, but she had no hope of ever seeing him again. It was a subject she and James had ceased to discuss because nothing could be changed and talking about it only led to sadness and acrimony.

She pushed an errant curl out of her eyes, catching the glint of gray among the chestnut. Where had the time gone? It seemed only yesterday when James had returned to the valley from medical school and they had started courting. Now they were both beginning to show their ages. While she detested the signs of age she saw in the mirror, the gray at James's temples and the lines around his eyes simply gave him a more distinguished air. If anything, he was more attractive now than he had been when they married. She shook her head at the unfairness of it all and turned her attention back to the cake she was icing.

The final step was something she had never tried before and it was taking considerable concentration. The layers were iced and ready for the final decorative piping, the part Mary Alice had been dreading since she agreed to do this. She made one final survey of the cake and set to her task with great care. Sally and Joe deserved the prettiest wedding cake she was able to create.

When Joe and Sally announced their engagement three months ago, Mary Alice and Sarah Sinclair agreed they would take charge of the wedding preparations and host a small reception in Sarah's front room. This cake was the final step and Mary Alice was looking at a picture from the newspaper, copying the flower design she saw there. She had done this with clothing since she had first learned to sew, but the cake was proving more of a challenge. Joe was due from Atlanta any minute now and she wanted the cake ready by the time he arrived. He was driving up from Ft. McPherson in his new Model T, purchased as a wedding present to take his bride on their honeymoon up in the cool Great Smokey Mountains in Tennessee. The sound of boots running up the Sinclair's front steps announced the bridegroom's arrival.

"Hey, is anybody here?" Joe's voice rang through the house as Sarah and Mary Alice went to greet him. He was in uniform as usual but carried a clothes hanger over his shoulder. It was covered by a cloth bag and looked like it had received great care to protect it on the dusty ride up from the army base south of Atlanta.

After welcoming hugs were exchanged, Joe uncovered his burden with a flourish and held it out for the ladies to admire.

Mary Alice rubbed the fabric between her fingers. "It's really very handsome and made of excellent cloth, but what kind of uniform is this? You've never worn one like it before."

"It's a dress uniform for formal occasions. If getting married isn't a formal occasion, then I'll never be involved in one. Do you think Sally will be pleased?"

The ladies exchanged knowing glances then Sarah said, "You could wear a croker sack and I don't think that girl would notice. But I think it will add just the right touch to the ceremony and the day. Charles bought a new suit, so he will look proper to walk Sally down the aisle. She's going to be a beautiful bride."

Mary Alice nodded. "She is indeed. James bought a new suit too for when he stands up with you tomorrow, and it's about time. He's been wearing the same three-piece for years. Now if you'll excuse me, I've got to get back to a very important job before the frosting gets too hard in the tube."

Joe and Sarah followed Mary Alice into the kitchen where Joe was given coffee and pie to tide him over until supper. After the normal casual conversational exchanges among friends looking forward to an exciting event, Mary Alice asked the question she had been dreading, but to which they needed an answer.

"Joe, I don't want to bring up a painful subject, but we're wondering if someone should go to Pine Log and get your mother to bring her to the wedding. Whatever you want is what we'll do and no one will say or think any different."

Joe paused as a sad expression crossed his face. "I went by the house before I came over here to try and get her to come, but she said she would be too embarrassed to be here with respectable folks. Pa's beat her up again and she's still wearing the marks. I guess it's for the best. Sally and me are going by there on our way back from the Smokies."

Sarah's eyes grew wider. "Did you say anything to your father about this?"

"Nope. Didn't see him. Pa stays away when I come around these days. I guess he knows when he's met his match."

***

The wedding day went off beautifully and the whole community enjoyed the reception. Mary Alice's cake was much admired and several remarked that it looked like it had come from a fancy bakery in Atlanta. The new couple went away after the reception and weren't expected back for two weeks, but less than a week later a familiar car pulled into the yard.

"Hello, Joe, Sally." Mary Alice tried to keep the surprise from her voice as she greeted them with hugs. "We didn't think to see y'all for some time, but I'm glad you had time to stop here. Come on in and have some tea. Aren't you returning from your honeymoon earlier than you thought? And who's this sweet girl?"

After placing a kiss on Mary Alice's cheek, Joe placed an arm around the small girl's shoulders. "This is my little sister, Ruby, the one that was born after me and Pearl left home."

Mary Alice extended her hand and smiled down onto an angelic face with big blue eyes and a mop of golden ringlets. What she saw reflected in the girl's eyes was something that could only be described as fear. She gave the girl's hand a maternal pat before releasing it. "Hello, Ruby. Joe's a favorite around here so we're always happy to meet anyone he brings."

When they were settled around the table, Joe's expression sobered. "I got called back to Fort Mac because of all the trouble over there in Europe. We aren't at war, but the army brass says we're needed on base anyway. Lord only knows why. We went by home to see Mama and Ruby like I promised. We can't stay too long, but I'm hoping Dr. James can see Ruby. She's been sick for a while now with her stomach. Can't seem to keep her food down."

Mary Alice was relieved. Shyness and a tummy ache must be the cause of the girl's troubled expression. "James should be home any minute now, and I'm sure he'll be glad to see Ruby."

When James arrived, he, Sally, and Ruby went to the front room so James could examine the girl.

As he checked her, his mood darkened. "Ruby, have you experienced any changes lately? Like weight gain?"

The girl nodded. "I'm getting fat. Cain't get my skirts fastened sometimes. Don't know why. I ain't changed the way I eat none."

"Ruby, have your monthlies stopped?"

"What you mean, Doctor?"

"Your monthly bleeding."

"I don't know what you talking about. I ain't got hurt lately."

James and Sally exchanged worried expressions. Sadly, it was not surprising the girl was so ignorant of her own developing body. Many mountain families still believed talking about human growth and reproduction would lead to wayward behavior, so they simply let their daughters discover what nature had in store for them when the event first occurred. Many a terrified girl had gone crying to her mother with soiled undergarments only to be shocked to find out this would be with them for a goodly part of their adult lives, along with cramps, childbirth, and the rest that goes with being female. James frowned. No wonder it was called "the curse."

He finished his examination and sat down on the nearest chair. "Ruby, why don't you go back to the kitchen. I'll bet Mrs. Buchanan might find some teacakes and milk for you. And ask Joe to come up here."

After the girl left, Sally turned worried eyes on James. "What's wrong with her? She looks healthy enough, but they say she's been throwing up for about three months now."

James waited to answer until Joe was seated with them. "I have a diagnosis for Ruby's stomach trouble. It's not very good news, I'm afraid. Do you know if Ruby has a boyfriend?"

Joe was the one to answer. "I'm sure she doesn't because Pa always said he'd kill any boy who came sniffing around a daughter of his. I'm sure he thought Pearl, and then Ruby, should give up their lives and any chance at happiness they might have to stay at home and take care of him in his old age. He's always been selfish and mean that way."

James thought about how to explain Ruby's condition. Straight on was probably best. "I'm afraid Ruby is pregnant. About three or so months, I'd say."

Joe turned ghostly white. "That's . . . it's not possible. She ain't got no boyfriend. She's just a child herself. Are you sure?"

"Quite sure, but she seems completely ignorant of her condition or any other facts of life. There are many decisions that need to be made and soon. I'll leave you and Sally to yourselves. Stay for supper. There's no need trying to go back to Atlanta tonight. You and Sally can stay here in the front bedroom and Ruby can bunk in with the twins and Lizzie in the side room. It won't kill Tot and Buster to sleep in the same room for one night."

Since Randy, Hiram, and Nancy had left home to continue their educations, Lizzie and Tot had shared the front room and Buster had slept alone in the side room, which suited him just fine. Randy would soon be ready to sit for the bar exam and the middle twins were enjoying life at Reinhardt. Lizzie had postponed her marriage so that her intended could earn enough money for them to buy a house. They hoped to marry in the coming year. After Archie's departure, James had managed to find the money to pay for all his children needed by selling some land and taking on patients far beyond the valley. This plan kept him gone from home for longer periods than in the past, but at least he was solvent again.

The following morning, James and Joe talked with Ruby, trying gently to pry the baby's father's name from her. At first, she continued to say she didn't understand what they were asking, but after much persuasion, she finally broke into tears and sobbed out a very clear understanding of how babies came to be in the world and that she had suspected she was with child but had been terrified to tell anyone.

When her story was finished, Joe's face was a fiery red. Through clenched teeth he asked, "Who's the father? Tell me, Ruby. Who's responsible for your baby?"

Ruby looked at her brother with terrified eyes and shook her head.

"Ruby, you've got to tell me." Joe softened his approach. "Maybe the boy loves you and would want to marry you if he knew."

"No, he wouldn't. He couldn't."

"Why? Is he already married?"

Again, she answered with only a movement small of her head.

"You're just a child, Ruby. Whoever did this will pay for it. Did he force you?"

Ruby nodded and cried all the harder.

"Who is it? Ruby you've got to tell me. What he did is against the law. He'll go to jail and never hurt you again."

"I can't tell you. He'll kill me. He said he would."

"Who said he'd kill you. Who, Ruby?" Joe shouted in frustration.

James placed a hand on Joe's arm. This approach was getting them nowhere. "Ruby, is the father someone we know?"

The girl's big blue eyes seemed to fill her entire face as she stared at James. She opened her mouth to answer, but no words came out. Her head dropped so that her golden curls covered her face and her shoulders heaved with silent sobs. Her brother looked at James with a depth of pain and despair equaled only in bereavement.

"Please tell me, Ruby." Joe's voice was filled with pleading. "I know I've been gone from home since before you were born, but I still love you and I want to protect you from whatever it is you're so scared of. Please tell me who did this to you."

The girl listened to her brother whom she really had never had a chance to know. She looked up at him with a gaze so intense it seemed she was seeing into his very soul. She drew breath to speak and stopped. After another stalled attempt, she finally uttered a small, whispered reply that was nearly unintelligible. "It was ..."

James thought he had not heard her correctly. "Who did you say?"

The reply was a little stronger this time. "It was Pa."

James's eyes flew from the girl to her brother. Joe's face turned ghostly white, then flushed a deep angry red. His first attempt to speak came as only a straggled whimper. When he at last found his voice, it was venomous. "That sorry son-of-a-bitch. His daughter. His own child. How could he?" Joe stopped mid-tirade and fell into a gloomy silence. He seemed to be puzzling over another issue that no one else saw. His eyes narrowed. "I wonder if . . ." He stopped short, as though the thought was more than his heart could bear.

When the silence in the room was no longer tolerable, James cleared his throat. "Something must be done. Ruby can't go back home as long as your father lives there and it would be better for her and the child if she was away from the community until after the birth. There's a facility in Marietta run by good people who'll give Ruby and the child very good care. Once the baby is born, they'll place it with a good family, if that's what Ruby chooses to do. Would you like to see the place for yourself?"

Joe stood and put his hand on Ruby's shoulder. "The first thing I've got to do is get permission for more time away from the base, and then I can start thinking about what to do about Ruby. Does the Waleska store have a telephone now?"

CHAPTER 29

To everyone's relief, Joe was able to plead family emergency and got a few extra days. James decided their next move should be to remove Ruby's things from the Harbin house and then go straight to the sheriff. Joe hoped he could persuade his mother to leave as well, never to return.

James recruited Newt to go with them, who in turn went after Johnny Blalock. When the party was assembled, the four men piled into a big farm wagon and headed for Pine Log Mountain. They left Ruby at the house with Mary Alice, Sally, and Lavinia. The girl had cried and begged to go with the men to see her mother and to gather her doll from Pearl's Glade, as James always thought of the place by the creek where the older girl had played as a child. Apparently, it was Ruby's refuge as well.

All was quiet when the quartet arrived in the Harbin yard. As Joe had predicted, Joss did not show himself, but James had no doubt he was lurking in the woods somewhere above the house. Nothing had changed in the way Joss Harbin took care of his place. The only difference seemed to be additions to the piles of trash and debris. As was her custom, Azaleigh twitched the sackcloth curtains over the front window before throwing the door open and rushing into Joe's embrace.

The effects of living with Joss were written across her face in a deep purple bruise. She clearly was not getting sufficient nutrition either, for she was nothing but skin and bones. James had never been sure of her exact age, but her face was now deeply lined and her hair, tied in a tight knot at the nape of her neck, was almost completely gray. She could pass for a woman over seventy, but James was quite sure she couldn't be more than fifty or so.

Azaleigh looked beyond Joe expectantly. "Where's Ruby? Ain't she coming home?"

"No, Mama. Ruby's never coming to this house again as long as Pa's in it."

"What you mean? She ain't been took terrible sick, is she?"

"No, Mama. Let's sit at the table and I'll tell you everything."

Out of respect, the other men remained on the porch while Joe talked with his mother. After just a few moments, a grief-stricken howl erupted from the house and after a few more, Joe came to the door, inviting the others to come in. Johnny declared, if it was all the same, he'd rather stay on the porch just to make sure things stayed quiet.

It took very little time to gather Ruby's clothes and place them in an old wooden box. James went to Pearl's glade and retrieved Ruby's little handmade rag doll which he found lovingly wrapped in an old oilcloth and placed far back in the dugout hollow beneath the hillside rock shelf. Her entire life fit into one small box.

As they were placing the box in the wagon, Joe called to his mother who was standing on the porch, "Mama, where's your stuff? We need to be getting on back to Salacoa. Dr. Buchanan says you can stay with them until we can get things figured out."

"I ain't going to Salacoie."

"But Mama, you can't stay here after all that's happened."

"I ain't going and you cain't make me. This here's my home and I'm staying right here."

No amount of pleading, shouting, or cajoling could move Azaleigh from the porch. Joe's final demand was met with an angry reply. "I ain't a going and it don't do no good for you to keep going on at me 'bout it. Now you folkses just get in that there wagon and head on down the road."

Resigned to leaving his mother behind, Joe got into the wagon and the quartet left for Canton and the sheriff. Maybe Ward Hamilton would at last have what he had been looking for—a provable serious violation of the law and reason enough to lock Joss Harbin up for a long time.

As they covered the bumpy sixteen miles to Canton, Joe was silent and appeared in deep thought until they were near the river crossing. He sounded almost wistful when he spoke. "I just can't understand why Mama wouldn't come with us. She can't possibly want to stay there now that she knows what Pa's done to Ruby. I know she's terribly afraid of him, but he couldn't hurt her if she was in Atlanta with Sally and me. I've never heard her so much as raise her voice, but today she acted like she was going to fight me if I tried to put her in the wagon. I just don't understand what's gotten into her or what she can be thinking."

James had the same thoughts, but he kept them to himself. No need in making a bad situation worse by voicing what they all could plainly see for themselves. "When your father is arrested, the house will finally be a safe home for your mother, and maybe, your sister. Your mother knows better than to tangle with him over this. It'll all be over soon."

They reached the courthouse and went around to the sheriff's office. Ward Hamilton was at his desk doing paperwork.

He looked up and grinned. "Well, what brings this deputation to my door? Come in boys and have a cup of coffee."

After observing the distressed expressions on his visitors, the sheriff adopted a more businesslike manner. "You boys look like this ain't a social call. Tell me what's happened on Salacoa to bring four of you to town."

It took very little explanation to get Hamilton on his feet and calling for his deputy. After the sheriff distributed rifles, they left for Pine Log as the sun was hanging high above the western mountains and arrived just before it was full dark. James looked around from the height of the wagon's bed and felt a chill crawl down his spine. Not a candle glowed from within and the curtains lay ominously still. Something wasn't right.

Hamilton asked Newt and Johnny to act as lookouts while he, Joe, James, and the deputy went into the eerily silent house. The men stood peering about the darkened room. As their eyes adjusted to the dim interior, Azaleigh appeared by the fireplace, gently moving a rocker back and forth.

Joe rushed over and spoke in a hoarse whisper. "Ma, are you all right? Where's Pa? Sheriff's come to take him to jail."

Azaleigh looked at the men with an odd expression. She jerked her head, indicating a location somewhere to her right. "He's out there in the yard. You cain't miss him."

The sheriff drew his pistol and went to the open back door. "Joss, come on in the house. Show yourself and keep your hands where I can see them. You're outnumbered and you ain't gonna get away with it this time."

There was no response from the yard. All was silent. No movement stirred the soft night air. There was only a sliver of new moon, which in no way cut through the darkness created by the thick forest surrounding the house.

Hamilton called again. "Come on out, now. Let's not do this the hard way."

Silence.

Hamilton turned to his deputy and whispered, "Well, I guess it ain't no surprise he ain't gonna come easy. Let's get this over with. You come with me and shoot him if he don't come quiet." The sheriff pointed toward a ramshackle building at the edge of the yard. "He's probably hiding out behind the shed, if he's still on the place. Joe, stay with your mother. James, stand here in the door in case he gets past us."

The pair went through the backdoor and onto the porch. James tensed as he watched them search the darkness for any signs that Joss was about. All was quiet. Not even a breeze stirred. The deputy nodded to his right, drawing Hamilton's attention toward a shotgun oddly propped against a porch post. They looked at each other. Joss Harbin was never without a firearm. They moved closer to the porch's edge and stopped. An inert form sprawled at the bottom of the steps. Exchanging wordless warnings, the two descended, halting beside the quiet mound.

Hamilton nudged the form with the toe of his boot. "Get up, Joss. Game's over. You try anything and we'll blow you to kingdom come."

There was neither movement nor any other response. The sheriff bent down by Joss and whistled softly. "Would you look at this? Thay's a hole in his chest the size of a basketball. I don't think we're gonna have to worry about trying to arrest him. Somebody's done finished him off for us."

The pair retraced their steps, stopping near Joe and Azaleigh. Hamilton called to Newt and Johnny through the front door. "Y'all can come in. Thay's no more danger from Joss Harbin." He continued in a gentler tone, "Miz Harbin, you want to tell me what happened here?"

Azaleigh looked around at each man, her gaze finally coming to rest on the open backdoor. "He done hurt my childern for the last time. He shouldn't ought'n to a done it. He's her Pa." Her gaze dropped to her lap as though she was trying to gather strength from her hands' ringing motion. "When Joss come down the mountain just 'fore dark, I asked him 'bout what he done, and he just acted like I was talking nonsense. I tolt him what Joe said, and Joss, he called my sweet girl feebleminded and a liar."

Azaleigh looked up at the men surrounding her with a hardness shining in her eyes of which James would never have suspected her capable. He thought all the spirit had been beaten out of her long ago.

Her eyes narrowed and her mouth turned down. "He said she's just putting on, looking for attention from men. He said if'n she was in the famibly way, it was 'cause she's a whore and been running with the neighbor boys. Well, I mayn't know much, but I knowed he was the liar. He done ruint all my boys 'cept Joe and I'm purtty sure he run Pearl off with his mean, sorry ways. Now, he's ruint my baby girl. She ain't got no chance for a happy life with what he done to her."

Azaleigh's voice became eerily quiet. "I made up my mind he done hurt my babies for the last time. I'd done already got the shotgun and was a holding it behind me when he was coming up the steps. When he was close enough, I just pulled it up and blowed a hole in him."

She paused and drew in a long breath. She shook her head and said almost in a whisper, "He ain't never gonna hurt nobody ever again."

A stunned silence filled the room. Of all the possible ends Joss Harbin might have met, this would never have been anticipated by anyone. James watched Azaleigh in amazement. There must be some small vestige of the once smart, willful girl remaining deep within her to have stood down her abusive husband and bested him at his own game.

Ward Hamilton holstered his pistol. "This is clearly a case of self-defense. I'm sure you shot your husband because he was going to beat you again. Knowing Joss, he probably would have killed you for bringing charges against him for raping Ruby. This is self-defense and that's the end of it." He glared at every man in the room, fixing them with a stern gaze, communicating that he would not tolerate contradiction. Each man nodded in agreement. A silent pact was made that night in the Harbin's main room.

Hamilton's plan would have worked, too, if Jeb Harbin had not raised the hue and cry regarding his father's untimely death and therefore, the loss of his livelihood. With Joss gone, the hold the Harbins had on the county's northwest district's gambling and moonshining operations was broken. Jeb had no concern for his mother's fate as Joss had long ago trained his older sons to believe she was mentally defective and deserved the treatment she suffered at his hands.

CHAPTER 30

A week or so after Joe and Sally left for Atlanta with Ruby in their care, James made a dash for Canton upon hearing some very bad news. Jeb Harbin had gone to the district attorney with a tale of murder covered up. The DA, Jacob Cumming, was up for re-election in the coming year and had been searching for a case to disprove his opponent's allegations that he failed to enforce the law, or rather, enforced it only when it suited his purpose. This case was just what he needed. No one would care about the fate of someone like Azaleigh Harbin when her own son wanted her tried and convicted. The DA conveniently overlooked the fact that Jeb Harbin was himself known to be a criminal. Fortunately, Jeb had not been present when the death occurred and would not be needed as a witness for the prosecution.

The sheriff was ordered to arrest Azaleigh and given a warning that he would be brought up on charges of dereliction if he failed in the matter. Ward Hamilton did as he was ordered, but not before dispatching his deputy on a mission of mercy. The deputy first placed a call to Ft. McPherson with an urgent message for Joe and then rode for Salacoa in search of James.

When James arrived in Canton, his first stop was by his uncle-in-law's office in the county courthouse. There was no hope the judge would or could take the case for the defense, but maybe Mary Alice's uncle might be able to direct him to a good criminal lawyer. The judge's secretary greeted James with the news that the judge was still in court, but he was welcome to go on into the office if he cared to wait. James thanked her and made a quick decision.

Randy was clerking for a local attorney while he waited to take the bar exam. The gentleman had a very good reputation as a trial attorney, but James had no reason to believe the man would take on a case like this. On the off chance that Randy might be able to help, James went to the law offices of his son's employer and mentor, Samuel A. Barrett. Mr. Barrett was a renowned barrister whose services were sought by the high and mighty from as far away as Atlanta. Randy had been lucky to get the job with him. Having a great-uncle who was county judge probably played more than a small part in his good fortune.

Randy came into the reception area shortly after James's arrival. "Papa, it's good to see you. If you'll wait for thirty minutes or so, I'll you take to dinner. My treat."

James smiled in wonder, as he always did after a separation from any of the children. He couldn't help remembering a little boy with grubby short pants and scabby knees instead of this confident grown man before him now. "I've come with a professional request. Is there somewhere more private we can talk?"

"Come on back to my desk. Is it about anyone in the family?"

They went to the back of the office suite where Randy had a small desk, mounded with files and papers, in a corner of the law library next to a dusty window. James smiled to himself as he observed the professional manner his son assumed when they were seated. No matter how old his children became, James would always partially see them as the babies they used to be.

He told Randy about Azaleigh's plight, asking for suggestions on how to proceed in acquiring good legal representation for her.

Randy's eyes widened. "That's a truly tragic case. Papa, if you would like, I could talk to Mr. Barrett about the case. I happen to know there is no love lost between him and the DA. He might be willing to help us in some small way. Let me see if he's free."

Randy returned and asked his father to accompany him into Mr. Barrett's office. As they walked along the corridor separating the law library from the main suite of rooms, Randy explained that Mr. Barrett seemed unexpectedly interested in Azaleigh's plight. He supposed it might be because his boss secretly disliked the politically ambitious DA with a passion. Through office gossip, Randy had learned that Mr. Cumming and Mr. Barrett had once been law partners early in their careers and that the DA had essentially committed legal robbery in his position as executor of an elderly lady's estate. He had unduly influenced the woman to leave him a portion of her considerable fortune, effectively giving him half of everything she owned. It may have been legal, but it was immoral and unethical in Mr. Barrett's view. The pair parted company and dissolved their partnership with considerable rancor and bitterness on both sides, according to Randy's source.

They came to a door marked private which Randy opened without knocking, ushering James into the room before him. James looked around the large, but plainly furnished office. Mr. Barrett apparently was not a man consumed with making impressions with his money or surroundings, but rather, with his prowess in the courtroom. They had met from time to time since Randy had gone to work there. Mr. Barrett appeared to be James's senior by at least twenty years, if the white fringe surrounding his freckled bald pate was any indicator. James had found him a plainspoken, kindly country gentleman who just happened to have the reputation as a force of nature when pursuing justice.

Mr. Barrett greeted James and gestured toward his desk. When they were seated, the lawyer came straight to the point. "Dr. Buchanan, I understand you have a bone to pick with the DA over a friend's arrest."

James told Azaleigh's story in a fully detailed account, including the events of the night Joss was killed. Mr. Barrett formed a tent with his fingers upon which he rested the bridge of his nose, listening intently and peering at James over his wire-rimmed spectacles in the manner of a kindly grandfather.

When James finished his account, the lawyer tilted his head and raised a quizzical brow. "So, you believe there is a case for self-defense, even though circumstances could be interpreted as her having planned to kill her husband?"

"Mr. Barrett, I've seen Miz Harbin after at least two of her husband's assaults and I truly believe she had good reason to fear for her life when she confronted him about his rape of their daughter. There're others who can support that view as well."

James had doubts about the complete veracity of his statements, but he kept them to himself. This situation demonstrated that sometimes the law had a limited acquaintance with justice. With a shock, he realized he didn't care whether Azaleigh had planned on killing her husband or not. James had always held a firm belief that the law should be followed as closely as the correct protocol for treating an illness. If Archie hadn't been under a death threat, James would have made him turn himself in to the sheriff and would have stood by him as he was sent to prison for forging checks at Jones's, if it had come to that. But Joss would surely have killed Azaleigh when he realized she was going to thwart him in the continued violation of their child. That was really all anyone needed to know.

Mr. Barrett asked a few more questions then fell silent, staring quietly into the dust-motes swirling through the stuffy air. His expression was akin a medieval knight's just before going to do battle with the dragon.

"Dr. Buchanan, young Randy here is gonna make a mighty fine attorney, and I've asked him to stay on with us once he passes the bar examination. We have a wide-ranging practice. We pride ourselves on taking cases big and small, as long as we can make a difference on the side of justice. Miz Harbin sounds like she's long overdue for some of that precious commodity. I'm happy to offer our firm's services pro bono." Mr. Barrett turned twinkling eyes on Randy. "Young man, this case will give you a chance to cut your criminal law teeth against a wily opponent. Are you ready to put in long hours in the law library?"

James was taken off guard by the pro bono offer, but was flooded with relief when the idea had a chance to sink in. The gossip about the rift between Barrett and Cumming might be truer than anyone realized. Whatever his reason, a barrister of Mr. Barrett's stature taking the case was a godsend. Over the next few weeks as James observed the vigor with which Mr. Barrett and Randy prepared their case, he marveled that the work was gratis. Mr. Barrett forewarned that it would take much longer to prepare for this case than to try it, and as the months of preparation proceeded, he assumed the demeanor of a Crusader readying himself to defend Jerusalem.

The trial began just after the New Year with a courtroom unusually crowded for the trial of someone whose social worth was so limited. The DA's political machinery had done its job in whipping up interest in the case, casting the DA in the guise of the guardian of law and order. Murder could not be condoned regardless of the circumstances and Azaleigh Harbin had clearly committed cold-blooded murder of the most serious kind, the murder of a family member.

James squeezed past several men to a place directly behind Randy at the defense table. With grumbling and shuffling, the men made room on the bench. Randy glanced over his shoulder and nodded but did not smile or speak. Judge Campbell, Mary Alice's uncle, raised his gavel and banged the court to order. The DA stood and looked over the packed room, pausing to make eye contact with anyone of importance. Apparently satisfied that he had the room's full attention, he strode to the jury box to make his opening remarks.

"Gentlemen of the jury, we bring before you a most serious case of willful murder. An act of the most heinous kind—the murder of a husband by his lawful wife, with forethought and intent. The shooting of a man in his own home by the woman who had promised to love, cherish, and obey him, his wife of forty years, the woman you see sitting here today . . ." DA Cumming glared and raised an arm, gesturing at the defense table. ". . . one Azaleigh Harbin. We will prove that on the afternoon of August 5th, 1914, Miz Harbin lay in wait for her husband to return from working on their farm, a man looking only for the evening meal due any hardworking husband, and that she did willfully and intentionally fire a loaded double-barreled shotgun at close range, emptying both barrels directly into her husband's chest, killing him instantly. In fact, she does not deny having committed this murderous act. She fully admits that she killed her husband in just the manner as has been described."

DA Cumming paused and turned wide eyes upon his captivated audience. He then gestured again toward the defense table. "Now, my honorable opponent, Mr. Samuel Barrett, is going to try to convince you honest, law-abiding citizens that there were mitigating circumstances, that Mr. Joss Harbin was an abusive husband, who had beaten his wife on numerous occasions. They will bring forth witnesses who will tell sorrowful tales of how Miz Harbin suffered at her husband's hands. They will try to tell you that she was in fear for her life. But I ask you, if he was so abusive, why were there no marks upon her face or body on August 5th? Why was her murdered husband found not to be armed with any weapon, not a gun, not a knife, not even a club or belt with which to defend himself? Why was his body found in the back yard, murdered before he could even set foot in his own house? I'll tell you why. It is because this woman, who had promised before God to love, honor, and obey her husband of forty years, no longer wanted to perform her wifely duties. She wished to deny her husband the lawful and God-given rights of a husband in relations with his wife. She had come to find his loving attentions repugnant and she wished to ensure his attentions stopped forever, so she took up his own shotgun and used it to end his life. The commission of this crime is not only against the laws of the State of Georgia, but it is against the laws of nature and the laws of God Almighty Himself."

Silence thundered in the courtroom.

Mr. Barrett rose quietly and looked each juror directly in the eye, smiling on each man with a gentle expression. "Gentleman, what Mr. Cumming said is true, but only in part. My client, Miz Azaleigh Harbin, did in fact shoot her husband on the afternoon of August 5th, last year, but it was not because she no longer wished to perform the duties of a wife, but because she feared for her life at the hands of a man who had beaten and abused her for the entirety of their forty-year marriage. She found it necessary to confront her husband over a grievous injustice, the nature of which will be revealed during this proceeding and which you will find as abhorrent as I do. Joss Harbin was an abusive husband and an even worse father. Azaleigh Harbin did the only thing she could do to preserve her own life and the safety of her child in the face of monstrous evil." Mr. Barrett paused and again looked into each juror's eyes before returning to the defense table and sitting down.

The DA resumed his position in the center of the courtroom. The first prosecution witness called was the county coroner, who confirmed what Cumming had already divulged regarding the cause of death and went on to add, "The shot pattern, or rather lack thereof, indicates the shooter was standing no more than a few feet, no more than five feet at most, from the deceased when the gun was fired. I'd say from the amount of shot I removed from his chest, Mr. Harbin caught the full blast from both barrels directly in the area of the heart causing instantaneous death."

Since the facts could not be disputed, Mr. Barrett had no questions for the coroner.

Mr. Cumming next called the sheriff, who recounted the condition, position, and location of the body with as little assistance to the prosecutor as possible. The DA then asked, "And in what condition did you find Miz Harbin?"

Ward Hamilton responded with a sullen stare. "I don't know what you mean."

"Did you see any marks, bruises, welts, or any other signs that she had been struck or abused by anyone before you got to the Harbin home? Surely in your capacity as an officer of the law you would have noticed such signs."

During the months preceding the trial, it had become clear that Ward Hamilton had no great affection for Mr. Cumming due to how the DA chose whom to prosecute and to whom he gave special favors. James was not surprised when the sheriff took a contrary stance.

Hamilton frowned. "It was dark and I didn't look for such."

"I ask again, did you see any signs of harm to Miz Harbin when you were at her home on the day she shot and killed her husband?"

Ward looked at the jury for a long moment and then slowly turned back toward the DA. He answered Cumming's question honestly, but his tone managed to convey that there was more to the story. "No, I didn't see any signs of harm right then."

"Did Miz Harbin say anything about what had happened to her husband?"

The sheriff had no choice but to answer. "She said she shot him."

It took prompting the sheriff several times and calling the deputy to establish Azaleigh's exact words and the events that occurred after the group arrived at the Harbin place. The deputy was the day's last witness and he was asked to review for the court where the body was found.

"Joss, Mr. Harbin, he was lying at the foot of the back steps."

"Was there any sign that he had gone into the house and then left again?"

"Not that I could see."

"So, would it be your belief that he had not gotten as far as the porch before he was shot?"

"I suppose so."

"He was killed without so much as having been able to get a cool drink of water from the well after putting in a long hot day of work? He didn't have time to even remove his boots?"

The deputy frowned and sought his boss's approval. Ward Hamilton nodded and his deputy answered, "I guess not."

The first day's testimony ended with what appeared to be a strong case for the prosecution. There were several witnesses remaining for the next day before Mr. Barrett could begin the defense. James feared the jury related far too well to the plight of a husband murdered by an ungrateful wife. He had watched their faces as each witness testified. The twelve men did not look on Azaleigh with sympathy or compassion. Instead, they peered over at her from time to time with speculative gazes. What they saw was a thin, old, shabbily dressed mountain woman who apparently stirred nothing but contempt, for they looked at her as though they had already made up their minds about her guilt. James left the courthouse worried and slightly depressed. When they gathered in Mr. Barrett's office to prepare for witness testimony, he expressed his concerns.

Mr. Barrett rested his nose on the bridge made by his fingers, a now familiar gesture that seemed to help his thought process. "We haven't presented our case, and I have faith the jury will listen to reason. Cumming hasn't and cannot present an airtight case. The law calls for him to prove her guilt beyond the shadow of a doubt, and I don't think he can. No one could. Azaleigh's chances rest on how well we can plant that seed of doubt. I know we don't want to do this, but we may have no choice but to put Ruby on the stand. Her being asked to testify will hinge on how well Azaleigh does. It would be very difficult to convince any jury that Azaleigh is innocent without them hearing her intentions from her own lips. I don't see how we can get away with not putting her on the stand, as much as I would rather not."

James shook his head and leaned forward. "Cumming will tear her to pieces. The man hasn't shown a shred of compassion. I pray she has enough of whatever made her stand up to Joss left to save herself a second time."

CHAPTER 31

The low-hanging clouds that hovered as they mounted the courthouse steps the following morning matched James's mood. Azaleigh had been less than eloquent in her own defense as Randy played the part of the DA in the practice preparing her for court. James could only hope she would do better with a good night's sleep and big breakfast under her belt. Despite her situation and being locked up each night, she was gaining weight and losing the haunted look that had been her normal expression for as long as James had known her. The stress of living with Joss had apparently been greater than being on trial for her life.

The judge's gavel brought silence, and the DA called his first witness, a gentleman of questionable veracity according to the gossip in Salacoa due to his rumored association with Joss as a customer and sometime distributor for Joss's product.

DA Cumming approached the witness stand then nodded at the jury with a conspiratorial smile. "Please relay what Joss had told you not long before his death."

The witness glanced around the courtroom with a self-importance smirk. "Well, now I don't go asking about people's private life. Joss, he just up and volunteered like. What he said was that his woman, her what's sitting over yonder . . ." He pointed toward the defense table. ". . . had done quit his bed and went to sleeping in the shed room. He said he might need to find hisself another gal."

"What did you think he meant by getting another woman?" The DA seemed pleased with this witness. Anticipation of even more damning words was written on his face.

"Well, I reckoned Azaleigh, she wasn't letting him . . . You know. Be a husband to her."

A slight murmur rippled through the courtroom.

The DA glanced around the courtroom to gage the testimony's effect and nodded. "Thank you, sir. I know you would rather not have been put in the position of having to relate these facts. I have no further questions for you."

Mr. Barrett rose for cross-examination. He strode to the witness box. When he spoke, his voice was quiet but filled with authority. "What, sir, was your relationship with the deceased?"

For the first time since he entered the box, the witness's confidence wavered. "What you mean, relationship?"

Mr. Barrett turned just enough so that he could see both the witness and the jury. "How did you come to know Joss Harbin?"

The man clearly had not expected the question. He hemmed and hawed before finally replying, "Well, now, I guess you could say we done business with each other from time to time."

"And what type of business did y'all engage in?"

"Well, Joss, he did this and that."

"Could you explain so that we can have a better understanding of his business?"

Cumming called out, "Objection. How and with whom Mr. Harbin did business isn't relevant to the crime."

The crease between the judge's eyes deepened. "Sustained. Mr. Barrett, you will have to find another line of questioning."

Mr. Barrett nodded and smiled at the judge. "Thank you, Your Honor." He then returned his attention to the witness. "Were you ever a guest in the Harbin home?"

"No, Joss, he didn't like folkses coming 'round his place. Never went in the house."

"So you were never a guest for, say, a meal or an overnight stay?"

The witness smirked. "I got my own house. What would I be sleeping over at Joss's for?" He didn't seem to recognize that a trap's jaws were closing.

"So you have no absolute knowledge of where Miz Harbin did or did not sleep?"

The man squirmed in the chair and tried to look at the DA for guidance. Mr. Barrett positioned himself to block the witness's view of anything other than himself. He asked again, "Did you or did you not have personal knowledge of the sleeping arrangements and intimate relationship between my client and her husband?"

"Well, Joss, he was the one what said it." The man seemed to think the truth might serve him better. "I ain't seen it one way or t'other."

Mr. Barrett smiled reassuringly. "Have you ever known Mr. Harbin to exaggerate or maybe stretch the truth?"

The witness returned the smile, looking relieved at not being accused of lying under oath. "Now, Joss, he could spin a yarn when he'd a mind to, but I cain't see why he'd make something like this up."

"Was Mr. Harbin given to talking about his personal life in such intimate detail?"

"I don't reckon I ever heared him talk about stuff like that before." The witness's eyes began to fill with suspicion.

"What was your reaction to Mr. Harbin's admission of failure in his marriage?"

"Well, I guess I's right surprised, Joss being such a big, fine figger of a man and all." The witness squirmed once again.

"How surprised would you say you felt?"

"Well, I . . . real surprised, I guess." The man was now craning his neck toward the prosecution table while Mr. Barrett moved in closer.

"Exactly when and where were you when this conversation took place?"

"I don't rightly remember."

Mr. Barrett smiled knowingly and cast a collegial glance at the jury. "You don't remember? A personal confidence of such an intimate and surprising nature and you don't remember where you were when the statements were made?"

"I already told you." A slight edge entered the witness's voice. "I cain't remember."

"Well, if you don't remember where you were, is it possible you don't remember the conversation as clearly as you supposed?"

The witness looked uncomfortable. "I suppose so, but he did say it."

"Thank you." Mr. Barrett turned and took a few steps away from the witness box, as if he had finished questioning the man. The witness was halfway to his feet when Mr. Barrett, with a classical dancer's grace, suddenly wheeled around. A simple question drifted across the courtroom.

"Why?"

"Beg pardon?" The witness, appearing confused, sat down again.

"Why would a man like Joss Harbin tell such deeply intimate details of his married life to someone whom he had never even invited into his home to sit down for a chat, much less to break bread?" The questions were no longer quiet. In fact, they were building in volume with each word Mr. Barrett spoke. "Why would he talk to such a casual acquaintance about something that would have caused him much embarrassment if it had become common knowledge that his wife refused his bed?"

The witness turned blood red and mumbled, "I reckon I ain't got no idea."

"Why would he choose you with whom to share such a personal burden?"

"I told you. I ain't got no clue as to why."

"Had he ever told you anything so personal before? Was he in the habit of telling you things of a personal nature?"

"No, I already told you." The witness's eyes widened and he glanced at the jury.

"And yet he chose you to whom he told this embarrassing secret."

The witness squirmed in his seat and replied weakly, "Yeah."

"I ask you again, why did he choose you in whom to confide such personal information?"

The witness was clearly feeling cornered and answered with more vehemence. "I told you, I ain't got no idea why he done it."

Mr. Barrett paused and looked around at the jury before placing himself within a few inches of the witness and thundering, "This supposed conversation never took place, did it?"

The witness visibly jumped in his chair. Mr. Barrett now moved aside so everyone in the courtroom could see the man's face.

"Remember before you reply that lying under oath is a crime punishable by time in prison."

The witness's pained expression puckered his lips as though he had sucked on a lemon. He looked from one attorney to the other and then at the judge. He turned again to Mr. Barrett and wilted like a weed starved for moisture. "Like I said before, he told it to me."

It wasn't a total victory over what was so obviously a lie, but it may have made a small dent the prosecution's case. As the witness testified, James had begun to wonder if the man had a stronger connection with Jeb Harbin, rather than Joss. It could account for the yarn he had tried unsuccessfully to spin.

The next and final witness in the prosecution's case was a man who lived on Pine Log, not far from the Harbin place, and was their closest neighbor. He was also known to be one of Joss's long-time customers. The DA asked the man to tell where he lived, how long he had known the Harbins, and other details to set the scene. With these preliminaries concluded, Cumming came to his real point.

"Tell us, where were you on August 5th of last year at about four o'clock in the afternoon?"

"I's on my way to see Joss."

"Did you see Mr. Harbin after you arrived?"

"Naw, I ain't got as far as the back porch when I heared Azaleigh and Joe talking about Joss."

"Were you in the habit of calling at the back door?"

"Naw, but thay was three men on the front porch, and I didn't hanker to have no truck with 'em. If'n Joss weren't to home, I's just gonna set down out back and wait for him."

"Did Joe and Miz Harbin know you were present?"

"Naw, they didn't know I's there."

"And what was it that Azaleigh Harbin and her son Joe were talking about?"

"They's talking 'bout Joss."

"Could you tell us what you heard?"

"Azaleigh, she was moaning and crying and saying how Joss didn't deserve to live after what he done to her baby."

"Do you know what Mr. Harbin was supposed to have done?"

"Ain't got no idea."

"You are sure you heard Miz Harbin say that her husband did not deserve to live?"

"Yes, sir. She said it loud like and I could hear her real clear. She said he didn't deserve to live after what he done to her baby. That's all I heared."

James stifled a gasp. The witness had clearly been on the back porch just as he described. How could he have approached the house without being seen? He must have slipped down directly behind the house, coming from the liquor still when he didn't find his moonshine supplier at work.

Mr. Barrett chose to release the witness without cross-examination. Joe had already told him that his mother had made the statement as reported by the man and the lawyer probably saw no benefit in dwelling on it. Instead, he chose to begin his defense.

The first witness he called was Joe, who gave a detailed account of life as he remembered it during his childhood and up until the time he joined the army. The jury was clearly disturbed by Joe's description of his parent's relationship. He reported in-depth the numerous times his father had threatened to kill his mother and the beatings he had administered over the most minor things. When Mr. Barrett thought the jury was primed and ready, he began his most provocative line of questioning.

"How many siblings do you have, Mr. Harbin?"

"I have four brothers and two sisters."

"And do they all still live in the county?"

"Two do. My brother Jeb and the youngest, my sister Ruby."

"And where are the others?"

The DA rose. "Objection. What do Mr. Harbin's siblings' places of residence have to do with this case?"

Mr. Barrett turned to the judge. "I am trying to show the effect that living with Joss Harbin had on his wife and children."

The judge nodded for Barrett to continue. Joe explained why and where his two eldest brothers were imprisoned, but he made no mention of Pearl. The time had now come to reveal what they suspected to be the reason for Pearl's disappearance. Mr. Barrett had saved this for last and hoped to work it in before he was stopped by a sustained objection.

Barrett drew a deep breath and stepped back so the court had a full view of the witness. "I believe you said there was another sister. Do you know her whereabouts?"

"No, sir. She left almost fourteen years ago when she was just thirteen."

"Have you had any communication with her since she left home as to why she left at such a tender age? Do you have any idea where she might be living?"

"No, sir. I don't know where she is, but I'm very sure she ran off because our pa was raping her like he did our little sister Ruby."

There was an audible gasp throughout the courtroom and the DA jumped to his feet. "Objection. This is mere speculation. Mr. Harbin has already admitted not knowing where his sister is, so how can he possibly have firsthand information about her reasons for leaving home?"

The judge agreed with the DA and asked the jury to ignore Joe's last statement, but the words, once said, could not be called back, and they had had the desired effect on the twelve men sitting in judgment.

Mr. Barrett called James next. James recounted Azaleigh's injuries and the threat he had heard Joss make against Azaleigh's life. He told how his own family and life had been threatened and how his barn had mysteriously burned shortly after his last confrontation with Joss. Once again, Mr. Barrett had saved the best for last.

"Dr. Buchanan, did you have occasion to treat Ruby Harbin in the summer of the previous year?" James then gave a detailed description of Ruby's condition.

"And did Miss Harbin tell you who had fathered her child?"

James glanced at the jury as he gave his reply. "It took some time to extract the name, but she finally said it was her father, Joss Harbin, who had fathered her child and that he had done so by raping her repeatedly from the time of her twelfth birthday."

Once again, gasps and whispers erupted in the courtroom. The judge banged his gavel and called for order. The DA objected that this was hearsay and that Ruby should be produced in person to report the alleged rapes. As he observed the uproar his testimony had produced, James feared the revelation had strengthened the prosecution's case against Azaleigh, but he had looked directly at the jury while speaking and had seen the disgust and horror clearly written on their faces. The jury's appalled reaction to Joss Harbin's rape of his own child coupled with the reports of Joss's threats to kill Azaleigh might be just enough to get an acquittal.

Mr. Barrett's last witness for the day was a neighbor who often passed near the Harbin cabin. "Can you tell the jury what you witnessed?"

"I was headed out to go hunting last fall when I heared a awful outcry coming from the Harbin place. It sounded like somebody was hurt bad, so I went to see about it. When I walked up to the edge of the yard, I seen Joss whipping Azaleigh with his belt, hitting her with the buckle like. He was saying over and over how he'd kill her if'n she was to ever go agint anything he said ever again. She was hollering that she was sorry and begging him to stop. That just seemed to make him madder and meaner. I guess his arm give out 'cause he stopped, but what I saw next just 'bout made me sick. He throwed her on the ground right there in the open daylight where anybody who come up coulda seen and he looked like he was gonna have his way with her right there. I couldn't stand no more, so I left real quiet like. Joss, he'da killt me if'n he'd knowed I's there."

Mr. Barrett thanked the witness and returned to his seat. "I have no further questions for this witness."

The DA was primed and ready. He strode over to the witness box and leaned on its railing as he began his cross-examination. "Well, that's quite a tale. Tell us, if things were so bad for Miz Harbin, why didn't you step in and help her? You must have had a gun with you if you were out hunting."

The man looked straight at the DA. "Yes, sir, I had my gun all right, but I care 'bout my life and my wife and childern. I's afraid I'da had to kill him if I didn't stay quiet or he'd come after me and mine. I don't need that kind of trouble. Besides, I didn't have no hankering to have my barn burnt. Everbody knowed if'n you crossed Joss, your barn was good as gone."

James looked at the jury to try to catch their reaction. Apparently at least two men in the jury box had some knowledge of Joss's reputation, for their heads were nodding in agreement.

The day ended on a high note for the defense, Mr. Cumming having decided against questioning the neighbor any further. As James left the courthouse, a sense of relief spread through him. It looked like they were almost home. The last witness would be Azaleigh herself because Mr. Barrett believed the jury wanted and needed to hear her say that she feared for her life when she killed her husband. He also hoped her near blindness would elicit sympathy.

The greatest fear was that she would not stick to the prepared responses drilled into her by Randy. Her life with Joss had left her with what was surely some form of brain damage. Her mind just didn't function as well as it once must have and she was easily confused. It was a gamble to let her testify, but it seemed a necessary one.

CHAPTER 32

As Azaleigh took the stand the following morning, James saw her hands trembling. She was clearly nervous and she peered about the courtroom, trying to make out the jury's faces. He was beginning to doubt the wisdom of having her speak in her own defense. Cumming was no fool nor was he a kindly paternal figure. He was a cunning and lethal inquisitor. Azaleigh would be no match for him if he were able to get her confused and doubting herself. James smiled reassurance and nodded, but he was not sure Azaleigh could see him.

Mr. Barrett put Azaleigh at ease, and she told a sensible but harrowing story of life as Joss's wife. When the moment came for the climactic question, Azaleigh was speaking with confidence and clarity.

"Miz Harbin, the prosecutor, Mr. Cumming has suggested that you willfully killed your husband, that you planned the shooting and then carried it out with the intent to kill Mr. Harbin. Now, tell us in your own words what was in your mind when you confronted your husband on the afternoon of August 5th."

"Joss, he ruint my baby girl, and he had to say what he done. He had to be stopped 'fore he done more harm to anybody. Last time he went at me with the belt, he told me he'd kill me if'n I's to ever go agint his word again. I done seen our son, Joe, and Joss couldn't abide him coming about the place. Joss had done tolt all us not to have no truck with Joe 'cause he's a traitor to the family, but he's my baby boy. A mother cain't just give up a child 'cause his pa don't like him, can she? When I's thinking on how to get Joss to leave Ruby alone, I decided I'd better be ready for him. He don't take no guff off'n nobody. So I got me the extra shotgun from behind the front door and I met him on the porch. I told him he had to quit the house so's my baby girl could come home. He said my Ruby was feebleminded and a liar. She ain't no such thing. Then he said he was gonna kill me for sure this time, so when he was coming at me, I pulled up the gun and shot him. It was me or him."

"Thank you for telling us about what is so clearly a painful episode in your unhappy marriage to the man who abused you and your children for so many years." Mr. Barrett released Azaleigh to the DA.

Mr. Cumming strode across the room and now loomed over the small bent form in the witness enclosure. "Tell us, Miz Harbin, if you were so afraid of your husband, why did you stay with him for forty years?"

"He told me almost from the first night we's married that he'd kill me if'n I was ever to leave him, and he'da hunted me down and done it too. Wouldn't have mattered where I gone. Didn't have no place to go anyhow."

"But isn't it true that your son Joe was in the community at the time? I'm sure he would have taken you away from danger if you had asked him."

"He asked me to leave, but I knowed Joss had to be tolt first."

James groaned inwardly. He had specifically told Azaleigh not to admit to Joe's asking her to leave with him. Joe certainly would never tell it and there was no one else who knew except those who had made a solemn vow to keep it a secret. Not even Mr. Barrett or Randy knew about Joe's begging his mother to leave with him. The light in the DA's eyes told James that what he feared most was about to happen.

"So you had the opportunity to get away from your husband, but you chose to stay. Why was that?"

The first clouds of confusion descended. Her eyes widened and she then squinted at the DA. "He hurt my baby. He had to own up to it."

"Was your husband a man with whom you felt you could have such a conversation?"

"What'cher mean?"

"Did you believe your husband would be willing to talk peacefully with you about Ruby?" Mr. Cumming asked gently.

"I knowed he wouldn't."

The DA raised an eyebrow, but in all other ways acted as though he were a kindly father questioning a beloved child. "So, knowing that he would not want to talk about Ruby, you stayed anyway?"

"I couldn't take it no more. He done ruint my last baby."

"So when he was coming to the house, what did you do?" Sympathy dripped from the DA's every word.

"I got the shotgun, like I said."

"And what happened next?" Cumming nodded encouragement.

"He said Ruby was a liar."

"Did that make you angry?" His eyes widened.

"Course it did. She's the sweetest girl. She wouldn't make up something like that."

"Did your husband have a weapon with him? Did he have, say, a pistol or an axe?" Cumming glanced at the jury and winked.

Azaleigh seemed unaware of what had just happened. She simply replied quietly, "No."

The trap was about to snap shut on her and Azaleigh seemed to have no idea. She appeared to think the DA was just making conversation or asking for her side of the story. James dreaded what was coming next. What had they been thinking in putting this poor soul on the stand? She was no match for Cumming.

"Did you raise the gun before or after he came near you?"

"I . . . I raised it 'fore he got close. I knowed he'd be mad."

"Did you ask your husband to leave after he called Ruby a liar?"

"No. He just kept coming at me."

"And so you did what?"

"I pulled the triggers."

"You intended all along to kill your husband, didn't you?"

Azaleigh squinted hard. Her hands began a rhythmic circling motion as though she were trying to clean them. She looked frightened and confused. Azaleigh sought Mr. Barrett's approval through eyes squinting with faded vision, but he could only communicate with a slight head shake, which James knew she was unable to see. She remained quiet so long that the DA asked the question again. The jury, which had been growing in sympathy for Azaleigh, began to peer speculatively at her.

She drew a shaky breath and finally mumbled, "I didn't want to. He just kept coming at me."

She gave the answer Randy had drilled into her, but in such a way that it sounded like a lie. Powerful men in authority clearly terrified Azaleigh. She became meek and submissive before them. She had told Joss what he wanted to hear for so long that she no longer had much in the way of verbal self-defense left in her. She had denied her own desires and opinions for their entire married life. The effects of forty years of burying and subverting her true self were stronger than the ability to defend herself. James didn't know or care what her true intent had been. He knew beyond doubt that Joss would eventually have killed Azaleigh and it now appeared the jury might finish the job for him.

The DA wasn't finished. He rounded on the hapless witness and thundered, "You killed your husband in cold blood, didn't you? He came to the house expecting his supper and you met him at the door and shot him before he could step foot in the house, didn't you? There was no conversation about Ruby, was there?"

Mr. Barrett was on his feet shouting his objections to badgering the witness, but the seeds of doubt had been planted with the jury and there was no turning them back. It all lay with Azaleigh's shaky sense of self-preservation, which seemed to be shrinking before their very eyes.

"He called my baby girl a liar. He had to own up to what he done. He'da killt me. He said he was gonna. I had to shoot him."

"So you have said. I have no more questions for Miz Harbin. She has said enough." Cumming gloated, satisfied that he had convicted Azaleigh with her own words.

Azaleigh had been on the stand for most of the day and was clearly at the end of her tether, but Mr. Barrett could not leave the jury with the DA's words being the last they heard. He did his best to repair the damage through re-direct, but there was no way to completely erase what had been planted in the jury's minds. The defense team left the courtroom that afternoon knowing there was only one witness remaining who could sway the jury back to their side. Azaleigh's fate now rested with a fourteen-year-old child's ability of to stand up to a grown man who would give her no quarter. He would take advantage of her youth and inexperience and turn them to his own purposes.

The next morning broke sunny and beautiful. The air was crisp and invigorating. A front had moved through during the night and freshened everything. Even the winter mud along the edges of the roads looked more appealing. Everything looked brighter, newer, clearer except the proceedings at the Cherokee County Courthouse. Despair accompanied James as he arrived in the courtroom. A very frightened and visibly pregnant fourteen-year-old girl was about to take the stand with the terrifying knowledge that her mother's life rested in her small, delicate hands. James watched Ruby enter by the double doors at the back of the room and awkwardly make her way through those still standing in the aisles looking for a seat in the crowded room. Joe walked with her, holding her hand, whispering to her. They paused by the defense table so Ruby could embrace her mother, then they took the seats directly behind Mr. Barrett.

The trial resumed and Mr. Barrett called his next witness. Ruby rose from her seat and began to walk the distance to the witness stand. James watched her square slender shoulders and he wondered how well his own girls would stand up under such intense pressure. He had observed Randy and Mr. Barrett preparing her. She had the desire to help her mother, but did she have the skill? That was certainly the question.

As James observed this brave little girl crossing the expanse of courtroom between her seat and the witness stand, he heard the door at the back open and then quietly close. He would have thought nothing about it except for the soft whispering that began and grew in volume as light footsteps sounded on the courtroom's floorboards. Someone of importance or of great interest was approaching. The person drew up beside the bench upon which James sat. He glanced over to see who was causing such a stir. He looked at the newcomer, narrowed his eyes, and looked more closely. Everyone in the room was looking from Ruby to the new arrival and back again. They were commenting on the remarkable resemblance between the child about to take the stand and the woman who had just entered the room. James stared. Could it possibly be?

CHAPTER 33

James watched in awe as the woman approached the defense table and tapped Mr. Barrett on the shoulder.

Azaleigh must have felt the woman's presence, for she turned and looked behind her. Her eyes widened and she gasped. "Pearl? My baby, Pearl? Is it really you?"

The woman bent and wrapped her arms around Azaleigh's shaking shoulders. "Yes, Mama. It's really me, and I have something I want to tell this court."

Mr. Barrett requested a recess so he could assess the information this unexpected witness might provide. They all rushed to his law offices to hear what Pearl had to add to the already sad story of life with Joss. When she finished, the room was deathly still. No one spoke.

Mr. Barrett ushered everyone back to court at the appointed hour. "I have a change, Your Honor. I wish to call Miss Pearl Harbin next."

Pearl took the stand and Mr. Barrett began. "Tell us, Miss Harbin, why have you come forward so late in these proceedings?"

"I live in Savannah. It was only by pure chance that I read about my mother's trial in an Atlanta paper. I pick up *The Atlanta*

Journal once in a while to see what's happening back home. I got here as fast as I could."

"Miss Harbin, I could stand here asking you question after question to draw out the information you have to share with this court, but after hearing what you have to say, I believe your words are far more eloquent than anything I might add. Would you please describe for us what living in your parents' home was like for you and your mother and what event or events caused you to leave that home at the tender age of thirteen?"

Pearl told about the times she had seen her father beat her mother and threaten her life. She told about having to hide her few playthings because her father believed everyone should work to earn their keep from the time they could walk. She told how she feared her father and how she tried to hide whenever he was in the house. She told how her brother Joe promised to protect her and fought their father over her right to go to school. She told how Joe was ultimately unable to keep his promise, no matter how hard he tried.

Before she began the last part of her testimony, Pearl looked first at her mother and mouthed the words "I love you." She then turned so she could make eye contact with every juror. "When I turned twelve, Pa said he had a birthday present for me. He said it was hidden in the woods so I wouldn't find it before my birthday came. Mama was in the garden and the boys were all out of the house. He took me to the woods far enough from the house so nobody could hear or see us. When I asked what the present was, he opened his pants and said, 'This.' That's when he raped me for the first time. He said a girl was her father's property and he had a right to do whatever he wanted with me. He said if I told anyone what he did, he'd kill me. The day I ran away was the day he put a pistol in my mouth and pretended he was going to pull the trigger. I had just told him he'd gotten a baby on me. Here's her picture. She doesn't know who her father is, and I'll never tell her. As far as she knows, I'm an orphan who has no idea who her parents were and that's the way it's got to be. I'm sorry, Mama, but she cain't ever come here. She's a good girl and she's happy. I cain't have her life ruined by Joss Harbin. He's done ruined enough lives already. If Mama killed Pa, it was because he was going to kill her."

A collective whooshing disturbed the courtroom's deathly silence as whispers erupted. James observed the drama's main players closely. Mr. Barrett beamed at Pearl and Randy patted Azaleigh's hand as he whispered animatedly in her ear. The DA's shoulders hunched slightly and he seemed to double up. Maybe the will to win the case at all costs had simply gone out of the man like air from a punctured balloon. A wave of shame washed over James as he considered his doubts about having helped these people. The loss of his barn and animals seemed such minor things compared to the pain these women had suffered.

They left the courtroom and went back to the law offices to await the verdict. Azaleigh couldn't seem to sit still. She paced the room, wringing her hands. "What you think they gonna say? I done the bestest I could. Are you disappointed in me, Mr. Barrett?"

The lawyer looked on his client with fondness and compassion. "I don't think anyone could have done any better against Mr. Cummings. He's a hard man to stare down. I have high hopes that things'll turn out all right. And even if they don't go completely our way, the judge will surely take into consideration all you endured with your husband before passing sentence. If the worst happens, we'll appeal the verdict, but don't worry. I really believe we have a good chance for acquittal. Pearl couldn't have arrived at a better time."

Azaleigh looked at Pearl and patted her hand. "She always was a good girl."

The quiet afternoon was disturbed by a page from the courthouse, calling into the depths of the offices, "Mr. Barrett, y'all got to come back to the court. The jury's done finished. Judge says come right now."

As the group moved toward the office door, James tugged on Randy's sleeve. "Is this a good sign or a bad one? It seems they made their decision awfully fast."

Randy shrugged. "I just don't know, Papa. It could go either way."

The tension in the courtroom was palpable as they sat watching Mary Alice's uncle read the slip of paper handed him by the bailiff. Word had gone around town about the jury's quick return and the room was filled to capacity.

The judge looked at the jury foreman. "Is this the verdict of you all?"

"It is your honor. We all agreed it is right and true."

James unconsciously held his breath as the jury foreman opened the paper to read the verdict. "We the jury find the accused, Miz Azaleigh Harbin, innocent of all charges by reason of self-defense."

A collective sigh floated through the silent room. The judge thanked the jury for their time and wished Azaleigh well. It was all over so suddenly after the long months of preparation and worry. Azaleigh was released and went home with Ruby to await the birth of the child at the center of all the trouble. Pearl planned to stay with her mother for a few days and then return to Savannah and the life she had built for herself and her child. Joe and Sally returned to East Point and military life. James went home to Salacoa and the sanity of the world he understood, a world he cherished more than words could adequately express.

When he reached the yard, he bounded up the porch steps and raced into the kitchen where he found Mary Alice putting the icing on a cake. He swept her into his arms and kissed her as though they had been separated for years, not days. As they sat at the table over supper, James told Mary Alice all that had transpired during the trial, ending with Pearl's story.

Mary Alice listened in silence throughout James's recitation. When he finished, her brow wrinkled. She studied him for a moment. "What do you think? Did she plan to kill him or did it just happen?"

James placed his fork on the edge of his plate and sighed. "When I was younger, I believed there were no questions where right and wrong were concerned, especially the law. I wouldn't have said this then, but that was before I encountered Joss Harbin. Now, I'm not so sure about the absolute letter of the law anymore. I truly believe he would have killed her eventually. She just got to him first." James paused and stared through the kitchen window at the mountain beyond. "You know, for a long time after Jeb Harbin's visit and his revelation about Archie, I wondered if I had made a terrible mistake in taking on the Harbins and their problems, but watching Azaleigh, Joe, and especially Pearl, I was struck by how much the human spirit can endure and even overcome. Watching Pearl face down Cumming, I felt maybe it was all worth the price."

James stopped talking and took Mary Alice's hand, kissing it as though they were still in their courting days, instead of old married folks. In response, she caressed his face with the tips of her fingers, pushing his hair from his eyes, before leaning in as he pulled her close. They wrapped each other in arms tingling with the mellow desire of long years of loving and being loved in return, of working and building a life together, of knowing they would rather grow old together than have all the riches the larger world might provide. They didn't have many of the material things other doctors with rich patients had, but they had each other and their children, which was more than enough.

Giving Mary Alice one final squeeze, he released her. "I'm just sorry I didn't see Archie for what he was sooner. Maybe then I could have put him on the right path." A sudden sadness engulfed him and he rubbed the bridge of his nose before shaking his head. "Enough of the Harbins and sad things that can't be changed.

Let's talk about something happy, like our daughter's wedding. Have Lizzie and that boy set the date?"

Mary Alice grimaced and shook a finger. "That boy's name is Cecil, as you well know, and they have chosen the first Sunday in June. They want a reception here at home like the one we had for Joe and Sally at the Sinclair's. I'm looking forward to making a wedding cake for one of my own this time."

CHAPTER 34

Lizzie and her young man were married in a beautiful June ceremony and immediately left for Dallas, Texas, where her husband had a new job. Lizzie's maid of honor, her sister Nancy, went looking for adventure and found it in a job offer from Pillsbury to join their staff of traveling home demonstration agents. In August, she moved to Boston, just before Hiram left for the University of Georgia where he was registered as a premed student. Randy accepted Mr. Barrett's job offer, passed the bar with flying colors, and was well on his way to becoming the firm's youngest partner. Life for James and Mary Alice became quieter with only Tot and Buster at home. They were contented in the way only people who have been married for a long time and understand each other deeply and passionately can be. The war in Europe, which filled all the papers, was a mere speck on a very distant horizon.

The only cloud in their personal sky came with the constant ringing of the recently installed community party line telephone system. Their ring, two shorts and a long, was usually for James who then left on the run to help someone in need. Since the doctor near Jasper had retired, James had more work than he really had time for. It just seemed he never was able to complete a meal in peace these days and when he did eat, he often complained of his stomach, asking for oatmeal or cornmeal mush instead of real food.

It was on Monday, April 9, that James made his way to Randy's office to seek his counsel regarding the purchase of a Ford Model T to help him make his rounds with greater speed. The crease between his eyes deepened as he stood at the reception desk waiting for the girl to finish a telephone call. What he heard on her end made him prick his ears.

"Oh, Johnny, what if we got married now? Do you think it would make any difference?"

The girl wiped her eyes as she returned the receiver to its cradle. "Hello, Dr. Buchanan. Are you here to see Randy?"

The girl's distress seemed caused by something other than a tiff with her beau. James put manners aside. "Is your young man thinking of moving away from Canton?"

The girl looked at him with wide eyes. "Haven't you heard? We're at war. Congress declared against Germany and her allies on Friday. All the young men are going to be called into the army, including my fiancé. I'm just sure of it. At least that's what the newspapers are saying. We just don't know what to do about our wedding."

James's spirits plunged. "My goodness. I'm sorry for the trouble this may cause you and your young man. I feared it might come to this when I read about President Wilson's speech before Congress on April 2, but the mail with Friday's edition of the *Tribune* wasn't delivered before I left home."

The blood drained from James's head, leaving him lightheaded. He slumped into the nearest chair—two sons of military age who were just beginning to find their purpose in life. Pray God there would not be a draft as there had been during the War Between the States.

Randy came into the reception area with a smile. "Are you ready to go, Papa?"

James blinked in confusion. "Go where?" The talk of war had driven all else from his mind.

Randy looked at his father as though he was surely suffering from the onset of senility. "Why, to look at the new Fords, of course."

James selected a new automobile, but his pleasure in learning to drive was greatly diminished by the war and by his old stomach complaint's return. He attributed the intestinal ailment to trying to meet the needs of his growing patient list and worrying about how the war might affect his boys.

They heard from Joe, who wrote to ask them to keep an eye on Azaleigh, Ruby, and Sally now that he was due to be sent to France with the first wave of American troops. Sally was to move to the Harbin home, since she would have to give up her base housing. Ruby's baby, some said by the grace of God, was stillborn and the girl eventually began to heal from the horror her life had been while her father lived. No one had heard from or seen Jeb Harbin since the trial. Some said he moved to Atlanta, others said he went west. Joe certainly made no effort to discover his whereabouts. It was good riddance as far as he was concerned.

As James struggled with learning to drive, thoughts of the impending draft distracted him. Boys were being called up from all over the state, and Cherokee County was no exception. Clashing gears and the engine stalling accompanied murmured prayers for a quick solution to this foreign entanglement.

On a Sunday afternoon in early August, Randy unexpectedly drove into the yard and strolled to the porch where his parents were entertaining the Sinclairs and his grandparents.

After an exchange of greetings, Randy caught his father's sleeve and spoke quietly. "Papa, could I speak to you?"

When they were out of earshot of the others, Randy withdrew a letter from his pocket. "This came from the draft board last week. I'm to report for induction in three weeks. After that, I'll be sent to Ft. Gordon in Chamblee. I've applied for Officer Candidate

School after basic training. I should know soon whether I've been accepted. I'm worried about telling Mama. How do you think she'll take the news?"

James's stomach cramped. Randy was just getting his career started and now he was being asked to leave it for God only knew how long to fight in a war that was not of America's making and which would surely not be worth all the American lives it would probably cost. Voicing these concerns would be of little use to his son, however, so James said the only thing that seemed right.

He put his hand on Randy's shoulder. "Son, I know whatever is asked of you, you will do it with honor. Your mother and I will be proud for you to serve your country. And as for Officer School, I can't imagine they will turn down someone like you who has a useful profession. We'd better tell your mother now. I'm sure she can't bear the suspense any longer."

Mary Alice outwardly bore the news of Randy's impending military induction stoically, but privately she expressed her terror for him. She and James read the newspapers every day. The descriptions of what was happening in the trenches were beyond belief and they agreed with the general sentiment, expressed in Georgia's newspapers, that America had no business getting involved in Europe's efforts to destroy herself.

Europe had lost its collective mind in 1914 and now America had joined them. Everyone had such high hopes when the new century arrived. It was like being granted a fresh start in life, but those hopes were being killed every day on the battlefields of Ypres, Verdun, the Somme, and places with unpronounceable names. The world was suddenly becoming a very dark and frightening place.

Randy left with others from Cherokee County three weeks later for Ft. Gordon and basic training. After crawling through mud, running up and down hills with fully loaded packs for weeks on end, bayonet and rifle practice, he was sent on to OCS and left for France just after Christmas as a second lieutenant. His first few letters home were full of tales of his comrades and the excitement of seeing exotic locales. That all changed after his introduction to trench warfare and hellish months spent living in holes in the ground.

James massaged his aching midsection as he tore open the latest letter.

March 15, 1918

Dear Mama, Papa, Tot, and Buster,

I hope this letter finds you all well and not suffering too much from rationing. I'm doing as well as I guess a man can living ankle-deep in mud. I can't tell you where I am or what I am doing because the Hun has spies everywhere, but I can tell you I'm somewhere in a trench on the Western Front. I have dreamed of seeing Europe, but never like this. When this war is over, maybe I'll come back some day and see the sights, if there's anything left to see. Right now, all that's visible to the horizon on all sides is mud, barbed wire, corpses, and the stumps where trees once stood. Every so often, we're ordered over the top and get to see the enemy for a second or two before he opens fire and we have to hit the dirt. If we make it all the way to the Boche trench, then the real fighting begins hand-to-hand.

Last week we captured two Germans in this manner. It sometimes seems like we're just trading the same few feet of land back and forth, over and over. It's a crazy way to fight a war, but we Americans are making a difference in the outcome, which is a good thing.

It's cold here, but we're getting rain instead of snow. I worry about the enlisted men because they have little choice but to endure the elements in the open. The trenches are over ankle deep in water. The mud underneath sucks at our boots and keeps our feet permanently wet. The worst is the gas. It burns the eyes and lungs with a ferocity that is unimaginable. The men that thought up this kind of weapon have earned a special place in hell, as far as I am concerned. We've already sent too many men to the hospital at the back of the lines with trench foot, gas exposure, and shell shock.

Yesterday when we went over the top, the men all around me, including my sergeant, were killed. He took a direct blast from a shell and all that was left of him were pieces. I dread writing to his family. I certainly will not describe his condition. It was too awful to think about. I don't know why I was spared, but I guess God has a purpose for me that I can't yet see.

I guess you are surprised I am writing so candidly, but it helps me to share what we are living with. They don't censor officer's letters, so I feel safe in writing what I have. I am going to close now because we will shortly be on the move again. Despite the conditions, I stay strong and healthy. Knowing I have a loving family to return to helps me stay strong mentally, as well. Until next time.

All my love,
Randy

James read the letter twice over while trying to decide whether to show it to Mary Alice. He certainly would not let the twins see it. In the end, he concluded Mary Alice would worry more not hearing from Randy than by the letter's contents.

Their worry over Randy did not in any way abate their concern for Hiram, who had so far not been called up. He was in his first year of medical school, and they prayed his training for such a critical profession would put him lower on the draft list, but this was mere hope on their part. It had little evidence to support it other than sheer heartfelt desire.

On the first Friday in April, James looked up from mixing medicines to see Hiram getting out of an unfamiliar auto, which left as quickly as it had arrived. He went to the door and called to his son to come into the office. He had a dreadful premonition and he wanted a moment alone with the boy before they went in to his mother.

James tried to appear relaxed and to keep his tone casual. "What a pleasant surprise. I didn't think we'd see you until after the summer term was over. Come in and sit with me for a minute while I finish this mixture."

James and Hiram talked about the usual topics—neighbors, family, local politics, and such—while James sought a way to ask the question that tormented him.

Hiram finally solved the problem for him. He stood up from the stool and squared his shoulders. "There's something I wanted to tell you and Mama in person. I didn't want to just send it in a letter. You know we're fighting an important war."

James's heart felt as though it had stopped. He met Hiram's gaze and nodded for him to continue.

"Randy's over there doing his part, making us all proud. I'm of military age, and I feel guilty that I'm here at home safe and sound while so many other boys from here are fighting. I've volunteered for the Medic Corps."

James looked at his son through narrowed eyes with something bordering on anger. His reaction was fear-driven, of course, but he couldn't keep the edge from his voice. "Hiram, there's no need for you to voluntarily put yourself in harm's way. Randy had no choice. He was drafted, but you have no reason to feel guilty because you aren't living in a trench and being shot at every day. And what about your studies? You're almost finished. How can you just give up at this point?"

Hiram shook his head. "Papa, they desperately need medics on the battlefields. Our boys are dying needlessly because they aren't getting adequate care. I'm going to do my part. I won't be able to live with myself if something happens to Randy while I'm sitting here just waiting it out." He paused and put his hand on his father's shoulder. "I thought you, of all people, would understand why I feel I must do this. When the war's over, I'll go back to medical school. The Dean has already promised everyone who volunteered that our places will be held for us."

James felt the sting of Hiram's words as though he had been slapped in the face. Of course, he understood. That was the problem. James understood all too well the price a man paid when he became devoted to an unshakable cause.

He tried once more to convince his child that there was no dishonor in safety. "Son, I don't think your mother will be able to bear it if something were to happen to you. She has accepted that Archie can't come home and that Randy had no choice in going to war. I'm not sure how she will take your volunteering. Have you given any thought to how she feels?"

Hiram's jaw muscles bulged slightly before he spoke again. "Of course I've thought of Mama, and of you too. Why do you think I'm here instead of simply writing this in a letter? And I think we both know Mama better than that. She may not like it, but she'll understand. She's understood with you all these years, hasn't she?" A mettle James heretofore had never seen shone in Hiram's eyes. "I'm reporting to the induction center on Monday."

Because James saw he had no choice in the matter and was fighting hard not to show his deep fear, he simply enfolded his child in a fierce embrace. He hoped his arms conveyed the support he knew his voice could not.

By September, there were two Buchanan boys fighting to make the world safe for democracy, and shortages were being felt in every commodity at home. Allied successes filled the newspapers, however, making the hardships seem worthwhile and easier to bear. When Bulgaria surrendered and signed an armistice on September 29, the end seemed to be in sight and families with sons in the war rejoiced as the weaker enemy nations began to drop out as well.

Everyone said that the War to End All Wars could not possibly last much longer. James and Mary Alice felt as though the world was poised on the brink of regaining its sanity and becoming safe again.

What no one anticipated was the emergence of a new and deadly enemy that was about to explode onto an unsuspecting public. In Georgia, it started in the military training camps at Augusta and Savannah and spread across the state like a river at flood stage. It descended on Salacoa without warning in the second week of October.

CHAPTER 35

James and Mary Alice were just sitting down to supper when the first call came.

"Dr. Buchanan, you gotta come fast. My childern's all suddenly took real sick and they's burning hot and coughing to beat the band."

As James gathered his medical bag and some extra medicines, two more calls came from other families, all describing the same symptoms. He did not return home until noon the next day and stayed only long enough to gather additional supplies and grab a quick meal. While he was gulping down a little dinner, another call for help came and he was off again without giving Mary Alice any indication of when he would return.

By afternoon, the county school superintendent sent word to close Salacoa School until further notice. Too many children were already infected and the young were being hardest hit by what was now being called an epidemic. Spanish Influenza had arrived with a vengeance and had taken a stranglehold on the county.

James returned home just before bedtime, bringing limber pine cuttings into the house with him.

Mary Alice picked up needles as they fell onto her freshly mopped floor. "Why are you bringing that mess in the house? It won't burn well. It's got too much sap."

James shot her a weary look. "That's the point. Get me the fireplace shovel and some matches. Send Tot and Buster in here to the kitchen."

When everyone had gathered, he set the pine tips smoldering. "I want you to breath in the smoke. Pinesap is a natural sanitizer and breathing infected air spreads this flu. It'll make you choke some, but get the smoke into your lungs. We don't have much in the way of medicine to fight this once you're sick, so the best plan is to stay well."

Tot and Buster coughed and spluttered but did as they were told. After they had gone to bed, Mary Alice took James's supper plate from the range's warming area, but he stopped her. "Can you just make me some mush? My stomach's acting up, and I think mush and a little milk'll sit on it better."

James ate without enthusiasm. When a person is exhausted, even eating is a chore and it seemed everything he ate these days caused him discomfort. He had been meaning to see his friend, Dr. Fogarty, about the problem, but he couldn't take the time right now.

When he swallowed as much as he could choke down, he passed his plate back to Mary Alice. "I know you're very clean in your kitchen, but I can't be too clear about how important it is to not just wipe up. You've got to sanitize, as well." His voice hardened as his volume rose.

Mary Alice frowned and pursed her lips. "I already do that. You've said it—"

James held up a hand then ran it over his face. He was tired beyond endurance and did not try to govern his tone. "This is too important, so you will listen again. Scrub everything, every dish, pot, the table, everything, after every use. Use soap and water as hot as you can stand. Make sure the twins scrub their hands and arms often. They are not to put unclean hands near their mouths or noses. Period." When he saw the hurt in Mary Alice's eyes, he softened his voice. "If someone who's ill comes to the house, send them home and call me. I'll let you know where I am as best I can. I'm going to old Mr. Wilson's now. I'll be there most of the night. I'll call you before I leave to check in and tell you where I'll be next."

James gave Mary Alice a quick kiss and was gone. With all this coming and going, he just didn't have the energy to do battle with the Ford. It would just have to wait until after this crisis passed. As he rode the elderly, uncomplaining Searchlight through the night, James reviewed Mr. Wilson's chances. The old man was now well advanced in years and there was little hope he would survive the virulent hold the disease had taken. The best James could offer this long-time patient and friend was his presence at the end. Mr. Wilson had no family and was very alone in the world. He had always been so appreciative of the invitations to Sunday dinner and the small attentions others paid him. James would not leave him to die alone no matter the toll it might take on him personally. He was already feeling the effects of too little sleep, but he thought he could probably doze in the chair by Mr. Wilson's bed.

***

Withered bodies and haunted faces confronted James as they had during his medical school days. They implored him once more to help them, but instead of joining him as they had in the past, they simply watched as he alone pushed with all his might against the object barring their way. It moved a little, but the faces were still not satisfied. They pointed to the unseen barrier with stick thin arms and looked at James with sad, hollow eyes. He renewed his efforts, but the object only moved an inch or two. Failure stared at him from the other side. Its face wore an expression of condemnation, accusing him with a baleful stare of not doing his best. It seemed to be silently mouthing the words, "You promised. You promised."

James woke with a start to an unnatural quiet. He picked up Mr. Wilson's wrist and found it still warm to the touch, but not as warm as living flesh. James was preparing to locate someone to go to Waleska to call for the county to remove the body, when a knock sounded on the front door. He answered and found Charles Sinclair standing at the bottom of the steps with his truck idling.

"James, you gotta come now. Sarah is took real sick."

It had been a long time since James had seen actual fear darkening his friend's eyes. "If you'll go to Waleska and call the county to come get Mr. Wilson, I'll go to your house right now. And please stop and let Mary Alice know where I am."

James found Sarah burning with fever and having great difficulty drawing breath. He had no sooner finished making Sarah more comfortable and gotten her fever down when Mary Alice called to say that a family across the valley needed him. By the time he arrived at the distant farm, the entire family of parents and five children were very ill with high fevers and other influenza symptoms. There was no one to come in and help care for the family so James stayed with them until a call came from another family. He then divided his time among the three farms. As the rampaging epidemic roared into its third week, James had been home only a few times just to get clean clothes.

He stumbled wearily through his own back door for the first time in four days and greeted Mary Alice with a kiss on the cheek. "I'm only here for a few minutes. Could you make me some mush while I change clothes?"

Mary Alice looked with concern into her husband's face. "You are positively gray and hollow-eyed. You've got to eat more than just mush. Please stay long enough for a true meal. It won't take much longer to eat real food for a change."

James was too exhausted to put up much of an argument. "I'll stay for a little while, but mush is all I really think will set well. My stomach's up to its old tricks. Just mush." He stumbled toward the bedroom while rubbing his aching middle.

***

Mary Alice tallied the remaining clean shirts as James returned to the kitchen and began inhaling his food. If he continued eating like a starving adolescent, there would be one less shirt than she had counted on.

To distract herself and him, she shared family news. "Papa came by today. He and Mama are doing okay, but Uncle Moses died before anyone in the family knew he was sick. They say Cartersville's been hit real hard by the flu."

She stopped speaking for a moment when she realized James was only half listening to her. He hadn't even expressed sorrow about her uncle's passing, which was so unlike him. She surveyed her husband and was alarmed by what she saw. James was much too thin. The skin sagged over his skull's peaks and valleys.

Near tears, she begged, "Please stay home for a little while and get some rest. It won't do anybody any good if you kill yourself trying to treat everyone who's sick. You just can't keep going like this. Surely there's another doctor who can come in and help."

The black circles under his eyes gave James's already thin face the gaunt quality of a death mask. Impatience darkened his handsome face as he barked, "I can't and you know it. There is no one else if I quit, and I'll not leave our people without care at a time like this."

His words held a harsh edge and he must have immediately regretted being so short for he put his arms around Mary Alice as she wiped at the tears trickling down her cheeks. When he spoke, it was with tenderness. "I'm sorry, my love. Please understand. There's no one else to care for the community. I will not leave our people to suffer and die without medical care. This is what God called me for all those years ago, and I can't fail now."

Mary Alice answered in a small trembling voice. "I know that, James. I really do. But I don't think God expects you to kill yourself as part of your bargain with Him. Please, please try to get some rest."

James smiled weakly, kissed the top of her head, and was gone before she could comment further.

October leaves flamed into November, bringing frost nearly every morning and the reopening of the school. In the new month's second week, Mary Alice stood stirring a pot of soup as her youngest came tumbling through the door, dumping their books and lunch pails with a clatter onto the kitchen table.

She held a finger to her lips and shushed them. "You two be quiet now. Your father's home for the first time in days and he's trying to sleep in the front room."

Tot looked at her mother thoughtfully. "Do you think he'll have to go out again?"

"I'm hoping not."

Tot's eyes narrowed. "Did he eat anything?"

Mary Alice's heart jumped. "He ate a little mush. Why do you ask?"

"Because that's all he ever eats anymore. Is Papa sick?"

Mary Alice's heart dropped. Her eyes flew to her youngest daughter's face which she searched while she thought about how to answer. Tot was such a pretty girl with huge blue eyes and a head of thick chestnut curls, but she was also a very perceptive sixteen-year-old.

Mary Alice hoped her answer would allay the girl's fears. She also desperately hoped it was true. "I'm sure he's just plain worn out. He'll get better when he's caught up on his rest. The Health

Department is finally sending nurses from Atlanta to help, and it looks like the flu may be calming down."

***

The flu epidemic, in fact, roared to an end as suddenly as it had begun. One day it was raging, the next it simply vanished. While the valley collectively sighed with relief, the toll the pandemic had taken was accounted by most to be the worst in their lifetime. Sarah Sinclair recovered, and for that they were all grateful, but so many others had been lost. It was a terrible irony that mountain boys had died in their stateside military camps without ever seeing action.

The announcement of the cessation of hostilities and the signing of the armistice on the eleventh was met with a joy so fierce that some described it as delirium. People were starved for something to be hopeful about.

Late in the month, James and Mary Alice learned that Randy and Hiram expected to be demobilized after the New Year.

James kept his concerns about their possible mental and physical health to himself. He had already seen the effects this war could have on young men when he was called over to Jasper to consult in the treatment of a recently returned infantryman. The boy didn't seem to have any serious physical injuries, but he simply sat and stared. He wouldn't or couldn't speak. His mind seemed to be completely shattered. James prayed his boys had escaped this fate. Surely, they would have let him know if they were suffering. Joe wrote that he would stay on in Europe as part of the occupation force charged with keeping the peace, but he expected to be home by summer's end. Perhaps if they were very fortunate, life might soon regain some vestiges of normalcy.

CHAPTER 36

The train puffed to a stop at the Canton Depot with only minutes to spare, which was good because James was in danger of pacing a hole in the platform floorboards. He paced, Mary Alice jumped at every sound, and the twins looked at one another with wide, anxious eyes. Bud and Nancy stood quietly behind the twins with their hands on their grandchildren's shoulders. Everyone was anxious for this day to arrive, but also a little terrified to see the marks the war may have left on the boys.

After an eternity, for which there seemed to be no reasonable explanation, two familiar forms in army drab stepped down from a passenger car, carrying everything they owned in bulky, beaten-up kit bags. James's heart turned over watching silent tears stream down Mary Alice's face as the pair approached. Neither had seen their twenty-fifth birthday, yet both could have passed for men in their mid-thirties. When they were finally within reach, Randy and Hiram swept their mother and sister up into their arms, literally lifting them off the ground. Buster hung back, following his father's lead with awkward handshakes, still caught between the worlds of boyhood and adulthood, never quite sure in which he was supposed to exist. Randy and Hiram, winking at one another, tousled their little brother's dark auburn hair and punched him on the shoulder like a comrade. They then bent down to embrace their grandparents.

A parade of vehicles departed the depot for the return to Salacoa. When they pulled into the yard, Lavinia flew from the kitchen flapping a dishtowel in greeting and calling for Newt to come and see the returning heroes. The Buchanans and Locklins had lived and worked together for so long that they felt more like extended family than landlord and tenants. Lavinia had supper on the table almost as soon as they had all gotten through the door.

Randy and Hiram piled their plates then gulped the food with the table manners of men who were accustomed to having their meager meals interrupted by mortar fire and hand-to-hand enemy attacks. They inhaled it before someone or something could snatch it away. When a vehicle passing on the road backfired, both boys dove to the floor, turning over chairs and breaking dinner plates, escaping an unseen enemy. Wide eyes stared at them when they crawled from under the table.

Bud broke the startled silence. "Boys, you got every reason to still feel afraid. Ain't no one here who thinks bad about you diving for cover. It's gonna take time before you're gonna be able to not search for the enemy behind every tree or hear a shot without your heart beating real hard. You'll get over these feelings after you been home for a while. One morning you'll just wake up and you won't feel so afraid no more. At least, that's how it was for me."

Randy and Hiram seemed to visibly relax when Bud finished speaking. Randy smiled weakly at his grandfather. "Thank you, Papa Campbell. You've never talked with us about what it was like for you during the War Between the States."

Hiram slumped down onto his righted chair. "I thought the reactions to combat would be gone by the time we got home. Obviously not. Maybe you could talk to us about what to expect. The wars may be different, but I expect soldiers' reactions to what they've experienced haven't changed much over time."

Bud nodded and ran his hand through his steel gray hair. The lines in his face seemed to deepen, and it was clear Hiram's words had opened his own wounds. "Anything I can do to help you boys would make me proud. Ask whatever you need to."

Randy and Hiram sat down and filled the clean plates Mary Alice put at their places. James watched them shoveling down food once again in silence. He now knew their transition back into peacetime and normal family life might be more difficult than anyone had allowed themselves to believe. At least they had a grandfather who knew what they were experiencing and who was willing to guide them. James couldn't say for sure what his boys felt, but he was relieved by Bud's words. It seemed just possible life might one day be normal again for his beloved sons, maybe somewhat surreal after France, but at least they had survived hell and lived to tell the tale.

Randy helped himself to another biscuit but stopped with his hand hovering over the butter dish. "Papa, is that all you're going to eat with all this terrific food on the table?"

Lavinia replied before James could swallow his latest bite. "Wyy, that's all he eats these days. I ain't seen him eat a decent meal in months. Says it's the onlyest thing what sets on his stomach. Now nobody ain't asked me, but if'n I was him, I'd be seeing after taking some care for my own health for a change instead of jumping every time that blamed contraption rings."

"Now, Lavinia—" Newt began, only to be cut off by his wife.

"Newt, don't you shush me. You know what I'm saying's the truth. It's a wonder he's got the strength to see to all them patients since the doctor over at Jasper retired. Let them Jasper folkses get theyselves they own doctor. Maybe one of you boys can talk some sense into him. Cain't nobody else."

The normally taciturn Bud added, "Lavinia's right. Your dad, he don't eat enough to keep a bird alive. You boys need to talk to him. Hiram, maybe he'd listen to you."

James frowned at his friends and family as heat crawled over his cheeks. The conversation had gotten completely out of control. "Thank you for your concern, Lavinia, Bud. I know y'all mean well, but I really do think this will pass like it always has before. And the Jasper community is looking for a new doctor. Just as soon as they find one, I'll go see Dr. Fogarty, if I'm still having problems. Right now, I just can't leave. There are too many sick folks and not enough doctors."

As if on cue, the telephone rang and James was off with his medical bag at his usual pace before anyone could ask who needed help this time.

***

After he was gone, Hiram turned to his mother and asked, "Mama, how long has this been going on?"

Mary Alice looked from her son to her father with eyes reflecting the true depth of her concern. Bud was grim-faced, nodding for her to answer the boy's question. "Lavinia's right. Your father's always had stomach trouble, but this has gone on far longer than any time in the past. He's lost weight and can't seem to regain it. He just won't slow down no matter how much anyone begs. I thought things would improve after the flu epidemic ended last November, but they never really have. Maybe you boys can talk to him. He might listen to y'all."

***

James threw his medical bag onto the Ford's passenger seat and went around front to turn the ignition crank. Perhaps he should ride his saddle horse rather than wrestle the Ford's blamed crank handle. He really was extra tired today. It must be the excitement of finally having the boys home.

At first glance, it appeared they might have survived the war without scars, but only time would tell if this was so. He had tossed and turned last night in fear over what they would see today when the boys got off the train. The relief upon seeing them had made him weak in the knees and watching them at the dinner table had given him hope that any effects of all the horror they had seen might be short-term. They were much too thin, but they had managed to retain their senses of humor, which was a good sign. James knew there would probably be some bad days ahead as they adjusted to civilian life, but maybe the transition wouldn't be too difficult. The fact that they had a loving family and careers to return to surely would help ease their way.

James eyed the crank handle in irritation. Every time he struggled with it, which was several times per day, he wished he hadn't let Newt and Randy talk him into buying this infernal contraption. It did get him to his calls faster, but cranking it seemed like it was getting harder every week. Must be age was finally catching up with him. After all, what did he expect at fifty-four.

With several jerks on the crank handle, James finally heard the engine catch and felt the Ford shudder to life. As he stood up, he suddenly felt so light-headed he feared he might pass out. He put his hand on the Ford's hood to steady himself and mentally heard Lavinia's words echoing from the dinner table. He wouldn't trade Lavinia as a neighbor and friend for anyone else he knew, but right now he was put out with her. She just didn't seem to understand there was simply too much to do and too many in need for him to take the time required for a trip to Atlanta.

He opened the Ford's door and eased himself onto the driver's seat. A sigh unconsciously escaped, and he put his swimming head onto the steering wheel. He would rest here for just a moment before he raced off to attend the birth to which he had been called. Perhaps he really should go to Atlanta to see

Fogarty, but not this week. In any event, he would have no place to stay since Mrs. Wilkins had died during the flu.

She had been so kind when he was a medical student and then when he was searching for Dolph. In many ways, she had treated him as a surrogate for the children she had been unable to bear. James hadn't known about her death until their Christmas card had been returned with a note from a neighbor. It grieved him to think that she might have died without anyone who cared with her.

Sometimes, it felt as though time was an enemy with which he was doing constant battle and that he was losing, not only the battle, but the war as well. He would attend to his own problem later in the spring when things calmed down a little and warmer weather brought improved health among his patients. And when he had the strength for the trip.

CHAPTER 37

It was in March that the telephone rang late one night, waking James and the household from sleep with a frantic call from Sarah Sinclair. "Charles is bad sick. He's holding his middle and groaning something fierce. He started with throwing up right after supper and said it had to be something he ate, but I ate the same supper he did and I'm right as rain."

James struggled into his clothes, drawing his suspenders over his shoulders and buckling the belt. It took both to keep up his pants these days. In fact, his three-year-old suit hung on him like it belonged to another man. As he stood up from the chair where he sat to put on his shoes, he momentarily grabbed its back to keep from falling. It must be the late hour and too little sleep that caused him to feel so weak and dizzy. James held the chair back until the feeling receded then gathered his medical bag and was off at his usual roaring pace.

He arrived at the Sinclair house to find Charles in considerable pain and feverish. It didn't take but a moment's palpation of the abdomen to discern the pain's source. He sighed and turned to Sarah.

"We've got to send Johnny Blalock to Waleska immediately to place a call to Dr. Fogarty in Atlanta. Here's the emergency number at his home. Charles has a bad case of appendicitis and that appendix's got to come out. Atlanta is the closest surgeon and I know Dr. Fogarty personally. He's the best and I'm sure he'll come quickly. I'll stay with you and assist Dr. Fogarty when he arrives."

"James, if he needs to have the thing out, why can't you do it? There's no telling how long it'll take for the doctor to get here from Atlanta."

"Sarah, surgery is a specialty, not part of regular medical training. I've done a little over the years when I had to, but I'm just not able to deal with this. There's too much that could go wrong and I'm not up to it right now. I don't think I have the strength."

There. It was said. For the first time since this last round of stomach problems had begun last year, James admitted to himself there might be something profoundly wrong with him, the healer, the one who was always responsible for everyone else's health. After Fogarty finished with Charles's appendix, James would at long last seek his friend's advice. Only a fool undertook his own diagnosis and treatment.

Fogarty arrived with surprising speed considering the distance he had to travel and the condition of the roads. He drove into the Sinclairs' yard around ten o'clock the next morning and called immediately for the kitchen table to be scrubbed with boiling water and the strongest lye soap available. When the table was nearly white, James and Fogarty applied a strong disinfectant to the tabletop, sides, legs, and the floor surrounding the table. Sarah had every sheet she owned in pots boiling on the stove to be used as surgical drapes and curtains. It was the best they could do. James prayed it would be good enough.

Dr. Fogarty handed a metal can to James. "If you'll clean the area and administer the ether, I'll see to the instruments."

James looked into his friend's frightened eyes and squeezed his hand as he covered Charles's mouth and nose with the mesh anesthesia apparatus.

James caught sight of Sarah hovering in the kitchen door. "It'll be all right. Dr. Fogarty's the best, and he won't let a simple appendix defeat him. Sarah, if you'll excuse us?" Once Charles was completely under, James got up and closed the door.

Fogarty made his incision and then pulled back the opening to see what they were dealing with. He whistled softly. "That's badly infected all right. It's a wonder it hasn't ruptured. Well, let's get it out before it changes its mind."

Considering the extent of the infection, the surgery itself was over fairly quickly. The two physicians sat at the kitchen table discussing Charles's treatment and possible length for recovery, when Fogarty's eyes narrowed. "James, how are you doing? If I may say so, you look unwell. You've lost so much weight I might not have recognized you had we met unexpectedly on the street."

James bent his head and studied a spot of blood on his shoe. "I was going to speak with you about this. I'm glad you asked." James then described his symptoms and their duration. He finished by telling Fogarty his own opinion as to the diagnosis.

Fogarty looked at James with despair in his eyes. "You know as well as I do what the probable diagnosis is. How could you have waited so long? You know something like this must be dealt with quickly."

James was lost somewhere in the past as he replied, "Yes, I know how foolish this must seem, but until recently, I hoped it was just the same old problem. I guess I just didn't want to admit to myself that I could get sick. I've always thought nothing could touch me. I'm the only doctor for what are sufficient patients for two men. At first, I thought it would pass like it did all the other times, but when it didn't, I was planning on getting down to see you, but then the flu epidemic struck. Then the boys came home and with the doctor near Jasper retired and there was just so much to do. Have I waited too long?"

Fogarty shook his head uncertainly. "I just don't know . . . I just don't know. But of this I am sure. The Mayo Clinic in Minnesota is your best hope. I'm leaving as soon as I've spoken with Mrs. Sinclair. I'll put in a call to the clinic when I get back to my office to make an appointment for you to see them. You must get to Rochester without further delay."

James agreed he would follow Fogarty's recommendation and made plans for the long journey across the country by train. He contacted every doctor in the county who was conceivably close enough to help his patients and bought his ticket. Then, he waited. Fogarty was able to get him an appointment for the first week in May.

James spent the time between Fogarty's telegram and the departure date for Minnesota doing what he was able for his patients. His illness was taking a toll on his energy, but he refused to give in, stopping and resting during the day, something he had not done since infancy, and then going off again to answer a call for help. Time dragged as his strength ebbed.

Not long before he was due to depart, he went in search of Mary Alice. He found her in the kitchen peeling potatoes. "Mary Alice, come sit with me at the table. We need to talk."

The fear in her eyes cut him like a scalpel slicing through flesh. "I'm not going to Minnesota. I've made up my mind. I won't survive the surgery and I want to die at home, not hundreds of miles away among strangers. There wasn't much chance anyway, but I'm positive that if the trip doesn't kill me, the surgery surely will. I've waited too long, my love." As she gasped, he folded her into his arms. They held each other for some time before James asked, "What do you think we should tell the children?"

She was silent for several moments before she leaned back and gazed into his eyes. "Tell them the truth."

He gave Mary Alice a fierce embrace, turned abruptly, and fled to the sanctuary of his office where he slumped onto the tall stool at the clerk's desk where he worked on his patient records. His chin dropped onto his upturned palms as he struggled with Mary Alice's request.

How did a dying father talk to his children about all his hopes for their futures and what guidance could he give that would stay with them for the lifetimes he would not be there to witness? If they asked why it had come to this, that a man in his mid-fifties with a medical degree was dying from a disease that might have been eliminated with early treatment, what would he say? Had it all been worth the price he and they were paying? At this point, James wasn't sure of the answers for himself and he had no idea what answers to give his children. The only thing he knew for sure was that he would have to find those answers and he would have to do it quickly.

CHAPTER 38

June arrived warm and sunny. Each morning the birds greeted the new day with joyful trills and calls. Each morning the sun peeped serenely over the eastern mountains, gracing the earth with its warmth and painting Mary Alice's kitchen a pleasant buttery yellow. Everyday more flowers and shrubs added their bright blooms to an already glorious display. Everyday young animals frolicked in the pastures. The whole natural world conspired in ignoring her grief and Mary Alice's spirit was weighed down with resentment. Beauty held no joy for her this year while James slipped away from them on a bed set up for him in the front room. Each day he seemed further away as he slept for longer periods, waking only for a few minutes at a time.

It was a blessing he was able to sleep. The laudanum and other opiates prescribed by Dr. Fogarty were doing their job and keeping him comfortable, otherwise, the pain might easily be unbearable. The doctor came from Atlanta twice per week to check on James and ensure the dosages were sufficient, increasing them if James seemed to be suffering more than in the past. He was a loyal friend and colleague. Cancer is a painful death, literally eating away its victim until there is no healthy tissue left. Death becomes what the old folks called a "happy release" for the sufferer but leaving a gigantic hole in the grieving family's hearts.

With James so ill, Mary Alice summoned the older children home. Her greatest fear was that he would die before they would be able to say goodbye, a thought that haunted her dreams. One by one they arrived via train and were ferried home in the Ford by Newt, who sat hunched silently behind the wheel. No one felt much like talking anyway, so his silence was a welcome island of peace before the reality at home delivered its punch in the gut.

Nancy and Lizzie had taken up residence in their old room with Tot and Randy and Hiram bunked in the side room with Buster. James's sister Liz and Bud and Nancy came daily to help and offer what solace they were able. Lavinia kept meals coming, never complaining about how many were or were not there when she was ready to serve. The house was oddly and solemnly silent for having so many people in it, but there was little reason for the joyful conversation and shouts of laughter that had filled its rooms in happier times.

The normally outgoing Newt became strangely silent and took to roaming the mountains behind the house in search of only God knew what. He did his work preparing the garden plots or tending to some other plowing or planting task, and then simply disappeared without a word to anyone. Often, Buster walked quietly behind him. The boy, who now matched James in height and wore his features, missed his father's presence, or rather, his conscious presence. James was home now all day and all night for the first time in Buster's life, but he slept most of the time, and when he was awake, the adults crowded around him with medicine or efforts to attend to his other needs so that Buster and Tot felt pushed aside and ignored.

Even with their father so sick and often awakened by the pain that came before it was time for more medicine, he made the effort to call them to him for a kiss and a few words, which made it all the sadder for them because it brought home to them just how bad the situation really was. It was a very lonely time for the youngest twins despite so many people coming and going from the house all the time. They clung to each other or sought solace in the company of anyone who had time for them.

Late on a sunny afternoon, Newt noticed Tot sitting forlornly on the back porch, her deep blue eyes red from crying, and looking very much alone, so he began sending her brother to fetch her and the three would take off over the ridge, not to be seen again until suppertime. Their world was falling apart and they had no power to stop it.

One day after a particularly long sojourn, Newt and the twins turned up at the backdoor with a fresh honeycomb and a bucket of huckleberries, deep purple at the peak of ripeness. "We just thought these might tempt James to eat something 'sides mush. These here berries is from the bestest patch on the mountain, and I stole the honey from the bees not more'n thirty minute ago. Do you think he could get a little of this down?"

Mary Alice looked up from the table where she had been mixing a dose of medicine and smiled wearily. "I'm sure he can, Newt. It's mighty kind of you to bring them. Maybe Lavinia or I could make a pie from the berries. James has always been so fond of fresh huckleberry pie."

Mary Alice waited to cut the pie until James was awake and then made quite a celebration of it, hoping to entice him to eat. He attempted to swallow a few bites, praising the flaky crust and juicy berries, but the pie stuck momentarily in his throat, sending him into a coughing fit and leaving him weak with pain.

She jumped to get the medicine, but James stopped her. "Call the children and send them to me one at a time. I need to talk to them now, before it's too late."

***

As he waited for the children to gather, James pondered all the things he wanted to say and feared he might not have the energy to complete. When he began this journey all those years ago, he hadn't anticipated all that he would encounter and how he would be changed by it. He had discovered unknown strengths and things in himself of which he wasn't particularly proud. Mary Alice had recently asked if he would do anything differently if he had the chance and he now knew the answer.

He spoke briefly with each of the children in turn, saying the things each needed to hear and extracting a promise from each that they would always look after their mother and that she would never want for anything. He talked with Buster longer than he did the older boys, not because he loved Buster more, but because life had allowed him less time with his youngest. During his lucid moments, James had tried to think of what he could say that would stay with Buster and guide him when needed.

With his strength ebbing, he called the boy to his bedside. He looked up into his youngest son's eyes, seeing fear and despair where an impish light once shone. James used his little remaining physical strength to reach out and place his hand on Buster's arm. It tore at his heart to feel the boy trembling.

"Son, none of us knows exactly how life will turn out or what will be asked of us along the way. We find ourselves in situations we never anticipated, where no choice is without its bad side. When you're unsure, follow what your heart tells you is right, no matter how afraid you may be. I have regrets, but following God's call into medicine is not one of them." James had intended to say more, but his strength was gone and his eyes refused to remain open. To his surprise, the faces of his recurring dreams were suddenly surrounding his bed and beckoning. Their bodies were miraculously whole and their eyes were bright and happy. They were bidding him to follow them, but he couldn't go just yet.

***

Tot was in the yard when Lizzie called her into the house. She ran toward the front room with the hope that somehow a miracle had occurred and Papa had discovered he was going to recover after all. Lately, her older sisters had accused her of living in a dream world, but she had no idea what they were talking about. Just because she refused to give up hope didn't mean she was out of touch with reality. But when she entered the room where he lay, her heart dropped. Her twin sat slumped in a corner with his head on his knees as he rocked back and forth on his haunches. An awful silence filled the room. Tears ran down her cheeks and she wiped at them quickly with her dress hem. Papa had his eyes closed and he mustn't see her crying. That would upset him. She went to him and lightly touched his hand, which was warm and dry. Her papa roused himself long enough to say a few words to her and squeeze her hand, and then he closed his eyes and slipped into a deep sleep.

Tot joined Buster on the floor and they hugged each other fiercely for a long, long time, until someone shooed them away. Their safe, comfortable, happy world ended later that evening, not with a mighty explosion, but with a gentle sigh just as the sun was bathing the valley in its final golden rays.

Their papa lay in state in the front room for two days during which food poured into the kitchen from all corners of the valley, as was the custom when anyone in the community suffered bereavement. The family took turns sitting by his casket day and night, for mountain people have always known that loved ones must not be abandoned, even in death.

Tot and Buster kept each other company on the second night, holding hands and with their heads on one another's shoulders. As they sat motionless and grief stricken, Tot looked over at Buster, his tears mirroring her own. "Do you think Papa loved his patients more than us?"

Buster gazed at her as if he didn't understand her question, then he quietly shook his head. He didn't seem to want to talk. Unlike her, he must not want to think beyond this minute.

Resigned to her twin's refusal to be drawn into conversation, Tot said what was really at the core of her anxiety. "It's just so unfair. Papa was here for the others while they grew up, but he won't be for us. Who's going to take care of us now?"

Her question broke Buster's trance. "Mama."

James's funeral was conducted in the open air under the big oak near New Canaan's front porch. The congregation was so large that only a small portion would have been able to fit in the sanctuary, so the pastor and pallbearers hurriedly set up chairs in front of the steps for the family and moved the casket onto the porch before the service began.

When it was time to move up the hillside to the cemetery, Tot sat unmoving after everyone else departed, refusing to believe this was all they had left of their beloved father. If she didn't move, then it wouldn't be so—it wouldn't be real and they could all go home and Papa would be there, alive and waiting for them with his arms stretched out like he had done so often when they were little. He would catch them up and carry them around, one on each arm and they would search his pockets for candy. If she didn't move, time would stop and she would be able to turn it backwards.

She sat there unmoving and unseeing until Lavinia put an arm around her thin shoulders. "Tot, get up. You got to go up to the cemetery. Come on now. You just got to get up."

Blindly, Tot did as she was bidden, but she didn't process anything that was happening around her. One moment she was sitting in the chair at the bottom of the church steps and the next they were at home again with all their neighbors filling the house, standing around tables groaning with the food they had brought. Much later, she had to ask what was said and to whom she had talked when the friends, neighbors, and former patients visited with the family, paying their respects and expressing their sorrow.

***

In the days following the funeral, Mary Alice was beyond tears. Her grief was so deep, so painful that she kept it locked away in a secret place inside her and only allowed it to show itself when she was alone at night in the bed that only such a short while ago had been shared with James. The wound in her heart caused by Archie's leaving and then deepened when contact with him finally drifted to a stop, was torn open and mingled with her new sorrow until they became one. She knew she had to be strong for Tot and Buster, for of all the children, they felt their father's death the most keenly. The older children loved their father and would miss him desperately, but they had known him into adulthood. They had lives to return to now that the funeral was behind them. Lizzie and Nancy had already gone back to Dallas and Baltimore and Hiram had returned to medical school. Her babies had known their father for only sixteen short years. It was so unfair. It was all so unfair.

In her despair, she struggled with an anger directed toward her husband's greedy patients who had demanded so much and given so little in return. She hurled silent words at heaven so filled with anger that they frightened her and made her wonder if she was losing her mind, or worse, condemning herself straight to the fires of hell. Alone in the big bed intended for two, she poured out her grief not in tears, but in anger so intense it bordered on hatred. She became afraid of the night and the sleep her exhausted body demanded, for she dreamed angry dreams about people she had known all her life or imagined it was all somehow a huge mistake and James was just away from home and would return in the morning. There were times when she was quite sure she was going mad.

It was a Sunday afternoon a few months after the funeral and the boys were home for the weekend. Randy came every weekend and stayed by his mother's side while there. Hiram arrived on Friday evenings as often as he was able to get away from his studies. The Sunday afternoon had passed in the usual way during warm weather. Bud, Nancy, Mary Alice, and the children sat scattered about the porch, rocking and sharing small bits of news from the community. They discussed nothing important, just the normal things that happen in any rural community, when Mary Alice said something completely disconnected from the conversation.

She looked directly at each family member before saying through clenched teeth, "It was his work that killed him, you know. He worried so much about other people and in the end it killed him. Do you think God really meant for him to die in order to keep his part of their bargain? Do you think anyone he worked so hard to heal has even the slightest idea what he gave up for them?" She turned angry eyes on her third son. "Hiram, you can't do it that way. Promise me you won't. Promise me!"

The group looked on in stunned silence. Bud reached over and took Mary Alice's hand. He glanced away and ran his free hand over his grizzled gray head before drawing breath to speak. "My darling girl, you're just plain wore down with grief. If anybody hada tolt me all them years ago when you and James was married that we'd be sitting here talking about him being gone, I'd have said they was a fool, but it's what come to pass and we cain't change it. We do the best we can and then we leave the rest in God's hands."

The lines between Mary Alice's eyes deepened and she turned hard eyes on her father, but he held up his hand for silence. "James, he made the onlyest choice he knowed how to make. He was called to take care of sick folks and that's what he done. Thay's some things we ain't never gonna understand or agree with and that's all right. We don't have to understand it all now."

Mary Alice was determined not to listen to anymore and rose from her chair intending to go into the house, but Bud grabbed her arm and pulled her back into her seat. She gripped the rocker's arms until her knuckles turned white and bit her lower lip until she drew blood.

"Mary Alice, you got to hear me out. It's not just for you. It's for the childern too. We just do the best we can and what we have to. That's what James done and he couldn'ta done it no different. And neither can Hiram. We cain't sit here trying to second-guess what's already happened nor why things turned out the way they done. It don't do no good to keep asking what if. James, he's gone home and he's at peace. Do you think he'd want you all cut up like this all the time?"

Mary Alice jerked back from her father as though he had slapped her, but Bud would not relent and would not let her escape. "James'd want you to live your life and find what happiness thay is, not spend it being mad at everything all the time. He'd want you to go on for your own sake and the childern's. I mayn't know much, but this I know to be gospel truth—James loved you, your children, and his work. In that order."

Tears, the first she had shed since she knew what the future held, began slipping silently down Mary Alice's cheeks as her father's words seeped into the secret place deep within her heart. With the suddenness of a summer storm, all the tension and pent up anger drained from her like runoff from the mountains after a heavy rain. Life would never be the same, but it would go on. She and the children would find a new balance through their love for one another and with the support of friends and family. Their faith would guide and strengthen them as it always had.

Peace, that elusive quality which had hidden its face from her for so long, finally reappeared and wandered in like an old friend coming to sit and stay a spell.

ABOUT THE AUTHOR

Linda Bennett Pennell has been in love with the past for as long as she can remember. Anything with a history, whether shabby or majestic, recent or ancient, instantly draws her in. It probably comes from being part of a large extended family that spanned several generations. Long summer afternoons on her grandmother's wrap-around porch or winter evenings gathered by the fireplace were filled with stories both entertaining and poignant. Of course, being set in the American South, those stories were also peopled by some very interesting characters, some of whom have found their way into Linda's work.

Linda resides in the Houston, Texas, area with one sweet husband and one adorable goldendoodle who is quite certain she's a little girl.

OTHER TITLES BY
LINDA BENNETT PENNELL

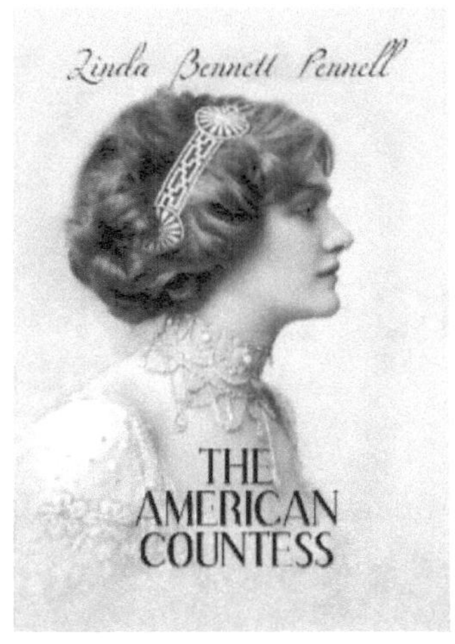

NOTE FROM LINDA BENNETT PENNELL

Word-of-mouth is crucial for any author to succeed. If you enjoyed *Gilead's Physician*, please leave a review online—anywhere you are able. Even if it's just a sentence or two. It would make all the difference and would be very much appreciated.

Thanks!
Linda Bennett Pennell

We hope you enjoyed reading this title from:

www.blackrosewriting.com

Subscribe to our mailing list – *The Rosevine* – and receive **FREE** books, daily deals, and stay current with news about upcoming
releases and our hottest authors.
Scan the QR code below to sign up.

Already a subscriber? Please accept a sincere thank you for being a fan of Black Rose Writing authors.

View other Black Rose Writing titles at
www.blackrosewriting.com/books and use promo code
PRINT to receive a **20% discount** when purchasing.